THE
KINGFISHER
AND THE CROW

THE
KINGFISHER
AND THE CROW

TIM DIAZ &
PETER MARINO

BookPress®
publishing • media

Published in Des Moines, Iowa, by:

Bookpress Publishing
P.O. Box 71532
Des Moines, IA 50325
www.BookpressPublishing.com

Publisher's Cataloging-in-Publication Data

Names: Diaz, Tim, author. | Marino, Peter, author.
Title: The kingfisher and the crow / by Tim Diaz and Peter Marino.
Description: Des Moines, IA: Bookpress Publishing, 2024.
Identifiers: LCCN: 2024915194 | ISBN: 978-1-960259-15-8 (hardcover) | 978-1-960259-22-6 (paperback)
Subjects: LCSH Politicians--Fiction. | Murder--Fiction. | Crime--Fiction. | Mystery fiction. | Thriller fiction. | BISAC FICTION / Mystery & Detective / Women Sleuths | FICTION / Crime | FICTION / Thrillers / Political
Classification: LCC PS3604 .I38 K56 2024 | DDC 813.6--dc23

First Edition
Printed in the United States of America
10 9 8 7 6 5 4 3 2 1

For our family and friends.

PROLOGUE

Sometimes, skipping school doesn't pan out the way you might think.

It was Friday, and D.C. families emptied out early to stretch the weekend. The boys wouldn't be missed. They were noodling around the Piscataway Creek shoreline, just enough distance from the road to be out of the way and not be bothered by nosy adults or cops. They found crooked walking sticks and trudged through the mud and trash that lined the rocks and deadwood to an open area facing the wide section of the Potomac before it turned back toward the city. After a brief pushing match, a rock skipping contest ensued. Who was the best? They didn't care all that much. Chucking rocks was better than being at school arguing over glue, sprinkles, and stupid costumes for the coming school play.

But after a few rounds of arguably the best rock-skipping in the county, a dull thud caught their attention. A wayward throw had struck a nearby lump of floating trash a few yards from shore. Blue crabs scattered into the water to avoid the assault.

Could they hit it again and sink the debris? Or hit a crab!

New contest!

A volley of bombs crashed into the river, with each toss getting closer and closer to their target. They were better at skipping rocks than chucking softball-sized stones. One found its mark. There was a loud thud and a bounce, and the rock splashed a few feet away. Direct hit!

The boys were celebrating with high fives while trying not to tumble into the river or lose a shoe in the mud when the tallest of the three stopped and forced the others to turn.

Their target had rolled over, and a ghostly face stared back at them, its mouth open and swollen tongue filling the hole. One eye was partially bulged out, the other pushed in a bit too far. The body bobbed but stayed put, snagged on a branch protruding from the river. Still too far to reach but close enough for another attack.

"Wicked! Did you see his eyes?"

The tallest boy dove into his pocket and tried to unlock the piece of shit phone that was his brother's two years ago.

"Camera. Camera. Before it floats away or sinks. Yes!"

"We're gonna be famous—we found a dead guy!"

Now they really had a target. Amid the squeals of delight and the jockeying for position, an onslaught that would have made the Navy proud rained upon the bobbing corpse. Who was going to be the man? Who was going to nail that guy square between his grotesque eyes?

They threw whatever they could find. Sticks, rocks, a few empty bottles, but nothing freed the body from the branch's grip. So the boys dared each other to free the man. But no one was brave enough to wade into the freezing water, let alone touch a dead guy.

With no profiles in courage, posing for pictures was the next best thing. Smiles beamed as they snapped a few with the head floating in the background and the crab mounted on it. Poses with the head peeking over their shoulders were fun too. They took turns pretending they were in a horror movie.

Even a dead body can get boring. It just sat there, glaring back at them. It was back to serving as a landing spot for crabs.

"The team is gonna freak out! Let's get the guys and come back tonight!"

The boys returned to their bikes and cranked off to their neighborhood. The mud was cold in the November chill, but the adrenaline kept them pumping through the streets.

Photos circulated, and by lunchtime, the three were instant celebrities. Some didn't believe them, a few were just jealous because they were stuck at school, and others asked about the body. They organized an expedition to show off their new find. Backpacks, flashlights, and a rope that might reach their treasure were collected.

But of course, there was that one kid. There always is. The one who showed his mother the gruesome pictures and caused things to come crashing down around everyone.

Before the kids could head out to retrieve the dead guy, the parents were all over it, and the cops were knocking on doors.

CHAPTER 1

Jerry Sharpe had his fill of fundraisers this week, but he was looking forward to this one. Tonight's third fundraiser should have been the only one. The evening's undercards were not worthy of most people's time. But over the course of the year, there were more than four hundred other Congressmen who had to have their moment and raise money from all the D.C. players, big and small. So three a night wasn't unusual—it was just absurd.

The Good Samaritan was perfectly positioned on Pennsylvania Avenue to attract big money and plenty of leg, and the Chairman was in rare form tonight, greeting all attendees at the door, thanking them for their generosity and glowing over their brides or "friends" for the evening.

Chairman Perry had his advance-man at his side whispering names and the roles of folks parading through the door to help his boss show his knowledge of all the important players at his event.

Jerry quietly lumbered along the bread line, inching his way to the door. Many slid in at the front, prolonging the wait for all the unfortunate rule-followers. The line skippers' punishment was just a belly laugh and slap on the back as the Chairman swept them in, after collecting a check, of course.

Jerry kept a watchful eye on the folks jumping the line—he hadn't seen them yet, but he knew they would show up for the big event of the week.

Jerry watched as Chairman Perry's turkey-neck wobbled back and forth over a shirt collar that was three sizes too small. The loosened, poorly-tied Windsor knot didn't appear to help stave off the choke hold his collar had on him. Jerry wondered which was tighter—the collar or the lobbyists' grip?

As the line shortened, Jerry's attention fell on a classy gentleman who emerged from the door like a cuckoo bird. The man was wearing a sharp blue suit and an impressive tie. It had a touch of orange in it, giving him just enough flair to catch a lady's attention. He swept out from under the canopy to offer sexy cargo escort under a massive black umbrella to avoid the occasional sprinkle.

Jerry listened to the banter as he came within earshot.

"Thank you, Ramon. It's always nice to see you." The ladies would roll their Rs to emphasize the romantic nature of his name.

"You look lovely, as always. You bring sunshine to an otherwise gloomy evening."

"You are too kind, Ramon. Love the tie. Handsome as always!" He was older than them, but he had an infectious smile, and the ladies soaked up the authenticity and attention. A pinch on the man's cheek or a quick peck would follow to greet their old friend who had made them feel special.

Jerry finally reached the front door, and cast a knowing smile to Ramon, who was scooting past to grab the door for a young lady. Ramon was on the job and didn't catch Jerry's gesture of support.

Jerry enthusiastically turned to the Chairman, who looked like he was about to choke out, and did the prerequisite two-handed double-pump handshake after he handed over his thousand to the sidekick.

The Chairman was getting tired even though he was only an hour or so in but smiled at his colleague. "Nice to see you, James. I appreciate your support. Go on in and have a good time."

"Thank you, Mr. Chairman. It's good to see you have a full house."

James? Really?

Jerry entered quickly to make sure others in line didn't hear the faux pas.

Jerry had served on his committee for almost a year, but he clearly had not caught Perry's attention.

Jerry dove into the room, miffed that his own party, his own chair couldn't remember his name. How he wished he were Ramon.

CHAPTER 2

As the evening sunlight began to fade on Pennsylvania Avenue, Skylar Nicholson squinted into the rear-view mirror of her Corolla. She had just landed an Olympic-caliber parking maneuver, and while this had improved her mood, Skylar could not shake the feeling that something was wrong.

She leaned forward in her seat, arched her back, and tilted the mirror down so she could see her face. *Shit*, she thought to herself. *Shit, shit, shit.*

She opened the glovebox and rifled through it. *Just one lipstick, that's all I need*, she thought. *There's got to be one in here somewhere.* Old parking tickets, pens, and an ancient registration form flew from the glove compartment. *Come on, universe, she thought, just one, any color. Just one freakin...*

Then she saw it—an old, respectable shade, hiding in the back corner under some loose change and an expired parking pass. "Yes!" she said as she dug it out from the corner. "Come on, now. If you're good, we can get a drink with the old, puffy men at the bar. Okay?"

There was just enough daylight left for her to finish "putting on her face," and like her mother, Skylar could do so in short order. As she passed the lipstick over her lips, she remembered how her ex-husband Chip used to say that she could go from sweatpants and a T-shirt to the belle of the ball in under five minutes.

A horrible, familiar feeling welled up in her heart. *Skylar Anne Nicholson*, she thought to herself, *it's over, and you ended it. Move on*. Her hands shook, and her thoughts shifted to the drinks waiting for her across the street. It wasn't fair. The Good Samaritan was full of men who could forget to wear their pants and the political circles would think it was cute, but if she forgot her face, no one would take her seriously. And if no one took her seriously, no one would talk to her. No talking, no stories. No stories, no paycheck, no trusty Corolla, no lipstick.

Skylar snapped the cap back onto the lipstick, threw it back into the glovebox for the next desperate occasion, and adjusted the mirror for her final inspection.

The woman in the mirror might have been stunning, but the girls of Fairfax County had made sure that Skylar couldn't see it. Until her freshman year at the University of Virginia, Skylar thought any-one who complimented her beauty was consoling her on account of her bad luck. Chip had changed this for a while, but despite years of trying, even he had failed to drain this poison from her mind.

CHAPTER 3

The Good Samaritan was in high gear. The slightly darkened chamber with paneling from floor to the ceiling had an old, polished look. It immediately made one feel unwelcome, despite the name's meaning. One could almost hear the curator turn and implore children not to touch a thing.

Even with the throngs of donors, the Good Samaritan still had room to maneuver. Jerry surveyed the crowds huddling together and asked himself his two favorite questions—who was on the prowl, and who was the prey? He viewed fundraisers as a place where one watched the food cycle in action. He took pride in watching *National Geographic* and *Planet Earth* and could describe any fundraiser as if he were narrating—with a deep English accent, of course, to really deliver the lines.

In his own mind, he began to narrate his own private episode of Planet Earth.

The first thing to understand when entering the fundraising ecosystem is its center—what attracts life and keeps it there—which, of course, is the bar. It is the coral reef that life hovers around to survive the night.

The variety of fish swirling around the bar were mostly lobbyists, with some staffers sprinkled in for good measure. Jerry had quickly learned that lobbyists come in three main species—sharks, barracudas, and baitfish.

The sharks were the old-school boys, the old hands, battle-scarred but experienced. When they swam toward the bar, others would buy them drinks or scatter to make sure they were not an easy meal, trapped in the wrong place at the wrong time. These men—and they were almost all men—knew each other well, and usually didn't mind when they bumped up against each other. They knew the pecking order, and they knew their colleagues were dangerous too. These were the guys who got shit done, but even among sharks, there were differences—the great whites drafted important legislation on behalf of Congress, inserted sneaky sections into boring legislation or found creative ways to kill threatening legislation. The blue sharks were always roaming about looking for ways to score easy meals for their clients, and yet there was always a hammerhead roaming about—the one guy who was the only expert on the one subject that was front and center for that specific session. He was useless outside of his one moment to shine. Sharks weren't concerned about networking—they were the network.

These guys did not know or ever approach Jerry, let alone come to one of his fundraisers. He could do nothing for them. He represented less than a small snack and was not worth chasing. Jerry recalled a biology class lesson—energy efficiency. These beasts would not consider him worthy of their effort.

Then there were the barracudas—Cudas for short. Slick, fast, and aggressive men and even faster, hotter, harder-drinking women. They could charm a bone from a hungry dog or sell ice to penguins. They wore fancy, fashionable suits, usually with pinstripes. The men accessorized with wet, slicked-back hair styles and goatees. These GQ types were slick enough to ensure they buttered up a passing legislator (or their staff).

The Cuda women would flash a smile, bat an eye, or provide a knowing squeeze from a hand on the arm. But this attention was only for those who had power, or maybe for those they intended to set up for a meal later. In some cases, this could be the same person. Jerry was neither.

And then there were the baitfish. They were the most entertaining, and in some ways, Jerry understood them the best. These lobbyists were the ones who had no record, nothing to lose, were inspired by watching too many *West Wing* episodes, and had absolutely no juice. To look busy, they hovered around the cheese and fruit tables in the middle of the room. If they were idle, they became bar runners for the Cudas. And oh, did they oblige, hoping they could avoid getting eaten, or better yet, maybe they could get intel in return or even perhaps a job as a junior lobbyist—become baby Cudas, a dream come true.

Oh yes, baitfish had been to school. They could recite each Congressman's name on sight, what committees they were on, their home districts, and what bar they liked to frequent in town.

Jerry was thankful for baitfish—he needed to look like he had someone wooing him. And he jumped in.

CHAPTER 4

Ramon smiled as Sky approached his station just inside the entrance to the Good Samaritan. She was his favorite. This was because she always looked him in the eye. No one else did.

Ramon came out to greet her. "Miss Sky, good evening. How is my *nieta*?" Skylar grinned and gave Ramon a warm kiss on the cheek.

"Wonderful, Ramon, especially now that I am an honorary granddaughter." She gave his forearm a squeeze, charmed by his Spanish moniker for her.

"Full house tonight," he whispered into her ear. "Chairman Perry fundraiser. All the families and tribes are well represented, with a sprinkling of eager little shits for comic relief. Try not to trip over any. O'Connor's at table five in the corner, marking his cards before the game starts, and Franchetti just opened his second pack of cigarettes. Helen and Frank are tending bar, and Perry speaks in thirty minutes. Sorry, Sky, but it doesn't look so good for you tonight. No real news, just the usual *putas* and bribery." Skylar pretended to blush and gently touched her necklace with her left hand.

"Shame on you, Ramon," she said with a wry smile. "How could you say such a thing? You know full well how much people like to read about bribery and prostitution."

CHAPTER 5

Jerry wasn't interested in sharks, Cudas, or baitfish. He was hunting for the kings and queens of the political ocean. He was stalking a particular queen and her offspring.

The Cudas and elected officials unabashedly referred to such people as whales. These folks were not registered—well, maybe they were on the Register of Historic Places—but these sea creatures carried tremendous power. Whales would never be caught dead visiting one of Jerry's fundraisers—the water would be too shallow, there would be nothing of value to eat, and Jerry was not significant enough to matter. Whales were the blue bloods. The real deal. The Roosevelts, the Van Burens, and their cousins who had built the railroads, the sugar industry, or whatever had brought them wealth a hundred years ago. For elected officials, whales do not represent a thousand a head. They were worth hundreds of thousands and more. The blue bloods stuffed PAC funds. If they liked you, the spigot would flow and no one could catch you. If they didn't, well, that would leave you borrowing markers from your Uncle Larry just to put handwritten cardboard campaign signs on lawns.

Jerry took a moment to observe the blue bloods. The old money was obvious to him. The elderly blue blood men, considered blue whales, dressed in 30-year-old suits, often with a vest, the pattern of upholstery popular in the 1970s. Ironically, they tried to portray an image of being of the people, often seen nodding to the common folk in the room and giving high fives to waiters. But they didn't care who they were. Their haircuts looked as unkempt as their tired dress shirts. Their bent, scuffed, and discolored collars looked like they were picked up at the Salvation Army. Their ties were chosen to look a bit low-brow to help downplay the money they were wrapped around. But Jerry knew what gave them away. Just look down—these men wore old, well-cared-for leather shoes that stood the test of time. Simply stunning.

The blue blood wives came from the same families, apparently working through a blue blood family exchange program. They glided effortlessly through the room and cast an image of Jackie O—old school prim and proper. The hair was never past the shoulder. Those with curls kissing the neckline were risqué for this crowd. They always had a handbag, but there was never anything but a real hand-kerchief in them, or, for the more daring, perhaps a polished der-ringer. They created a ring of personal space that was never invaded, even by their male counterparts. Most in the room were terrified of them, and rightfully so.

Then there were the newly minted, young male blue bloods. The rich sons that never had to work hard to earn their keep. They tried to dress the same as their fathers to imply they carried the same juice, but they were not seasoned and lacked their elders' fashion sense to pull it off. The young blue blood boys wore suits like the Cudas, and their shoes were more about a recent fashion statement than the tried-and-true, generation-lasting beauties their fathers wore. But what really gave them away were their ties. Jerry stroked his tie and hoped he offered a more authentic look than these young men.

The young blue blood women were a different sort. They were not blue whales—they were killer whales—lethal hunters with skills acquired under their mothers' and grandmothers' tutelage. They stuck to the classics—solid colors, simple yet elegant jewelry, and hair that was prim, proper, and just slightly suggestive with a gentle, youthful flair to catch an eye or two. Provocative. But these whales were absolutely ferocious. They were not afraid to kill and eat their prey right in front of terrified ocean-dwellers. Jerry was certain they disemboweled a hapless soul early at each event just to make that very point.

Jerry knew as a freshman congressman, you were lucky to stay one step above the baitfish and could be mistaken for one, like the embarrassment at the door. While he hated these whales with a passion, tonight he needed to swim among them. Like he belonged.

CHAPTER 6

Sky's eyes adjusted to the Good Samaritan's long, dark, ornate interior. It was part Victorian ballroom and part 1920s art deco bank lobby. The hardwood bar ran the length of the wall to her right for almost sixty feet, with con artists and thieves waiting in lines three deep to get a drink. The bar had hosted this scene every Thursday evening for more than a century. She loved the place.

She made eye contact with Frank, who motioned to Helen, who gave her the signal to make her way to the spot at the bar where her drink would be waiting. *Damn, Ramon*, she thought, *you're too good to me.* It took her a few minutes to find an approach to her destination, but her access to Helen was cut off by two rows of suits.

Helen gave Sky's drink to one of the suits with clear instructions, who passed the drink along to another, who managed to overcome his extreme intoxication long enough to give it to her without spilling it.

"So," the grey-haired, rotund gentleman said, "one brandy old-fashioned for the woman who has supernatural control over the bartender." Sky watched him sway, then watched him look her over, slowly, from the tip of her head to her toes, and back up again.

"Wait," he said, "now that I've gotten a better look, I'd bend the rules to get you a drink, too. Where are you from, hon, Wisconsin? Only place I know where they put brandy in an old-fashioned."

"Sorry," Sky said. "I'm from Virginia. But thanks."

"Staffer?" he said. He was leering now, with his eyes focused squarely on her chest. *Good Lord*, she thought, *this is going to be fun.*

"No, Senator Heilbronner, I'm a journalist—Skylar Nicholson with *The Thread*. We met last year at the RNC. I believe your wife Leslie and I spent a wonderful evening talking about our love for UVA."

The man blushed, and Sky noticed he was starting to sweat. "Well, of course! I'm so sorry, um, Skylar. Ms. Nicholson. I didn't mean to be so... forgetful. I do meet a lot of people."

"You do, Senator. You do."

"What do you mean?"

Sky went in for the kill. "Well, a lot of our followers send us pictures, and I have been meaning to ask you about one in particular."

"Yes, yes…" The Senator was frantically searching the bar area for someone. *Your aide is not here to save you*, Sky thought. *He stepped into the men's room two minutes ago.* She took her phone out of her blazer pocket and held it up to the Senator's face.

"Since we have a minute, I thought I would ask if you wanted to comment on this picture, taken in Miami at the Soybean Producers' Association convention. Because some of the people you met right here. Do you see? It turns out that they came all the way from the local escort service to join you for a meeting about tax policy. So I was just wondering, Senator, how did the meeting go?"

Before the Senator could respond, a young, well-built man forced himself between them and informed Sky that he had just received an urgent call summoning Senator Heilbronner to the Hill. By the time the aide had finished his interruption, the Senator was already out the door, hailing a taxi for an escape up Pennsylvania Avenue.

I'll probably pay for that, Sky thought, *but it was worth it.*

Sky took up her usual position at the end of the bar and scanned the room for more fun and opportunity. Ramon was right. The usual players were here, doing their dance and creating news as the night continued. She played with her necklace and rubbed the smooth pearls against her chin as she watched the droves of lobbyists storm the bar.

Finding a story in a place like this began by noticing something that looked out of place—a person, the tone of a conversation, even the tie one of these old men chose to wear. If anything was out of place in the external view of things, something interesting was likely simmering underneath. The key to success was to be objective, as her mentor once told her, and to watch the play without becoming a character in it. She had just finished this thought when tonight's "wrinkle" arrived, in the form of a man who divided the lobbyists at the bar like Moses before the Red Sea.

CHAPTER 7

Jerry learned quickly how to get through a crowd at a fundraiser—draft behind an old blue blood as they made for the bar. Kind of like pulling tightly behind an ambulance to cheat your way through traffic. He took advantage of the wake behind a rather large blue blood on the move.

Jerry arrived at the bar unscathed but had trouble making eye contact with the bartender as she was scrambling to get all the requests being barked over the heads of lobbyists who were not giving up their high-priced real estate at the bar's waterfront. She finally saw him leaning in.

"What can I do for you, sir?"

Jerry leaned in to read the nametag. "Helen, I could use a really fine cup of coffee right about now." *No drinking—dulls the brain.* Jerry was sure she was used to being hit on throughout a fundraiser and was glad she was gentle and tossed a smile at his harmless effort to connect.

As he waited for his coffee, Jerry was jostled from behind. A great white had bumped him and pressed him against the bar. Jerry recognized the man immediately. Sean O'Connor ran Housing and Urban Development (HUD) twenty years ago and got his start as a prosecutor somewhere in Georgia following in Daddy's footsteps. Likely Granddaddy's too.

O'Connor had not been the secretary of HUD—he was more powerful than that. He served as the chief of staff. As was always the case in the city, a powerful chief of staff called the shots. He was making it known to his colleagues along the bar that he was pissed because the housing proposal's funding levels were "prehistoric."

Slightly distracted, Jerry almost got stepped on by shark number two. Gus Franchetti was a chain-smoking, equally sized Orioles fan given his baseball cap. He was barking back at O'Connor, insisting his good friend was thinking like a ten-year-old girl, and told him that if he wanted to have the type of development he represented in Charm City, the funding had to be five times what had been proposed. O'Connor was clearly not happy that his comrade was outspending him there on the spot.

Jerry was enjoying the two circling each other and then heard a commanding voice behind him.

"Coffee boy!"

He turned and smiled at Helen as she slid his cup to him. Helen kept going to meet a young woman at the end of the bar wearing lipstick that wasn't quite right. It was an unusual shade of brown that made her look as if she had done her best to look put-together but just couldn't pull it off.

Well, he thought, *I guess even the ladies have their share of misfits.*

Jerry took a long draw from his coffee cup, enjoying the strong, unadulterated taste he needed to keep going. He turned and surveyed the two carnivores.

"Fellas," he said, "I agree with you. If we can get that kind of money behind this, I could even get my small public housing project done back home."

The two bowling pin men looked at each other and appeared to look underneath their shoes to figure out where the hell that voice was coming from.

They laid their dark, lifeless eyes on the Congressman squeezed in between them, and both turned their girth toward him to amplify their size.

Gus decided to break protocol and address the freshman Congressman. "Don't go too heavy on the coffee, dear boy. We don't want you getting out of hand tonight. Bold choice. But I am glad you are on board. We can make that happen if you do your part."

Sean winked at his longtime partner. He wanted a piece of this too. "Ah, Congressman. It is good to see the newbie is with us." He continued in a more formal voice. "I am confident our folks can help you get that off the ground and make your people happy back home. Let's get that appropriation up where it belongs."

Jerry nodded to the two goliaths and decided not to press his luck. With one last glance at Helen the bartender, who was still chatting with bad-lipstick-girl, Jerry scooted along. He assumed they were tasked to count noses. Not that they needed his vote, but insurance is always good if it didn't cost them or their buddy, Chairman Perry. The same chairman who had failed to remember his name.

That feeling of a successful engagement with the big boys evaporated when he saw the next wave of young blue bloods move toward the bar.

There he is. The prize. But wait, what? What is she doing here? He was supposed to be alone!

CHAPTER 8

Jerry's plan had become more complicated. Instead of a steady drive through the country, the evening turned into a lap on the NASCAR track at Watkins Glen. The roll cage rattled under the stress, and the tires strained to keep their grip. Jerry's heart was pounding, and he was struggling to keep his composure.

Abigayle Sullivan. Local girl made good. Jerry certainly remembered her from back upstate. But this was an unexpected development that could change his plans.

Why was she on his *arm? Please. Not him. Really? He was supposed to be alone.*

Jerry tucked himself into a small school of Cudas and peered through the crowd. The young blue blood commanded the room, stinking of old money. Jerry could almost touch him. He would take care of him soon enough. But Abigayle? He may need to recalculate. But this was supposed to be the night!

Jerry needed to refocus. He took stock of the man parading past him. The guy sported a beautiful, expensive suit, black, polished shoes, and a smashing shirt. But alas, the tie. The tie. Disappointing. They swept past the prying eyes and pulled up to a spot by the bar that magically appeared as they approached. Helen the bartender stepped up ready to serve when her male counterpart blocked her and smiled at the couple.

"Good evening, Mr. Hawthorne. You look well."

Only a slight nod was returned.

The barkeep swirled around and unlocked the private oak cabinet directly above the mirror behind the bar. As with the other Good Samaritans across the country, certain folks had their own stash, labeled for others to envy. The black chain and lock on Hawthorne's large cabinet made enough noise to prick one's ears and make them turn. The barman dusted off the bottle with the label adorned with an old man lighting a cigar and spun it in his hands so all could see the Van Winkle bottle clearly. Yes, he made a real show of it for all to watch.

The four-thousand-dollar bottle of scotch impressed Franchetti. Jerry watched him lick his lips and pan the crowd for approval of such a wise choice of drink. Others around the bar got the message.

Jerry heard Franchetti whisper under his breath. "Man is so freaking rich he can literally drink money and piss it away an hour later."

Jerry smiled. *Just a little fish now, aren't we, Gus?* He faded into the crowd. He wasn't quite ready to engage. He needed a moment to figure out how this was going to work with Abigayle in the picture. He drew a deep, calming breath and took stock of himself in the mirror. He was pleased—a decent suit with just the right tie. He glanced down to look over his shoes. They could be mistaken for old-school and generational. Back in the mirror, he gazed at his own blue eyes and smiled. Yes, the tie would rival the old blue bloods' ties. She would notice the tie—guaranteed.

Hawthorne was commanding a growing crowd, and he and his girl disappeared behind waves of blue suits. Jerry didn't have to worry about being noticed now. He needed to turn his attention to what he was here to do, and not to be distracted—even by her.

CHAPTER 9

It was the streak of red that caught Skylar's eye—a short, red dress on a beach-ready body topped with light, strawberry-blonde hair. Something deep in Sky started to jump, and she took a step forward before she knew what she had done.

It can't be, she thought. *She went home—back upstate—broadcast journalism or something.*

As if on cue, the woman driving the red dress turned and locked on her with sharp, dazzling amber eyes.

Skylar started to blush, for real this time. *Shit. It is you.*

"Skylar! Oh my god, Skylar Nicholson!" the woman squealed. She let go of her man's arm, ran toward Sky, and gave her a long, lingering hug. "How are you, sister?"

"Abby? I can't believe it! What are you doing here? I thought you were upstate."

"We just opened an office in Alexandria," she said. "I'm here setting it up. Oh my god, *it is so good to see you!*"

The two women were still in an extended sorority-sister embrace when Sky opened her eyes and noticed that Helen was giving her a concerned look from behind the bar. *Uh-oh*, the look whispered. *Are you okay?*

Sky squinted back at Helen with a confused look of her own. *Of course I'm okay. She's an old college friend. Why wouldn't I be okay?* Helen motioned with her head toward the other end of the bar as she scooped ice into a row of empty glasses. *Because*, Helen's eyes screamed, *incoming*.

As she relaxed her embrace with Abby, Skylar watched her ex-husband cut in front of both of them to tap Abby's date on the shoulder. The two men shook hands and started a little reunion of their own. Sky's heart fell from her throat to the bottom of her gut in an instant. *Him. Of course. I guess I'm part of the play tonight.*

"Sky," Abby said as she pulled her toward the bar, "let me introduce you to Tyler. Honey? Honey, I need to interrupt your bro-moment. This is Skylar Nicholson. We were Alpha Chi sisters at UVA. Sky, meet Tyler Hawthorne"—she paused for mock emphasis—"the third, or something."

"The original, actually," the man said, "but no introduction necessary. We go way back. Well, look at this! Little Sky, all grown up." Skylar's intuition shifted into overdrive as she made the connection. *Oh, Abby*, she thought. *You are in way over your head.*

"You two know each other?" Abby said. "That's wild."

"We sort of grew up together," Tyler replied. "Way back, our families used to share a house up at the lake every summer—for a few years, anyway."

He took a sip of his drink. Abby looked at Sky's face. Something inside of her winced.

"That's, um," she said to Tyler. "That's interesting. Small world." Her date rescued her.

"Oh, it was a long time ago. So Sky, what have you been up to? I'll be seeing Caroline in a few weeks, and when she hears I saw you, she'll want to know everything."

Skylar never had a chance to answer as her ex-husband joined their conversation, carrying three drinks. "You have before you, brother Hawthorne, the former Senior Washington Correspondent for *The New York Times*. I say 'former' because she was fired not too long ago for slandering a United States Senator. Hello, sweetheart. I would have grabbed an extra-large old-fashioned, but I figured you might have already blown through their brandy." Abby spun around and stared at Chip, appalled.

"It's okay," Sky said, "he does that sometimes on account of his very small penis."

Tyler Hawthorne laughed so hard that he seemed about to spit his drink across the bar. "Awesome," he said, shaking his head. "Haven't changed a bit."

"Abby," Sky said, "I'm sure you remember Chip Taylor, *former* husband of mine, *present* Metro section editor at *The Washington Post*, and an *eternal* burden to everyone he meets. If he didn't make a great brandy old-fashioned, he'd have been dead a long time ago. Hello, darling." Chip nodded at Abby.

"Yes," Abby said with a frown. "Of course." She looked him over with a cold, emotionless stare.

"Actually, Tyler," Sky said, "I'm now with a digital news service called *The Thread*. One hundred percent online content, zero corporate bullshit."

"Well," Tyler said, "that's where the industry is headed. Congratulations."

"If," Chip interjected, "you like gossip."

Abigayle Sullivan had heard enough. She handed her drink to Sky so she could use both hands for what came next. She thrust her index finger directly into the man's chest and started to poke it. Hard. "Is that so, Chip? Because I run one of the largest strategic communications firms in this hemisphere, and you people are at the bottom of the list whenever I need to recommend a news brand people trust."

"Sure you do," Chip said with a snort.

Tyler looked at his feet. "Um, Chip, be careful. She knows what she's—"

Abby shushed her trustafarian date, raised her left hand, and began to pick both Chip and his paper apart, using a finger to emphasize each of her points. "One, your reach sucks. Two, your subscription retention is pathetic. Three, less than twenty percent of your readers—your own readers, Chip—say they would turn to you first for information in a crisis. And finally," she said as she pulled a business card from the back of her phone, "fifty percent of the D.C. Metro section is gossip-ridden drivel. Sites like *The Thread* are where all the eyeballs are going. They're going to eat your lunch. Count on it."

Chip stared at her with his mouth open. Tyler smirked as he continued to check the tops of his shoes for scuffs.

Abby held her business card between her index and middle fingers and waved it in front of Chip's nose. "Abby Sullivan, Genesis Communications. Nice to meet you. Now, if you'll excuse us, I must give your ex-wife a scoop about the Secretary of Commerce that will make your paper look like it's fast asleep. Again." She turned on her heel and headed for the ladies' room.

"Sky—I'd go, if I were you," Tyler said. "Besides, I need to buy this poor Theta brother of mine another shot. Anyway, can you calm her down for me? I didn't sign up for an MMA fight tonight."

"Sure," Sky said as she turned to have a last look at Chip. He wouldn't meet her eyes, so she went up to him, gently put her hand on his shoulder, and whispered into his left ear.

"Good night, sweetie," she said, and made her way to the ladies' room.

CHAPTER 10

Sky's mind raced as she bolted to the ladies' room. She was getting light-headed, and for once it had nothing to do with how much she had been drinking. *Chip. Abby. Tyler Hawthorne. All in one night, Jesus. And now, a scoop about Commerce? What possible trouble could the Secretary be in? The woman is a former nun!*

When she came through the door, Abby had just finished checking the stalls. They were alone. Sky tried to be the first to speak, but Abby reached out with both hands, pulled her face in, and stared directly into her eyes. She was angry.

"What the hell are you doing here?" she said. "We had a deal, *sister*." Sky pushed her away.

"What are you talking about?"

Abby frowned. "My god," she said. "You don't remember."

"Don't remember what?"

Abby reached for Sky's purse, which she had left on the bathroom sink. Sky tried to stop her but was a split-second too slow.

"That's mine," Sky said. "What the hell are you doing?"

Abby quickly unzipped the purse, fished out a small prescription bottle, and checked the label. "You know," she said, "when you buy this stuff on the street, people who actually need it can't get it."

Sky made a swipe for the bottle with one hand but missed. "That's none of your business," she said. "Give it back."

"Really? Is that how it is now—*sister*?"

Sky had her hands on her hips now. "You're one to talk," she said. "Where'd you find Tyler? Didn't you learn anything in college?"

Abby smiled. "Plenty—most of it from watching you. Besides, is it so bad if I choose to play with someone who is both financially and physically well-endowed?"

"I suppose not. But it doesn't end well. You know that. For him, or for you. It never does."

It was Abby's turn to put her hands on her hips. "Look who's talking about bad endings—the *former* Mrs. Chip Taylor. Besides, it's not like I'm marrying the guy. It's only our second date."

Sky reached out and picked her purse up off the ladies' room vanity. "Sorry I mentioned it. Anyway, I'm fine, Abby. Just surprised to see you."

Abby shook the pill bottle until the rattling sound echoed against the bathroom's tile walls. "Not so fine," she said.

"They help me think in the morning," Sky said. "That's all."

"I'll bet," Abby said. "Especially during a monstrous hangover."

That was enough for Skylar Nicholson. "Oh, so you're swooping in to save me now—is that it? I don't hear from you during the worst two years of my life—and NOW you show up. To lecture and criticize while you're whoring your way from one end of D.C. to the other. Fuck you."

"Don't talk to me like that," Abby said. "I'm here because I care about you."

"Then mind your own business!"

Abby stepped forward and lifted Sky's chin with one finger until she could stare into her eyes. Sky was so surprised that she offered no resistance.

"Here's your scoop, Sky. We ran into each other just two nights ago. I told you why I had been out of touch. I told you about all the sisters in the area who called me to tell me you're spiraling again. I reminded you of how, all those years ago, you saved my life and that I would always be here for you. Always."

Sky didn't move. Tears began to stream down her face.

"So here I am. And you don't remember any of it, do you? What does that tell you?"

Abby dropped her finger from Sky's chin, and Sky let it fall until she was staring at the tile floor. The longest silence of their friendship filled the air.

"I tell you what," Abby finally said. She pulled out a business card from her pocketbook and handed it to Sky. "Put this somewhere safe," she said, "before you black out. The odds are better you'll find it tomorrow."

"That's not funny," Sky said softly.

"I'm not joking," Abby replied. "When you're ready to get real about what's going on with you, call me."

With that, Abby Sullivan walked out of the ladies' room and left Sky alone with her thoughts.

CHAPTER 11

Sky stood at the sink, trying to salvage what was left of her mascara and her evening. *To hell with fixing the makeup*, she thought. *Just get out of here before too many people see you.* She worked the escape route out in her mind—straight out of the bathroom, past the bar and three sets of tables, hard left, and out the side entrance. If Ramon saw her in this condition, he would demand to know who was responsible for it, and Chip didn't deserve what Ramon was capable of doing to him.

The plan almost worked—she made it past the bar and the second set of tables, but after she turned, a familiar voice called out from behind her.

"Well, well... Is that Skylar Nicholson? Yoo-hoo! Skylar!"

Shit, she thought. *Of course. Thanks for the warning, Tyler.*

Thirty years of training shot through Sky's central nervous system. If anyone else at the Good Samaritan had called out to her, she would have made a fool of herself trying to make conversation. But this was a matter of muscle memory—she could ace this one in her sleep, dead drunk, or even after having just seen her ex. She turned to face the voice with a perfect, poised smile.

"Aunt Millie! Millie Hawthorne, is that you? My goodness, it is!" She leaned down to give the old woman the same peck on the cheek she had given Ramon.

"Yes, hello, child! Please, come sit." The tiny, diminutive lady with steel-blue eyes sat at a circular table guarded by a few well-heeled women of her generation. *You don't have to greet all of them*, Sky reminded herself. *This isn't your début, and Mother is not looking over your shoulder.*

Skylar squatted down next to the old woman and took her hand. "Well, look at you. Looking brilliant, out on the town, and ready to break hearts! Aunt Millie, you amaze me. And I just spoke with Tyler. He looks *great*!"

"Thank you, dear. And look at you—you are simply ravishing. How is your mother? I wanted to call you before I came back to town, but she never returned my call."

"Oh, that's strange," Sky said, "it must have slipped her mind." *Or*, Sky thought, *she can't stand you.*

"Well, that happens sometimes," Mildred said. "We're not getting any younger. Anyway—sweetheart, I heard the news, and I'm so sorry."

What else does she know? "You are too kind."

"Now, dear, listen to me. I have something to tell you." The old woman squeezed her hand gently. Skylar braced herself.

"There's still time, darling," Mildred said. "Gerald and I married late in life and had three gorgeous children. Don't lose hope."

Skylar's heart sank again. *I have got to get out of here.* She gave the old woman's hand another gentle squeeze and put on a pained, grateful face. "Thank you, Aunt Millie. It means so much coming from you."

"Well, I'm sure your mother would agree." She leaned forward, winked at Sky, and pointed at the bar. "But watch out for men like that one over there—the one standing by himself drinking coffee at this hour. Do you see him?"

"Yes," Sky said, "what about him?"

"He's a dud. You can tell just by looking at him. As he turned around just now, I expected to see a sales tag dangling from the sleeve of his suit."

Sky grinned. "Aunt Millie, for shame! Look at his lapel pin. He's a member of Congress!"

"Nevertheless, it's true. And don't pretend you didn't notice."

"Well," Sky said, "He is probably new. It's the same with every freshman, Aunt Millie. They want to look like they have done it all before, but they haven't. The strutting around just makes it worse. Now, I'm sorry, but I'm afraid I do have to run."

"I know you do, dear. It's written all over your face."

Dammit, Sky thought. *The mascara.*

"Which one is your ex? The one in the gray talking to Tyler?"

"Yes ma'am, that's him."

"You can do better—trust me on that. Give my love to your mother, and—oh dear, the dud is heading this way. Better use the side exit. Oh, and one more thing, sweetheart."

Skylar leaned down to let the old woman whisper in her ear.

"If your ex-husband should ever need to be separated from his position at the *Post*, or separated from anything else, you just let your Aunt Millie know. She'll take care of him."

Sky kissed the Hawthorne matriarch on the cheek, left the Good Samaritan through a side door, and started looking for whichever bar might call out to her in the crisp November night.

CHAPTER 12

Jerry tried to blend into the gathering crowd as the good Chairman tapped on the mike and began his speech of "thank yous" and "attaboys" to his staff and key lobbyists. Perry had to make sure those guys got credit so they could continue to be relevant in their clients' eyes and generate great sums of cash.

I wonder how much Perry raised per word of his short, insignificant speech tonight? Did anyone even care what he had to say?

Jerry continued to scan the room. He didn't bother listening to Perry's speech but was glad that it was short and sweet. His mind wandered as his eyes caught a group of grandmotherly women all draped in black gathered over the Chairman's shoulder.

The group of women reminded him of a TV show about crows. Crows are extremely smart, solve complex puzzles and remember things from long ago. They are known to have a mob mentality to defend what was theirs and could be seen gathering in the hundreds to mourn a fellow member of their flock. *Mob mentality*. Fits. Jerry chuckled to himself, but not because he was amused. Centuries ago, people had dubbed a flock of crows a murder. He loved the turn of phrase, especially tonight.

There she was, milling about with her murder of crows. Mildred Hawthorne, the Hawthorne empire's matriarch, was the queen, huddling with her fellow scavengers.

Yes, a murder of crows. A perfect description. Better than a pod of whales. Yes, he liked it much better.

Some believe the crow is a symbol of death. Jerry's temperature climbed as he thought about how her turn at death was coming. But not tonight. Tonight, Jerry was on his hunt for another member of this royal family, starting with her favorite. To achieve that, he would need to offer some appetizing bird seed. With the right level of humility and with great delicacy, he gently entered the dangerous territory occupied by Mrs. Mildred Hawthorne.

The Hawthorne empire had a broad range of business interests but was at its core a mining company. It owned and operated more than half of the coal mines in the U.S. While her late husband traveled to exotic places, Mildred was stationed at the business's helm. She was the one with the brains and the balls to keep the company successful. She was tiny—she looked like you could pick her up, sling her over your shoulder and run a full sprint with ease—but make no mistake, she was made of granite. Maybe from the same slabs that came from her mines. Folks always underestimated her—without provocation, she might reach over and castrate you in front of her friends just to prove a point.

Mrs. Hawthorne despised environmentalists, especially those who touted clean energy. Those representing anything related to environmental issues made sure to steer clear of her at these events. She would eagerly point out that those same asses benefited from her coal every day. She was quoted, or maybe more like she was caught spitting, recently in the *Post*, saying "environmentalists should be gutted alive and fed to the fishes."

Jerry found that quote quite poetic. He also knew that for such a steamboat, she was also a staunch supporter of the arts. She refused to support art in other countries, especially in Europe. Her family had made their fortune in America, and that was where they would spend it.

CHAPTER 13

Jerry's target for the night was only a few strides away. Patience. Fortune smiles on the well-prepared. The art and science of broaching the inner circle of blue bloods was dicey. Jerry despised them and knew they were never to be trusted. He understood that someone like him should have no illusions as to his place in the world. One wrong step, and he was done. He would have to go through the motions and risk being bitten in half.

Jerry had missed an opportunity only minutes ago. The woman from the bar—the one with the funky lipstick—was chatting Hawthorne up. That was a moment he didn't recognize until it was too late. It would have been a lot easier to jump in there with someone of similar station in life. But the chance was gone before he knew it. Now there were two elderly women with her—swimming along in the shadow of their friend's clout. He didn't know either one, but as expected, he could tell by their coziness that they swam in the same circles.

The other women in the trio spotted his approach and tried to use their stern expressions to dissuade him. One pressed her hand on

Mildred's elbow to give a discreet heads up. But Jerry was shrewd enough to get there before they could turn.

"Pardon me, Mrs. Hawthorne." Jerry provided the respectful gesture of recognizing his intrusion to all royalty involved and that he meant no harm.

"I am Congressman Jerry Sharpe, and I was hoping to get your insight into a proposal regarding a new wing at the Johnson Museum of Art." Jerry didn't wait to be interrupted. "Your contributions to that museum have been generous, of course. They are interested in expanding their impressionist exhibit, and I was curious to know your thoughts on whether upstate New York would be the right location for these exquisite pieces?"

Yes, Jerry had gone right for her ego, and had thrown on extra butter. "I assure you I am not asking for any support." This brought quiet but discernible coughs from the ladies accompanying Mildred. "I know you have made tremendous investments in many exciting exhibits and institutions including the Johnson Museum, and I am aware of your fondness for the impressionists."

Mrs. Hawthorne seemed to perk up at his introduction and acted as Jerry had expected. He watched her contemplate his name and take a long gander at her new suitor of sorts. He assumed by her smile that the suit met her approval—not flashy, traditional, certainly new. She did not hide her gesture to look over his shoes, then Jerry watched Mildred center her attention on his tie. He had searched for weeks for the perfect one. It was a gentle blue that he thought made his eyes stand out.

Jerry knew she was quick to learn he offered neither wealth nor power, but to his relief, she nodded nonetheless, apparently indicating to her friends as much as to Jerry that he may stay for the moment until she decided to move on.

"Yes, young man, I am aware of their proposal. Their collection is moderately intriguing. My father was friendly with Herbert." But she threw in the jab. "His family has done a respectable job with the Monet collection, but the Renoirs are not particularly moving."

"Indeed, Mrs. Hawthorne. My sentiments exactly. I also find they have not taken advantage of other meaningful pieces from one of my favorites, Pissarro." He paused for the intended effect. He had found a tidbit in an artsy upstate wine and cheese magazine where she had revealed her love for his work and her desire to bring more pieces to America so others could see and appreciate her taste.

Mildred nodded with approval.

Jerry proceeded gently into the next layer to see whether she was ready to truly engage. "I would think, given the region's history and connection to the women's movement, that Pissarro's work would have a particular impact and meaning and be the right direction to pull the museum's entire collection together."

Her nose perked up and she took a sip from her champagne, studying his eyes as she spoke.

"I would certainly agree. If you can convince their team to pursue this direction, I think you would be wise to take advantage of their proposal, Mr. Sharpe."

Jerry understood the jab in her not using his title and watched her body language. She was getting ready to pass him off.

"Thank you, Mrs. Hawthorne. I hear that your son is interested in the arts. I represent the region, and he could…"

Her eyes peeked over Jerry's shoulder. "Oh, Tyler! Tyler! Come here and meet this interesting young man."

Yes, timing is everything.

CHAPTER 14

Tyler was rumbling toward them, and he did not look at all pleased. His jacket glistened—he clearly had gotten a drink thrown at him. He was storming out when his mother stopped him.

Jerry noticed he was missing a special accessory. Abigayle was not on his arm. In fact, she was nowhere to be seen. This was exactly what he needed. Perhaps the first problem had solved itself.

Tyler leaned into Jerry to immediately intimidate him in an attempt to scare him off. Jerry was surprised for a moment—the man was a lot bigger up close. His chest was the size of a whisky barrel, and his bulging arms looked like legs stuffed into his suit. He still had his rich man's drink in his right hand.

"Mister—I mean Congressman—Jerry Sharpe, this is my oldest, Tyler. And wait, where is your young lady friend? Didn't you two just get back from our little horse ranch?"

Jerry understood the message. The Hawthorne family was wealthy, your son and Abigayle are together, and he was a small fly on the ass of an elephant.

Remember your place, Jerry.

"Mother, never mind that gold digger. She was just a little fun for me. That's all. She's back there hanging with the waiters." Tyler seemed to regroup a bit from his apparently bitter end with Abigayle and kissed his mother gently on the cheek.

"A pleasure to meet you," Jerry interrupted politely and shook hands aggressively with Tyler, who juggled his drink rather effortlessly to engage with Jerry.

Jerry knew the clock was ticking now. He needed to get Tyler alone, and quickly. "Mrs. Hawthorne was providing her insight into some art investments to consider—we both seem to have an affinity for the more obscure impressionists. What is your take on Pissarro?"

This had the desired effect—Jerry wanted to get Tyler's defense systems online—he could tell Tyler didn't like his tone—and he would worry that a small-time Congressman was only hunting money.

"Jerry, my boy, I am not familiar with his work. I am more of a Van Gogh fan. You know, like the water lilies."

Jerry caught a knowing and warning eye from Mildred. He knew Mildred would not embarrass her son, but the look was more to remind Jerry not to embarrass him either.

He went for it anyway. It was the only way.

Jerry wanted to ruffle some feathers. Or better yet, steer the whale into shallower water—a bit easier to handle. He also wanted to return the spiteful tenor of Tyler's address to him.

"Tyler, respectfully, the Waterlily Pond is beautiful, yes, but it is the work of Monet, not post-impressionist Van Gogh."

As expected, Tyler was not pleased by the correction in front of his art-loving mother and immediately went on the offensive.

"Sharpe, right? Art is my mother's passion. Art is for women and gays. My passions are the finer things in life—things real men can appreciate. Beautiful women, expensive suits, antique cars, this bourbon." Tyler didn't wait for a response. "You know, things you might not have seen before."

Tyler looked over Jerry's suit with a cocked eyebrow and then directly into his eyes. "Brooks Brothers, perhaps? Well, it turns out that Tom Ford is a family friend." Then, taking a second to pat Jerry's shoulder, he said, "And he had this baby made just for me. What do you think?"

Jerry didn't have to look at Mildred. He knew she understood her part of the game was over, and she needed to leave this insignificant man to his doom with big, sweet Tyler. She gracefully excused herself and retreated to the safety of the blue blood circle behind her, away from the unfolding bravado.

Tyler turned to Jerry with an unexpected smile on his face. "Congressman Sharpe now, is it? I do remember you, you know. Moving on up from a deputy prosecutor to Congressman. I hope there aren't any hard feelings and that our family can continue to count on you and your support in your new role here. Your predecessor understood that very well."

Jerry steamed beneath his forced smile, but he tried to keep himself from looking weak and afraid. He knew exactly what kind of man was standing in front of him. He had to bury that case years ago when "the family" had his boss close down the investigation on Tyler. The two sorority sisters dropped their charges and transferred to another school, but the fraternity boy in front of him had never grown up, never changed. But of course, the county hospital had gained a new emergency intake center named after the Hawthornes.

Hawthorne knew he had struck a nerve, and was ready to launch a larger volley to bully Jerry. But Jerry had a plan. He could open up the engines a bit now. It was a familiar act, and exactly what he was counting on tonight. He needed Tyler to continue bullying him. He wanted Tyler to kick and spit at him the rest of the evening.

After another ten minutes or so, Jerry couldn't take another story about all the custom suits Tyler had personally picked up in London at Tom Ford's home over the years. He didn't want to hear about any more of his conquests either.

What a pompous prick.

The coffee was wearing off. Fast.

CHAPTER 15

If Tyler Hawthorne had put on a decent tie, Jerry might have let him off. Nope. He deserved so much for all he had done. The arrogant smirk Tyler cast to show he was playing with his food didn't help either. Jerry needed to set the hook.

While he managed to keep the conversation going with Tyler, Jerry reflected on his own life back at the Glen, the bottom of Seneca Lake, the bottom of New York. The region's bottom dweller. Not much to speak of, really. Jerry winced inside—winters sucked, summers were full of blue bloods who didn't care about the locals. His kind was the help, and there wasn't a whole lot to do with your time.

Then there were the likes of the Hawthornes. Tyler and his extracurricular activities at the College in Syracuse. *How do these people get away with everything? That's right—money and power. Lots of it.*

Jerry shook his self-pity away and dove in, trying to move the discussion forward to set up the bait. "I was lucky to learn about engines when I was a kid—cars, outboard and inboard motors for boats. Even smaller engines like snow blowers or generators."

Tyler was going down the dark path Jerry had hoped for. "A working man, huh? How on earth did you become a law man? Did you earn enough for community college? I bet you and your buddies know a lot about muscle cars."

Jerry knew he hadn't spent his summers frolicking on the lake like ol' Tyler here or even Abigayle, for that matter. He had toiled in the garages at the racetrack, fixed outboards for all the vacationing rich folks who had managed to break their drive shafts showing off on the wakes. "I worked on some great race cars at the track, and some fabulous boats—even your late father's boat a couple of times as a kid."

Tyler saw an opportunity. "Dad always said the help upstate was pretty good but complained about having to keep coming back to get it fixed. But you managed to get things fixed, didn't you, buddy?"

Jerry's rage was being replaced with excitement. Things were going as planned. This was the guy he had wanted to meet face-to-face for too long, and now here he was, in the flesh. He needed to get Tyler outside—to get this rich, arrogant fuck away from the pod of blue bloods so Jerry could take care of him.

"I did work on a few of your dad's cars too—I really liked that beautiful, perfectly preserved Mercedes. What an elegant car. That engine was amazingly tuned and was as tight as a German virgin— Guten tight." Tyler didn't get the joke. Or else he was saving his laughter for later with his buddies. "But the car I was never able to get close to was your father's '67 Jaguar. That was the coolest thing I had ever seen in my life. Would love to get behind the wheel of a car like that someday."

Jerry knew the blue blood in front of him had inherited the car. He'd seen Tyler enough times racing around town.

"Oh yeah, little buddy? You're in luck, then." Tyler's smirk showed Jerry that this was an opportunity to rub the pristine '67 Jaguar in his face.

Tyler slugged down the remainder of his drink. "A guy from your neck of the woods should see greatness at least once in his life." Tyler was no longer mincing words.

Ignoring the nasty comment, Jerry tried his best to indicate that nothing would be more thrilling than to be permitted to get close to the car. "Don't tell me you are driving that wonderful machine tonight!"

"Why don't we go around back and check my ride out?"

Tyler turned immediately and led the way out the back of the Good Samaritan to the rear parking lot. There were no lobbyists at the rear stoop—they were attached to the bar given the drinks were still free for another hour. The small lot was stacked up. Folks would have to wait a bit before they had a shot at getting their car out.

But not Tyler.

Jerry found himself with his mouth slightly ajar. Was it awe or envy? He wasn't sure which, but he was impressed. Muscle cars and 4x4s were his thing, but you couldn't help admiring the stunning green British machine sitting in its own spot, far from the door-dinging of the typical cars packed into the parking lot.

"Jesus."

"Fuck yeah, little man. Bet you never saw anything like this wherever the fuck you come from." He gently slid one finger along the Jag's leggy lines. "Hop in and check it out."

Jerry stood there for a few moments, taking the car in. It had been featured on the cover of *Cigar Aficionado* several years ago—Tyler's late father leaning against it after he had announced his retirement. The magazine did not do the British beauty justice. Not even close.

Jerry felt obliged to indulge in the magnificent car. He could not believe the interior. The leather was immaculate and original—blue bloods didn't buy anything they had to restore—and it was clear that this car had been in the family since the day it had come over from England in '67. Jerry caressed the dash and smiled. The leather was tender, which was a bit weird—almost felt like the belly of a catfish.

Tyler stuffed himself behind the wheel on the right-hand side. His body was built for a full-sized pickup or a Hummer, not a car designed for a tiny Englishman with a posh mustache. Jerry knew that the car was a way to attract the ladies, and given what had likely happened back at the bar, Tyler was going to have to start hunting again. But, as Jerry had planned, that wouldn't be the case ever again.

Tyler finished climbing in, and Jerry felt the car list to the right. Even with the strong scent of alcohol filling the car, Jerry pressed on. "How about you take me for a spin? I would love to feel the 260 horses under this beast!"

"Two hundred sixty five, and she is a lady, not a beast, little man. She will get up when she wants to."

The "little man" bit was starting to piss Jerry off. He watched Tyler crank the engine to life, and it did indeed roar like a big cat. The little wipers whisked across the windshield to clear the rain drops that had apparently dared to land on the antique. The whole effect was somewhat dampened by that stupid tie draped over the steering wheel as Tyler looked over his shoulder to make sure he was clear to stomp on the gas.

CHAPTER 16

For an owner of such a masterpiece, Tyler wasn't a very delicate driver. He slammed it out of the lot and ripped a right onto Pennsylvania Avenue. The White House disappeared instantly as Tyler got lucky and saw green at all the traffic lights. While 265 horses might be only slightly more powerful than a modern VW GTi, its engine had been a monster back in the day, and it still didn't disappoint.

Jerry managed to coax his new buddy out of downtown and onto 193 west along the Potomac to open it up. The car was quite impressive. Even though he wasn't driving it, he could tell how responsive it was to the ass behind the wheel. As he enjoyed watching the Jag gobble up the road, Jerry had a greater appreciation for what the blue bloods had—someone like Tyler, born into old wealth, got to enjoy the fine things in life. *Like this Jaguar. Like Abigayle.*

A jolt around a turn snapped Jerry into the moment. It was time to move on from this nonsense. He had his prey out alone and heading in the direction he had planned for. It was a lot easier than he thought it would be. Alcohol and arrogance were his friends tonight.

He was getting closer. He turned his attention to the item in his pocket calling out to him. He felt the weight of Old Reliable in his pocket. His beautiful folding knife pressed up against his thigh. It was well worn and broken in, but razor sharp as he was trained to keep it. Oh, how he loved the feel of the zebra bone handle—how it fit perfectly in his hand. The knife was making itself known, awakening next to him.

Jerry was watching Tyler out of the corner of his eye, catching him sneaking a peak at him to see if he revealed any envy. "Just the best, right?"

For a second, Jerry thought he might have wondered about the zebra bone out loud. But the shit-eating grin on Tyler's mug told him otherwise. Jerry cautiously slipped his hand into his pocket and palmed the knife. They were only a half mile from the turn-around at the entrance of Great Falls Park.

Scouts were always prepared.

"Absolutely—a real head-turner, Tyler. Up here on the right is an easy place to turn around—we need to get back."

"Getting car sick, little buddy?"

Tyler stomped on the brakes to try and demonstrate his driving skills but managed to bounce the beauty into the turnabout—certainly unflattering for such a lady.

"Not like driving your piece of shit Civic through the Glen, is it?"

Jerry nodded as respectfully as he could at the nasty little jab. "I am a bit woozy from the speed. Can I get out so I can catch my breath? Man, you're right, this is the most beautiful thing I have ever seen. You are one lucky man!"

Jerry eased out of the Jag and slowly worked his way to the front of the car and stood admiring the grillwork while attempting to look a little woozy. He knew Tyler would join him.

Jerry was glad there were no streetlights around—he didn't think he could hide his eager expression. He watched Tyler adjust the side view mirror before gently stroking the fender as he approached the front of the car with a grin the size of Montana etched on his face.

For someone slightly less bulky than the size of his catch, Jerry moved with the swiftness of a bird scooping up a frog in a marsh. He pretended to stumble and grasped Tyler's shoulder to steady himself.

Jerry gripped his trusty knife and drove it right into Tyler's groin, and with one gorgeous motion, gutted Tyler up and into his sternum, and swept his blood-covered hand down and to the right, and back where he'd started.

The blue blood's entrails burst from him and tumbled in front of the left headlight in a steaming pile. Blood sprayed over the elegant hood and sullied the silver cat ornament. Jerry could feel Tyler's hot blood on his hands, but Tyler held steady, gazing directly into the eyes of the man who had gutted him. For a split second, he almost looked annoyed. His grip on Jerry's forearm relaxed, then his eyes rolled, and then he drooled on Jerry's arm.

But the fun part? The blend of sheer surprise and horror in Tyler's eyes. All that wealth. His bloodline didn't matter now. He was just a slab of meat—*just like the rest of us*.

Jerry knew at that moment Tyler wasn't thinking about Abigayle. He was likely more worried about his precious lady that was now covered with his blackened blood. Jerry couldn't help himself and whispered to the dead man in front of him.

"Yes, that might leave a stain."

CHAPTER 17

Jerry's leather-soled dress shoes were not cut out for the icy Potomac. He had fished along this bend several times when wearing waders, but he now had trouble steadying himself in the current. Balance was also trickier given how the water played with his eyes in the dark.

He embraced the rush of cool air that swept down from the Blue Ridge and listened to the branches pick up their pace along the bank, dipping into the river like a rowboat's oars. He could see the rain coming—it was skittering from upriver, a shimmer in the darkness. Peaceful.

Jerry gazed down at the barrel-chested body's shocked face as he dragged it by the necktie.

Did this guy really think that accessorizing his custom suit with a cheap Chinese knock-off would make him look like the common man? Perhaps.

He scoffed, pulled the blotchy face closer to him and unceremoniously tightened the ridiculous tie around the corpse's cold, white neck. He leaned into the ghostly face and smiled as he recalled the last book he had read, a nature book about the hunting skills of the belted kingfisher—a crafty, patient ambush predator striking with such ferocity that it impaled its prey straight through.

Apropos.

Jerry peered into the eyes of his lifeless prize, smiling at the irony, or maybe just the play on words. He wiped his trusted blade clean on the so-called prince's sleeve. He was just as good a hunter as the kingfisher. Maybe better. He had just slain a member of "royalty" with precision and overwhelming power.

His train of thought was disrupted by the coming rain. First it fell softly, almost forgiving, then it started to pour. He tilted his face toward the night sky to soak it all in. The spray on his cheeks relaxed him, but not so much that it would water down the moment.

His feet were beginning to numb as the frigid water swirled around his stiffening legs. But he really didn't care. Neither rain nor icy water would spoil the orgasmic shivers bolting up and down his spine. He had waited for this moment, and he was going to cherish it as long as he could.

The limp body swayed in the rushing water and the remaining blood seeping into the water reminded him of the dark-roasted coffee he had sipped before discussing menswear with this piece of shit only a few hours earlier.

He admired the gaping midsection as the current's cleansing rush filled it to the rim. It was fine work, he had to admit—one swift, elegant move and it was done, just like he had learned as a boy. You didn't have to brutalize your prize like so many amateurs did in the field. You could quickly slice through the skin and separate it from the meat. The fats and oils made the job easier too.

You could even rip through the bone if you were an expert in how to field-dress game. You just needed two things—a steady, trained hand and a razor-sharp field knife. And he had both.

Many young kingfishers perished the same way they survived—their initial dives as fledglings would often result in their new feathers becoming waterlogged, drowning themselves before they were ready for the world. He needed to climb out of the river before he became one of them. He needed to get moving. His work was done for the night.

He let the tie slip through his fingers, then shoved his victim further into the current, just like one would when feeding bait fish with scraps left from a filet. He let the knife rinse a little more in the current, then folded the blade back into its handle.

What was left of Tyler tumbled further into the river, floating for a few moments, the tips of his Kiton shoes catching some dead leaves downriver. He smirked as he recalled a quote from earlier that night that ended with, "...should be gutted alive and fed to the fishes." The body rolled a few more times until the cavity captured enough of the river to sink it. The remains might not be found for days. They'd find only what the blue crabs failed to eat.

CHAPTER 18

When her alarm went off, Sky woke up with the taste of tequila, lo mein noodles, and vomit still mingling in her mouth. It was by far the worst hangover she'd had since finalizing her divorce, and while she had not planned on it falling on a workday, she consoled herself with the thought that the evening might have been worth it.

This was a small consolation. Every cell in her ached. Her bedroom smelled as if her body had been pumping tequila, sweat, and flatulence directly through her pores. Her contact lenses were still in, and when she tried to open her eyes, she realized that her eyelids were almost crusted shut. She could see nothing but fuzzy, bright shapes dancing in the dim shadows of her bedroom. *Well*, she thought as she plucked the lenses out of her eyes, *I finally did it. I drank myself blind.*

Skylar moved her legs off the side of the bed and used gravity to help her rotate into an upright, sitting position. She decided that soon, quite soon, she would be ready to walk to the bathroom. But not just yet. For the moment, she would ponder a few pressing questions—how she had gotten back to Adams Morgan, how she had gotten into her apartment, and how all this pain could possibly have come from stopping for one drink at the Good Samaritan after work.

She heard her phone buzz from its position on the bedside table and realized with a mixture of dread and relief that it held the answers to these questions. She picked it up and scrolled through the notifications. The reckoning was brutal—debit card charges from bars all over the district, a midnight visit to an Asian restaurant in Arlington, and ten Uber rides. Easily a $500 night, and she didn't remember any of it. *Well*, Sky thought, *I didn't drive, and I was obviously too smashed to bring home an ax murderer. It could have been worse.*

Her relief was interrupted by a text message from Eric Zimmerman, her editor at *The Thread*: **You're on this, right? D.C. networks will lead with it tonight. Be first.**

A wave of adrenaline threw Skylar off the bed and she crawled across the floor toward her makeshift home office. *First with what?* she thought. She climbed into her desk chair and checked the time. It was 12:15. She opened Slack on her phone to gauge what her editor might be referring to but found nothing, which meant either that Eric was messing with her or what he had was so hot that he had kept it away from the rest of the team. She decided to cover each option and replied:

On it. Might need home page placement.

Ok, good. 1:00 at the latest.

So whatever it is, she thought, *it's big*. Sky set her phone down on the desk and started connecting her laptop to three large screens arranged in a semicircle around her chair. She had less than an hour. The hangover would have to wait.

CHAPTER 19

Sky arranged her work so that each screen displayed a different source of information—the first, to her left, was for the publishing software at *The Thread*; the second, at center, for its social media presence; and finally, to her right, a screen for her personal accounts.

Sky could do her job this way because *The Thread* was built for the digital age. At the *Times* and the other print legacy publications, reporters spent the day chasing down a relatively small number of sources, which limited what the paper could know about a story in a given day. In the long run, this meant that the biggest news stories tended to rely on the credibility of a handful of people, which led to predictable questions from nervous editors: *How can we be sure we have the right source here? Will anyone else go on record? What else do you have?* It was a bureaucratic, political, and slow machine which spat out the same answer to its reporters every day: *come back when you have more.* It drove Sky crazy.

At *The Thread*, Sky's sources came to her via the phenomenon of social media. She still sought out sources in person, but most of her scoops came from the fact that, as she was fond of saying, she had two million volunteer investigators in D.C. armed with a pocket-sized digital camera and the hashtag #TellTheThread.

She glanced at the time—12:20—and began to work the screens from right to left. It took less than a minute to figure out that the breaking story in question was a murder. The details came in via a text from a friend in the police force:

Heads up–approx 30 y.o. w male found dead in Potomac, downstream of Great Falls. Gutted like a fish when police found him. Fancy suit, no positive ID. Btw were you out last night?

Sky moved her focus to the center screen and Twitter. She scrolled through the usual #TellTheThread posts for a Friday morning—drunk bro selfies, sightings of drunken politicians, videos of drunk drivers needing arrest—when she saw she had a direct message from @threadskyfan:

Found this on my SON'S phone. He says he got it from a friend who said some kids found the body. Kids. Finding dead bodies. #WTF #TellTheThread #GuttedInD.C.

She clicked on the attached photo and immediately had to look away. It was a picture of the uncovered victim, taken at the site where the Park Police had found him. It was obvious someone leaked the photo. An officer was standing in a position that blocked his face, but she could see that the victim's belly had been cut wide open, leaving a large, triangular hole. An empty, gray cavity was all that remained of where his stomach and intestines had been.

My God, Skylar thought. *This is gold.*

Sky turned to her third screen and realized that this crime would allow her to do something she had been pondering for months. She opened *The Thread's* custom publishing application and briefly thought about the risk she was about to take. One did not just gobble up prime home page space for a story, even if one was a star hire from *The New York Times* with tacit permission from one's editor.

She checked the time—12:28—and made her decision. Speed was why she came to *The Thread*. It was time. She began with a title that she knew would keep her readers coming back for more:

Is D.C. Safe?

In the next twelve minutes, Sky moved the photography sent in on Twitter from the previous week, along with an archive of images from other violent crimes committed in D.C. that year, into what would become a permanent fixture of *The Thread's* home page—a news hub for all who cared to follow the details of violent crime in the D.C. area. A semi-blurred photo of last night's victim was the largest feature on the home page, with #IsDCSafe? covering the body in large block letters.

The lede wrote itself. While D.C. had long been dangerous in places, over the past six months, there had been an increase in crimes touching readers in *The Thread's* core demographic—young, well-educated, ambitious, and overwhelmingly white. Few had any personal experience with violent crime, but all were capable of thinking that one day, they, too, could be found floating face-down in the Potomac.

Sky's piece was a rallying cry and a demand for those in power to pay attention. The gruesome murder was the last straw, she said—*Thread* readers had a duty to one another and to the general public.

They would share what they knew, and use #TellTheThread and #IsDCSafe to do it. *Be our eyes and ears*, she asked, before ending her short piece with five hashtags:

#GuttedInthePotomac

#TellTheThread

#DemandAnswers

#WhereIsTheMayor

#D.C.StatehoodNow

Her army would know what to do with them.

Sky hit "publish" at 12:40 and found herself staring at an error message: *Please contact system administrator.* She hopped onto Slack and sent a direct message to Craig—it was the only kind of message he ever responded to.

Craig, it's Sky

Lol I know

I'm on deadline wtf

Ur trying to publish with no QA auth. What u doing?

My job. I have 5 min. Make the button work. Plz plz

Idk. Don't like this. Hackers

Cmon its me.

Maybe. Who won the 1957 World Series?

Milwaukee Braves. Push the button Craig

Winning game and pitcher?

You insult me. Game 7, 5-0 in NYC. Lew Burdette

Ok. Godspeed.

With this, Sky walked gingerly from her desk into her bedroom, vomited into an unlined wicker wastebasket, and collapsed into bed. It was 12:45, and the first of what would be thousands of direct messages had already hit Sky's Twitter account.

CHAPTER 20

When her phone rang, Sky knew exactly who was calling because there was only one person left in her life who called without texting first. She took a deep breath, tapped the green button on the screen of her phone, and closed her eyes. Her mother would speak first. She always did.

"Hello, Skylar? Are you there? Sweetheart?"

"Hi, Mom," she replied. "What's up?"

"Oh, thank goodness. I am so happy to hear your voice. Your father says I'm overreacting, of course—with him, everything is always fine. But everything isn't fine, is it? Watch the news, I tell him. You don't think I'm overreacting, do you?"

Here we go, Skylar thought. "That depends."

"Of course not." Sky's mother called her father in the next room. "Arthur! I've got Skylar on the phone. She says she's fine, but if you ask me, she sounds a bit shaky."

"Mother!" Skylar yelled back, as if her father could hear her out in Chantilly. "I'm not shaky. What happened?"

"Don't play dumb with me," her mother said. "I saw all of it on your blog this morning. And now it's all over the news."

"It's not a blog," Sky said. "It's an online news service. A blog is just—"

"Poor Aunt Millie. Can you imagine? In town visiting Tyler, and someone *kills* him! You remember Tyler. You met him when we went up to the Hawthornes' lake house. He cut his foot on a rusty soda can and had to get stitches. There was blood all over the floor. You were so upset."

"*WHAT?*" Skylar screamed into the phone. "Mom, did you just say—"

"Oh, you remember him. I know you do. You had such a great time. But to have your son killed so gruesomely... I just can't imagine. Millie called, and, well, my heart just broke for her. I just sat there and listened. I didn't say a single word for twenty minutes. Not a single word."

"Every cloud has its silver lining," her father said in the background.

Sky was speechless. *Tyler Hawthorne*, she thought. *Murdered. Holy shit.* Her mother's temper brought her attention back to their conversation.

"Arthur, shame on you! A person would be crazy not to be scared, and crazy to not call her daughter. That's all I was trying to say."

Sky couldn't believe what she was hearing. "Mom," she said firmly, "first of all, I'm 33 years old, and I can take care of myself. Secondly, why would you be scared? You lived in New York City by yourself before you met Dad, and you were ten years younger than I am now."

"That was different," her mother said.

Different, Sky thought. *Okay, time to wrap this up.*

"Sorry, Mom, I have to go. I'm at work. I'm so sorry to hear about Tyler. Please give my love to Aunt Millie."

"Oh, I did, sweetheart. When she asked for your number, I gave it to her right away. I hope you don't mind. Listen, before you talk to her, you should know something—the Hawthornes made a huge donation to the Natural History Museum for a new exhibit, and Millie has been begging me for weeks to come to some cocktail reception there in December. But I haven't had the chance to let her know we can't make it. Anyway, I'm sure she isn't thinking about that right now, but she loves you so much, and, well, she's staying downtown, so..."

Of course, Sky thought, *I get it now. Because the ten-minute drive from Chantilly is such a chore. And the phone is worse.*

"If she reaches out, I'll find the time to see her and let her know," Sky said.

"Oh, thank you, dear. Now listen. Before I let you go, are you sure we can't bring anything to Thanksgiving at your place? It's not that I don't think you can do it, sweetheart, it's just that—"

"I'm 33, Mother. Just bring Dad and your sunny disposition. I'll take care of the rest."

"Point taken," her mother said brightly. "I won't ask again. Anyway, I have to go. Please stay safe and call us if you need anything!" Then she hung up.

Sky sat in her office chair with her head in her hands. Something about the conversation filled her with dread. Her mother, once unfazed by one of the world's largest cities, was now scared of her crime-free Northern Virginia suburb. She would now have to take Aunt Millie to lunch and hear about all of this. *I was four feet from him*, Sky thought. She began to reconstruct their conversation at the Good Samaritan in her mind—what he looked like, what he said—when a single thought made her freeze.

Oh my God, she thought. *Abby.*

CHAPTER 21

Ramon picked up her call on the first ring. "Skylar—are you in trouble or something?"

"No, Ramon, I'm fine."

"I was worried, Sky. You left last night without saying goodbye. And now you are calling me at lunchtime, so…"

"I'm sorry, *abuelito*. It was a long night. I had to leave in a hurry."

"You forget that I used to be a policeman. I saw bad things happen to people. Please send word to me through the bar next time."

"I will," Skylar said. "I'm sorry. Thank you for looking out for me."

"Especially now, right?" Ramon said.

"What do you mean?" There was an awkward silence.

"Now that you're famous. You went viral! That's what they call it, right? Congratulations, my friend. I am happy for you."

Silence again. Ramon started to laugh. "Wait a minute," he said. "Did you just wake up?"

"Maybe," Skylar said sheepishly. "Is it so horrible to take a short nap after posting a story?"

"Well," Ramon said with a chuckle, "call your office. They have news for you."

"And I have news for you," she replied. "The man they found in the Potomac River was at Perry's fundraiser. I would be ready for a visit from your former colleagues if I were you."

"Ugh. Horrible," Ramon said. "And that new detective they hired is a total pain in the ass. We'll be ready. But how can you know all this?"

"Sources," she replied. "Ramon, do you remember a guy who came into Perry's fundraiser, a bit full of himself, with a pretty lady on his arm?"

Ramon laughed. "I don't know," he said. "You just described all the men who come to the Good Samaritan. What was so special about this guy?"

"His date. Red dress, blonde hair, total knockout."

"Oh, yes," Ramon said, "She was here. Nice lady. I can see why you would want to look after her."

Sky's heart filled with dread as her worst fears were suddenly made visible in her mind. "Well," she said, "she's one of my best friends, so—"

"She didn't leave with him, so don't worry about that," Ramon said with a playful tone in his voice. "They had a big argument at the bar. She threw a drink in his face and got an ovation as she stormed out, even from the old guard. She's a catch, for sure."

"That's kind of what worries me," Sky said.

"Sorry, Sky, I have to go—Carmelita has an appointment at noon in Falls Church. Will I see you tonight?"

"Maybe. I'm thinking about taking the night off."

"In other words," he said, "you'll come if you can find your friend first. That's why I like you, Skylar. You look after your friends." Ramon ended their call just as a new Slack message arrived from Eric Zimmerman:

50K retweets and 5,000 comments since 1:00 pm. Mayor's office called. Apoplectic. Say we are reckless. Threatening to sue. Nice work.

Sky tossed her phone onto her bed and started frantically searching her apartment. Her living room was an eclectic mix of second-hand furniture covered in a decorative layer of laundry, junk mail, and empty take-out containers. *My five minutes of fame can wait*, she thought. *Where is it?* As she tried to clear the remnants of last night's take-out from the living room, the lo mein noodle container's smell summoned a new wave of nausea, so she went back into the bedroom and threw herself on the mattress.

As she turned her head away from the light shining through her bedroom window, she found it. It was inside the bra she had worn the night before, which she had managed to tuck between the mattress and headboard before she passed out. Sky grabbed her phone with one hand, and the card out of the bra with the other. The card read:

Abigayle Sullivan

Partner

Genesis Communications

703.555.6312

abby@genesiscomms.com

@abbygenesis

***

When her phone rang, Abby hit the red button on her screen to forward the call to voicemail. *I don't care what that piece of shit says*, she thought, *we're through. Nobody talks to me that way—not even Tyler Hawthorne.*

The phone rang again. She forwarded it a second time. *How could a country-club kid have such bad manners?*

When her phone rang a third time, Abby lost it. She snatched the phone from the corner of her bed and began the tirade she had been preparing since she got home.

"Is this some sort of joke? I thought I made myself clear, asshole!"

There was a pause, followed by a voice she didn't expect to hear. "Abby! It's Sky. I'm so glad you picked up."

"Sky? Wow. I didn't expect—"

"Listen, I only have a minute. First of all, are you okay?"

"Sure. I'm fine. Why? What's wrong?"

"Now I have thirty seconds. Are you free for dinner tonight?"

"With you?" Abby replied. "Of course."

"Great," Sky said. "I have to sit for an interview downtown at 6, but we could meet at the Cactus Cantina at 7:30. Does that work? I can send you a link."

"Don't bother. It's right around the corner from me. Wait, did you already know that?"

"Abby, I'm a journalist. And I have Google."

"Then it's officially a girls' night," Abby said with a playful tone in her voice.

"Ugh," Sky groaned. "Abby, listen—"

"What's wrong with that?" Abby snapped.

"No, no," Sky continued. "That's all good. It's just that, well, there's something I have to tell you. Are you sitting down?"

"Did you give me permission?"

"Don't start. You may be getting a visit from the police."

Abby Sullivan gasped. "What have you done, Sky?"

"Very funny," she replied. "But this news isn't. Listen, Abby. Tyler Hawthorne was killed last night. Murdered. Brutally. I'm sorry to be the bearer of such horrible news, but I couldn't stand the thought of you hearing about it in the press, and it's everywhere now."

Sky waited a few seconds for a response. "Abby, are you there? Abby?"

"I'm here."

"I'm so sorry about this," Sky said. "Is there anything I can do to help?"

"Yes. Meet me at the Cactus Cantina at 7:30."

CHAPTER 22

The man in the mirror had grown into his looks over time, maturing out of his awkward Eagle Scout and engine geek phase to his now underestimated six-foot-plus frame that filled an Armani suit quite nicely. Jerry liked sporting the '50s look, and even occasionally donned a fedora in the rain if he remembered to grab it. He thought a fedora could be his thing, but it wasn't catching on. Outside of his trusty intern, no one commented on it.

The suit was classic in style, a nice gray with gentle blue pinstripes that you would only notice when taking a closer look. The double-vent jacket gave him a more sophisticated look, or at least he thought.

Jerry looked deep into his own cool blue eyes, reflecting on the previous night and all that had happened. Or, as he would often say as a "friendly amendment to that last comment," what he had *made* happen.

He didn't mind ditching his suit last night, given it was a Macy's special, and after spending time in the river, it was useless anyway. The only things he would miss were the shoes. He had adored those well-worn, old-school cap toes.

Jerry glanced down at the new, black wingtips, then gave the lapels a nice tug to straighten the lines along his chest. He nodded to himself, pleased with how his hard-earned track star body filled his expensive suit.

He evaluated his small office and was disappointed that the only thing on the walls that might impress his constituents was the news coverage of his win just a year ago. He didn't appreciate the fact that his victory story in the *Review & Express* shared the top fold with a picture of two men draped in floppy-eared winter hats, smiling back at him with a pair of coyotes strapped over the pickup's hood. "Local boy goes to Washington" was placed right next to "Schuyler coyote hunters exceed quota."

No charges for those two knuckleheads, and no other coverage of my victory.

Given that the rest of District 23 included Ithaca, Corning, and a splattering of small towns across the Finger Lakes' southern tips, he should have expected as much. He had competed for space with the obits in the *Ithaca Journal* last November.

A rap on the door woke him from his quick mental trip upstate. "Jerry? Christopher just showed me that story about the man killed last night. The one they found in the river this morning. Did you know it was Tyler Hawthorne? Terrible, even for that horrid family."

"Yes, Jane. Chris showed it to me a few minutes ago—he almost lost his lunch when he saw the pictures. Those crabs crawling all over him were super gross."

"Who would do such a horrific thing?"

Jerry nodded without looking at her. "Quite right, Jane, who would do such a thing to such an upstanding citizen?" He cleared his throat. "What time do we expect our friends from upstate? We have work to do."

Jerry watched as Jane considered him for a moment. She was a snappy dresser too. Always looked put together. Her eyes gave her away. She was a bit concerned over his lack of empathy for anyone left in the river like that. She flashed three fingers at him and turned to return to her desk. Jane, his mother's best friend, had taken care of Jerry in his darkest hour, taking him in after his mom's death. He was grateful she had volunteered to come to D.C. to work in his office when he won because there was no one else he could trust. For all purposes, she supported him as his mother would have, but he could never bring himself to call her Mom. They agreed long ago that Jane would be enough.

Jerry checked that his office door was closed then turned to the shadow box on his coffee table displaying scouting awards. He opened the glass cover and returned his trusted bone-handled knife to its rightful place—center-stage among the awards and merit badges, the last gift his mother had given him.

The display reminded him that he came from Nowhere, USA. Upstate New York was rural and poor. He had lived a small-town life. But Jerry knew he was different from the rest of the townsfolk. His mother's unsolved murder in a town with little scandal made him feel like he was in a movie. He didn't miss the quick glances from folks on the street when he was a kid—to him, the whole town seemed to know what had happened to his mom, and they never wanted to look him in the eyes. He didn't want to look at them either.

Last night was a long but successful hunt. Jerry rocked forward in his chair and leaned down to open the steel fire safe under his desk. He pulled out its contents, which included an old picture and a three-ring binder. He sat quietly as he held the picture up where the light was better. His mother's gorgeous and loving eyes looked back at him. The picture was from her senior year in high school, a few years before he had come along. She was stunning and full of life.

He returned the photo and plopped the binder down on his desk, considering whether he should flip through it again. He already knew what was in it. He had memorized it. He called the binder his murder book. It was a copy of the file on the investigation of his mother's death. It had taken years to get his hands on it, and months before he could gain the courage to look at it, especially the pictures. After several tries, he was able to get through it and understand what it meant. Each time he looked it over, he trembled as he remembered that awful day.

No one had ever been able to explain what happened. The file was lacking in any real evidence, and it did not offer any theories or motives, let alone any potential suspects. Anything of real substance had been redacted. That in and of itself implied there was much more to this story. But there was no proof. Nothing concrete, and it was clear there was little follow-up to the investigation. Jerry suspected it had been a cover-up, and he'd been unable to discover anything more when he'd been a prosecutor back in the day.

The evidence was limited. No fingerprints, and while the wounds were consistent with a .38 caliber pistol, no gun was found at the scene, nor had one ever been recovered. The locals had pored over the house with nothing to show for it. Hundreds of pictures were taken, but nothing had materialized, and the murder remained unsolved.

A few months ago, Jerry found what he thought was the smoking gun, so to speak. He was reviewing several copies of the list of individuals interviewed after the murder. Most names were those of neighbors in the area to ask whether anyone had seen or heard anything. Not a peep. The list included Jane and her husband John, several employees at the hospital, and two redacted names. The heavily redacted notes implied there had been an incident at the hospital before her death, but no details followed. Having Jane and John on the list was curious enough, but neither had offered anything helpful to the police. They were both always uncomfortable discussing what had happened, but he knew there was more to be discovered.

It was the two redacted names that were of most interest. It had occurred to him that he had multiple copies of the list of interviewees. As he compared the copies, one of them had only one name fully redacted from the list. The other name was M. Hawthorne.

Jerry's juices ran hot again. The Hawthornes either killed or arranged for his mother to be killed. The blue blood family's power and money made sure none of it came to light. But why would they care about Mom? At this point, did it matter why? They had to go.

The rush of last night was gone, and it was replaced with rage that burned in his stomach. He needed a release.

CHAPTER 23

Jane's voice chirped from the intercom. "Mr. Dominico and Mr. Savage are here for your three o'clock, dear."

"Thank you, Jane. I'm just finishing something up. I'll be out in a few."

"Are you okay? You sound… Well, you shouldn't keep our boys waiting too long."

The tiny waiting room was poorly decorated. There was a torn couch, two chairs, a wobbly coffee table, and a slim receptionist's desk, where Jane sat quietly greeting the two or three guests he received each week.

He thought about the two turds waiting in his lobby. Francis "Frankie" Dominico, the only guy who seemed to own property in Montour Falls, was joined by Mr. Jim Savage, who ran the seedy Clipper Inn on the town's border with Watkins Glen. Jerry had more than his fair share of run-ins with Jim over the years. There was even an evening when they exchanged blows over a comment Jim made about his mother. Well, one blow, really. Jerry had crumpled Jim's nose in front of half the town, and it had pointed slightly to the right ever since. While the two men were by no means the most upstanding citizens in his district, they had made the trek to D.C. to see Jerry about the public housing project they were so desperate to get done. He felt like this visit showed that he was somebody. But he was having trouble controlling himself. These two morons were visiting to plead with him to get something they wanted. This was the first thing he was able to complete for the district. He finally could bring home the bacon. But he didn't really care today. Someone else was top of mind.

The Congressman strode through the entrance and reached down deep for his well-practiced smile. He leaned in with an open hand to greet his guests.

Frankie was fat from frequent visits to the donut shop built less than a year ago, and he was popping out of his ill-fitting suit as he took Jerry's hand. Frankie's tie was poorly knotted and may have been used as a napkin earlier that morning.

Jim took his time getting up, much to Frankie's dismay, and gave his typical limp-ass handshake, clearly not wanting to spend a second more than necessary on this visit. Jerry gave him a hefty squeeze, just enough to hurt. Jim's nose was still bent—it hadn't healed right and he'd likely never seen a surgeon to fix it. Now it was starting to lose its color. That gave Jerry a little comfort.

Jim was dressed as if he were selling a Yugo on a screeching hot day in August. Crumpled khakis, a belt at least three sizes too long, a shit-brown corduroy sport coat with elbow patches that smelled of his pack-a-day habit, and a yellow, short-sleeved golf shirt, unbuttoned. One button was hanging on by a thread and dangled at the bottom of the "V."

Jerry got the message. He wondered if another jab might knock some sense into him, or better yet, fix his nose. "You boys find the office okay? They're still renovating the upstairs to move us into a permanent space, you know. I'm just glad we could squeeze you both in today. The calendar keeps getting out of control."

"Well, we found the cafeteria three times as we screwed around upstairs, but we got here." Jim waved his arm toward the hallway. "I guess it is nice to have those vending machines right there."

Jerry ignored the cheap shot and gestured his guests inside. Jerry knew that freshman Congressmen got the worst real estate in the building.

Frankie spotted a plaque on the wall and pointed at the black-and-white picture next to it that included him at the donut shop groundbreaking. "I have that same picture on my office wall. That donut shop, especially those damn Boston Cremes, have not been good to me. Oh! By the way, sir, I love your tie."

Clearly ignoring his colleague and the brown-nosing, Jim threw the blueprints on the small, round coffee table, knocking over the shadow box. While the glass didn't shatter, the collection of badges and the knife tumbled onto the floor. Jim was not happy about his self-created distraction and found himself embarrassingly falling to his knees to clean it up.

From what felt like a secret room, Chris, Jerry's valiant intern, swooped in the moment he heard the crash. The recent college grad was down on the floor collecting the awards and scout paraphernalia and casting a knowing smile to Jim, his grin saying, "Don't worry. I got this."

Jim stood up, thankful for the rescue, and turned his attention to the Congressman.

"Sorry, Jerry. Your boy here looks like he has it under control."

Jerry considered crushing the prick's nose again for his continued insolence but hung in there and offered his best "no problem" smile and leaned over the plans now sprawled over his tiny table, but with a watchful eye on Chris, as he fumbled with the award.

While the two guests examined the blueprints with him, Jerry watched as Chris gently replaced the ribbons and badges into their proper spaces. His palms sweated a bit as he watched Chris stand up straight and palm the knife with a rather perplexed expression. He watched Chris roll the knife as he looked over the carvings in the handle, and he seemed to run his finger along the flat of the blade.

"Chris, I think we are all set," Jerry said, interrupting Chris's unfolding curiosity. "Put that stuff down, and I'll take care of it later."

His faithful intern seemed a bit confused as he was almost done with the shadow box. This was the prized possession in the room. He stood there with the knife in his hands, not sure what to do next. Jerry gave him a reassuring smile and nod. Chris gently laid the knife and a few badges on a side table and made a silent exit to provide the men privacy.

"See here, Jerry, we have everything ready to go. Permits done, surveys complete, and we even put a barrier of sorts along here and here to minimize dust at my fine establishment next door." His boney fingers traced the property lines between the site and the Clipper Inn.

Frankie jumped in, his tone respectful. "Yes, Congressman Sharpe, I think we have our ducks in a row. The only thing we need now is the HUD money to get this started."

"Well, boys, I'm working hard to make it happen, and I think I'm almost there. The vote is next week, and I think we'll have good news when it's all said and done. I've chatted with the Chairman and his people, and everything looks good."

The two men looked at the blueprints again. They had come all the way down here to do their show and tell. They took turns swinging from the Congressman to the blueprints, as if there were something they needed to do next to show it was a worthy project.

Jim broke the awkward silence. "Jesus, Jerry. You couldn't have told us that when we called last week? The drive sucked coming down here."

Frankie interrupted. "Congressman, we are grateful for your work and support on this project. Once you have secured the funding, we'll be thrilled to have you come home and host a groundbreaking."

Jerry turned his attention from the sweaty, fat man to Jim. He had had enough. The ass didn't know he'd gotten it done just last night. He leaned into Jim's space. Having five or six inches on him helped make the right impression. Jerry's face reddened, and he could feel a new fire burn inside. "Listen here, you little fuck. I could just as easily take that money and level your piece of shit crack shack and send you and your broken-down hookers to jail. Either way, you can get the fuck out."

Frankie moved faster than his body would imply, rolling up the prints and glaring at his business partner. He stepped between the two men and bowed his head and shook the Congressman's hand with the vigor of a man who just wanted to escape. "No matter the weather, we'll have a groundbreaking ceremony as soon as we get the good news. I'll arrange for your travel when we're ready. We'll take care of everything. Thank you so much, Congressman. Montour Falls will be so happy to hear this news!"

Frankie unceremoniously grabbed Jim's left triceps and with a surprisingly tough grip for a fat little man, led him out and through the waiting area.

"Jane—excuse me—Mrs. Robertson! It's good to see you. You look lovely as always! I'll be sure to give the folks back home your best!"

Jerry didn't escort them to the door. But he took great pleasure in overhearing Frankie say, "You are such a dumbass. You want him to bust you up again?"

Jerry made sure his door made the necessary crash to put an exclamation point on their departure. He spun around and could not wipe the grin off his face. Other than kicking around his one intern on Thursdays and bank holidays, he didn't get to bully people very much. Folks back home would hear about this one!

CHAPTER 24

OPINION

Fair Warning

We will not be ignored, Mr. Mayor.

By Skylar Nicholson

@skythread

I was face-to-face with Tyler Hawthorne at the Capital Grille on the night he was murdered, gutted, and dumped in the Potomac River. We spent some time doing the standard schmoozing and networking that people in this town do on a Thursday night. It was a nice evening, and I hope the only time I will have cocktails with a man hours before his death.

This one hurt, *Threaders*, I'm not going to lie, and not because we already knew each other before our conversation last night. It hurts more because if you think about it, any one of us could have been Tyler Hawthorne. Education is no protection. Proximity to power is no protection. Wealth is no protection. (And apparently, the Metropolitan Police Force is no protection.) **#DCisNotSafe.**

Earlier today, I laid out what D.C.'s finest know—and don't know—about this case and those that came before it. Thank you for your spirited comments, which have been met with shock and derision by both the Mayor's office and the few members of Congress who bother to think about the citizens of this city anymore.

You read that correctly. When pressed to explain the administration's lack of a coordinated response to the recent crime spree, a source high up at the Mayor's office, who has asked to remain anonymous, told me, "These were all sad and regrettable random acts. Try raising two kids in Anacostia with bullets flying around every single night. That's what the mayor and the police chief are focused on. Every day."

By all means, Mr. Mayor, protect that family in Anacostia. But with a $753 million budget and a team of 3,800 officers armed to the teeth, I think the average D.C. resident can be forgiven for expecting their city government to handle more than one problem at a time.

And—by the way—who pays for that government? It isn't the desperate family in Anacostia (thank goodness), and it isn't the Tyler Hawthornes of the world, or their accountants, or their tax lawyers. They live outside of the District and exploit a tax code which was largely written for their benefit.

Who does that leave? The people who are up in arms about Tyler Hawthorne's murder. Us.

You remember us, don't you, Mr. Mayor? We were your unpaid interns after graduate school. We got your coffee. We picked up your lunch order. We made your PowerPoint presentations. We stayed at the office into the early morning hours negotiating with other staffers so you could get that funding into that bill you've already forgotten about. (Some of us also said nothing when we got our asses pinched by men who controlled our careers.)

We all know that the little guy gets screwed in this country—in

Anacostia, in Flint, on the south side of Chicago, and in West Virginia coal country. It's not right, and many of us came to D.C. to fix it.

This week, though, thousands of well-educated, hardworking D.C. residents woke up to the realization that despite decades of hard work, they—no, we—are still the little guy. We did what we were supposed to do—pursue higher education, show deference to authority, pay our professional dues—but decades later, we are still the little guys. Disposable, debt-ridden, and shit-upon.

Mr. Mayor, you shut down the only working group between the District and Congress that could solve this problem. And now we're supposed to sit back and be silent as our friends are getting sliced up and gutted? While you do nothing? I don't think so.

This is a fair warning, Mr. Mayor. Pay attention. We are not as disposable as you think we are.

#DCGeneralStrike #WalkOutDC #IsDCSafe #DCisNotSafe #Resign

CHAPTER 25

Sky climbed into her Uber at 6:45 and headed up Wisconsin Avenue toward the Cantina. She was exhausted. The afternoon had been a blur of meetings, phone interviews, and real-time updates to *The Thread*. #IsDCSafe—the story and the hashtag—had exploded. A team of six people now sorted through thousands of messages from readers who were angry, scared, and demanding answers. The comments section alone was now a political hurricane bearing down on the mayor's office and Congress. *Thread* contributors started to use graphic usernames to emphasize their theories about the crime— names like *guttedinthe202*, *deadTy3606*, and *allknottedup* caught her attention quickly.

Sky had lost any desire to look at her phone, so she spent the ride admiring Georgetown and its inhabitants through the window of her driver's Prius. The neighborhood was, she realized, a lot like how she had come to see herself—quaint and confident when viewed from a distance, but gritty, crumbling, and unsafe if anyone bothered to take a closer look. Her phone buzzed. Before she could stop herself, her hand turned it over to check the text. It was from her father:

Nice job. Try to enjoy it.

By the time Sky arrived at the Cactus Cantina, Abby had been at the bar for over an hour, and, as often happened, a small semicircle of fans had formed around her. As soon as she saw Sky, Abby made a loud announcement to her newly minted friends.

"And here she is! Ladies and gentlemen, give it up for that star of stage and screen, Skylar Nicholson!" The bar erupted in applause, and Sky took a slow, self-deprecating bow. A man stepped up and handed her a drink.

"Brandy old-fashioned for Ms. Nicholson. We've been hearing a lot about you," he said. "Impressive." Sky's mind raced as she thought of what Abby might have said to half of northwest D.C. between tequila shots.

Abby gave her a long, tight hug. "We all saw you here, on the news, breaking the big story. God, how gorgeous you are when you're on the big screen!" She turned to the men surrounding the bar. "Am I wrong? Is this woman not the most gorgeous thing you have ever seen?" The bar fell silent, and Sky's heart was filled with a strange blend of panic and delight.

"I am," she replied in a loud voice, "and by the power vested in me as a gorgeous woman, I hereby order you to come with me to that table over there and eat something. All I need is a large plate of nachos—and two shots of tequila so I can catch up." It worked. The crowd laughed and turned away.

Sky made sure that their table was a good distance from the bar, and that Abby had her back to it when they sat down. Abby was not as drunk as she had pretended to be. In spite of this, she was unprepared for the grilling she got from her college roommate.

"Who are those people?" Sky said in a loud whisper. "Did any of them follow you here?"

"What?" Abby said. "No, they're just—"

Sky reached around and put her hand on Abby's shoulder to guide her to their table. She pushed more than she guided. "Are you sure? We can go somewhere else. Have you seen anyone strange more than once since you left the Good Samaritan last night?"

They reached the table, and Abby turned to face Skylar with one eye still on those watching them both from the bar. "I already spoke to the police," she said in a calm tone. "They gave me the whole speech. Said someone would come by in a few days to follow up. Calm down."

Sky sat down at their table and let out a sigh. "Okay. It's been a long day, and all I've been able to think about was how it could have been you last night. And then I came in here and... Well, it's like you're having a freaking party, Abby. And now those guys over there probably think we're a couple."

"Paranoid much?" Abby said with a smile.

"Yes, I'm a little jumpy. It's been a long day."

"I'm sorry," Abby said as she sat down. "I should have known you might not be ready for that. I just wanted to praise you to your face. You need to hear it. You always have."

"Thanks," Sky said. "You're right about that."

"Well," Abby said with a smile. "That's progress. Put a girl on television, and the next thing you know, she's being honest with herself."

"I have been on television before," Sky said softly.

"I know," Abby said. "Before—the whole thing at the *Times*."

"You know about that?" Sky asked.

Abby rolled her eyes. "Yes, I know about it," she said. "You're not the only one who knows how to use Google. But Sky—hey, look at me—I don't believe everything I read."

Sky stared at Abby, clenched her jaw, and made a tight frown. She did not like the direction this conversation was heading. A plate of nachos arrived, accompanied by four tequila shots—the two Sky had ordered, and another two from their fan club at the bar.

"Is this really what you had in mind after what you said to me last night?" Sky said.

"Tell me what's up with you," Abby replied as she picked up a shot glass. "We can discuss your choice of painkillers later."

Sky picked up a shot glass, and the two sisters downed the tequila. No lime. No salt.

"Tell me," Abby said, swallowing behind a sour face. "Tell me what happened. Then I'll do my bit. I'll tell you what I know about Tyler Hawthorne the third, or whatever he called himself."

Skylar gasped. "Oh my God, Abby, I'm so sorry. I didn't even ask. Are you okay?"

Abby gave Sky a weary smile. "Yeah, I'm okay. Sort of stunned, though, to be honest. He wasn't anything special, mind you. It only took two dates and a lot of his money for me to figure out that he was an asshole. It's just the first time anything like this has happened to me, and now I have yet another reason to carry pepper spray in my purse. But it's fine." They drank the second shot of tequila in unison.

"Fine," Sky said. "Really, do you want to talk about it?"

"Nice try," Abby said. "Tell me about what happened to you at the *Times*, then we can talk about me."

Skylar looked into Abby's eyes and knew that if she didn't look away, the tears and the truth would come spilling out of her. Abby's eyes were her personal superpower. Sky had never been able to figure out how to hide from them, or how to lie to them. "Well," Sky said, "there's not much to say that hasn't already been whispered, written about, or litigated."

"That's a start," Abby said. "Keep going. I'm going to need more if you want any of these nachos, and let me tell you, they are to die for."

Skylar gave Abby an icy stare.

"Hey," Abby said, "it's me. I couldn't judge you even if I wanted to."

"What's to judge?" Skylar asked. She could feel her face beginning to redden. "I had my dream job, a chance at a Pulitzer, and then some piece-of-shit boomer set a trap for me, and I stepped in it. He got a promotion, I got a pink slip, and now my life is a mess. I rest my case. Can we move on, please?"

"I see," Abby said. "And the Senator?"

Skylar threw both her hands down on the table hard enough to make the silverware jump. "I was right! And the asshole is in jail now, where he belongs. Why do you always do this?"

The fan club at the bar fell silent and turned its gaze toward their table. Abby looked over her shoulder, waved, and smiled at them as if to say, *no trouble here, gentlemen. Do carry on*. She turned her gaze back toward Sky and leaned into her. It was time to give Skylar what she needed, and Abby knew it would hurt.

"Why do I always do what?" Abby said. "Make you feel your feelings?"

"Watch it, sister," Skylar hissed. "I've driven the best therapists in D.C. to despair. I can handle a two-bit marketing consultant from Syracuse."

"I never said you couldn't. Now, back to the story. I hadn't heard anything about a boomer. What I heard was that you went around your editor's back, based on a tip from a bad source, and printed a story that was…"

"Temporarily wrong," Sky said. "Based on a source given to me by a colleague—a source he knew would lie. He set me up, and they fired me. Just as he'd planned."

"Back up," Abby said. "Temporarily wrong? What's that?"

"Senator Rollingsford was taking bribes. Daily. We all knew it. We couldn't back up the one I put in the story, that's true. But that wasn't the story—the story was the corruption. The pattern. My timing was off. That's all."

Two more shots of tequila arrived at the table. Abby waved at the crowd at the bar and sent them a million-dollar smile.

"Your timing was off? Sky, that doesn't sound like bad timing to me. That sounds more like benevolent libel. And I adore you for it."

"What?" Skylar hissed. "Fuck you."

"I know you're hurting," Abby said, "but if you say that to me again, I will leave you at this table with nothing but your tears and the bill."

The sharpness in Abby's voice hit Sky in a corner of her heart she had long abandoned. She was exhausted. The tears came.

"Calm down and listen to me. You were human. You made a mistake—with good intentions, for sure. That mistake hurt people, including you. But you can make a mistake and still be amazing. You can still be the same Skylar. You can."

Sky's whole body started to shake, and she tried to hold back a sob. "No," she whispered. "I can't. I blew it. I threw it all away. Everything is in pieces."

Abby got up, walked around the table, and wrapped an arm around Skylar. "Whoa, hey. I'm right here," she whispered into her ear. "I'm here. And so are you—Skylar Fucking Nicholson. The same awesome you."

Sky shook her head, trying to compose herself. Abby gave her a playful nudge with her hip and went to work.

"You remember her, right? The woman who was just on TV because she broke the big story?"

Sky shook her head again and reached for a napkin to dry her eyes.

"The one we all looked up to in college. The president of Alpha Chi Omega. Nobody did beer funnels like you, and you always managed to somehow make the Dean's List. I'm sure they're still talking about it in Charlottesville."

Sky started to chuckle and finally lifted her head. "I'll bet."

Abby handed her a wad of tissues. Sky blew her nose. Abby continued.

"The same Skylar who sometimes gets up into her head a bit too much. Maybe—could that be the one?" Abby gave Sky's shoulder a little sideways squeeze. Sky managed a smile.

"Yeah, well, maybe," she said. Abby took this as a sign that it was safe to return to her seat.

"And," she concluded, "who then punishes herself for things that aren't really her fault."

Sky raised her two hands in the air in a gesture of surrender. Abby smiled and reached forward to grab another chip from the basket in front of them. Then she waited.

"It's just that..." Sky said, "I feel so lost."

"Well," Abby said, "I'm here for you like you were for me—for as long as it takes."

Another round of tequila shots arrived from the bar. Abby waved.

"Oh, look! More numbing agents from our friends. Care to join me?" she said.

"No," Sky said, "I've been burping that stuff up since last night. I almost didn't keep that last one down. I'll pass."

"That," Abby said, "is the best thing I've heard all week."

CHAPTER 26

Sky did her best to be quiet as she got dressed. She really didn't have to—it was her apartment, and well past noon—but the sight of Abby asleep on her pull-out couch demanded silent reverence. The sunlight of this crisp November morning warmed her through the bedroom window. To disturb the scene was unthinkable. *It's not fair*, Sky thought. *No one has the right to look that good first thing in the morning.*

Sky turned to her mirror to finish her face, and promptly dropped an earring onto the hardwood floor. She leaned down to look for it, whispered a short scolding to herself, and realized that the spell of her Saturday morning had been broken.

"This is not okay," Abby said in a soft, sleepy voice. "You usually don't run off by yourself until the second day of a girls' weekend."

Sky walked over to Abby and sat down on the bed's edge. "Don't start," she said. "I'm running late. Besides, you were right last night. I could use the company."

Abby smiled. "Good," she said. "Because I'm staying until you're in a better frame of mind, whether you like it or not." There was an awkward silence.

"Thanks," Sky said. "So does your dedication explain why my Adderall went missing?"

"When you have your own prescription," Abby said, "it will be yours. Until then, I suggest you try a lot of espresso."

"Abby," Sky said. "I know what you're thinking, but it isn't a problem. It isn't."

"Good," Abby said. "Because I've had that kind of a problem. And I'm not going to stand by and watch you get one. Period."

Sky sat there, stunned. She decided they could talk about it later that night.

"So," Abby said quickly, "what is so pressing that I'm losing track of you on a Saturday? Is it business or pleasure—and don't you dare say pleasure."

"Neither," Sky said. "Karmic debt."

"I see," Abby replied. "Brunch with mother?"

"Close," Sky laughed, "very close. But not quite. I'm having tea with Mildred Hawthorne in Georgetown."

Abby sat up. "Hawthorne? Is that—?"

Sky let out a long sigh. "Yes," she said. "Tyler's mother."

"How did you know Tyler, by the way?"

"Our mothers went to college together. Aunt Millie would come and visit us in Chantilly, and we summered up at their lake house when I was a kid."

"Wow," Abby said. "You call her 'Aunt Millie.' That's creepy."

"It is," Sky said. "But it's on me to represent the family in her hour of need. Besides, she might come up with something I can use on *The Thread*. I need to get moving. One does not arrive late for tea with Aunt Millie."

"Okay," Abby said. "I approve your application for a Leave of Absence. Go shake Aunt Millie down. And when you're done, bring back some decent food. There's nothing here but kale chips and moldy pad thai. It's depressing."

"Yes, your majesty," Sky said with a grin.

"I like the sound of that," Abby said. "What time is tea with Aunt Millie?"

"One o'clock," Sky said. Abby looked over her shoulder at the clock on the bedroom nightstand. It was 12:30.

"What the hell are you waiting for?" Abby shrieked. "Jesus, Sky, no wonder you're always late. GO!"

CHAPTER 27

Sky was one block from Aunt Millie's Georgetown residence when her father called.

"Dad?" she said. "I didn't know you knew how to make phone calls on your iPhone."

"Hello, Sky," her father said. He sounded calm, but his tone was formal and serious. "Your mother told me that you might be seeing Millie this weekend. Is that right?"

"Yes," she replied, "and your timing is perfect. I'm due to have tea with her in five minutes, and at this rate, I'm going to be late."

Her dad laughed. "No, you're not," he said. "You're not late. Not even close."

Sky rolled her eyes. "Okay, I guess. So what's up?"

"Find a quiet spot. We need to talk about Millie."

Sky stopped walking. This was not a tone she had ever heard from her father. "Dad," she said, "can we do this later? I really don't want to be late."

"Skylar," he said, "listen to me. Aunt Millie will come down the stairs at 1:30 and pretend to be sorry about keeping you waiting so she can show you who is in charge."

"Have you and Mom both gone crazy?" Sky said. "This is Aunt Millie we're talking about. I am paying a sympathy call to a grieving mother, and you make it sound like I'm about to lock horns with Vito Corleone."

"That's why I called," he said. "You're closer to meeting a Corleone than you think."

"What is that supposed to mean?" Skylar checked her watch. 1:03.

"Do you know how Millie Hawthorne got her money?"

"By marrying Mr. Hawthorne, I presume, based on her age."

"An excellent start," her dad said, "but only half true. Her family made a fortune in the shipping business, with roots dating back to colonial times. His fortune was larger, and all in mining. Oil and coal in the United States, copper and tin in South America. It's a big business, and a dirty one."

"Yeah," Sky said, "not every family can say it destroyed a planet."

"That's not the half of it," he said. "The Hawthornes have had a huge influence on the Hill for over a century. Nothing that could hurt them happens—ever."

"Great. Anything else while you've got me?"

"I'm afraid so," he said. "There was a point when Millie suspected Mr. Hawthorne had eyes for your mother."

"Dad! Is this really necessary?"

"Yes," he said. "Gerry Hawthorne had a well-deserved reputation as a philanderer, so Millie was on the lookout. There were always rumors of a local girl here and there. There was nothing to it with your mother, of course, but once she got the idea in her head, things got catty between the two of them. I had to have a gentlemanly conversation with Gerry up at their lake house. He was complimentary of your mother but assured me she wasn't his type."

"That was nice of him," Sky snapped.

"Yes. What was I supposed to tell your mother after that? What was she then supposed to say to Millie? It was a mess, even by 1970s standards."

"That's enough, Dad," Skylar said. "I think I get it."

"You really need to, Sky," he said. "Millie Hawthorne is not above taking revenge on our whole family through you. And don't be fooled. Millie calls the shots within the Hawthorne empire, and she has for years. She's a force of nature. She likes you, and she can help you, but she is ruthless, so tread carefully."

***

The Hawthornes' Georgetown residence was somehow enormous, garish, and understated at the same time. Sky paused for a moment before she reached for the rather fancy knocker. *Okay*, she thought, *condolences, love from Mother, if there is anything we can do, please let us know...*

Sky was accustomed to representing her mother on social calls like this. She was a native Virginian and a debutante, just like her mother and her grandmother before her. This heritage came with undeniable benefits, but it demanded obedience to a strict set of social obligations in return.

Whenever her mother was unable to honor one of her own obligations, young Skylar did so on the family's behalf. The afternoon she'd gotten her driver's license, for example, Mrs. Nicholson was too drunk to drop off the cake she had baked for Mrs. Thompson, whose mother had recently passed away. Sky had taken care of it, and on that day had signed an unwritten contract with her mother that had bound her to this day.

Skylar knocked on Mildred Hawthorne's door fully prepared to serve a cause more important than herself. Again.

CHAPTER 28

A thirty-something, brown-haired woman in a long, black dress answered the door. "Ms. Nicholson?" she said.

"Please, call me Sky. You must be Shannon." The woman produced a weak but genuine smile, as though Sky had been the first guest who had ever bothered to say her name.

"That's right," she said. "Shannon O'Donnell, Mrs. Hawthorne's assistant. Do come in, Ms. Nicholson. I'm afraid Mrs. Hawthorne is delayed a few minutes, but she shouldn't be long. Right this way."

Shannon led Sky into the entryway of a home which looked like it could be used as an exhibit at the Smithsonian.

They walked from the foyer into a living room decorated in a colonial style, with a small table set for two in the middle of it. A fire was blazing in a large fireplace that took up much of the rear wall.

"Here we are," Shannon said as she motioned to the chairs at the table. "Please make yourself at home. Mrs. Hawthorne will be down shortly."

"Thank you very much, Shannon," Sky said. "If you don't mind me asking, how is she holding up? Such a horrible thing with Tyler.

If this is no longer a good time, I would be happy to reschedule."

Shannon looked at her in silence for a moment. "You are too kind," she said in a shaky voice, "but I can assure you that Mrs. Hawthorne honors her commitments. Regardless of the circumstances."

Shannon pulled her eyes away from Sky and aimed them at an undefined section of the hardwood floor. It was quite possible that she had not meant this as a compliment.

"Well," she said, "please do let me know if you need anything. I'll just be in the next room." As she turned to leave, a wave of reporter's intuition washed through Sky's mind.

"Shannon," Sky said. The woman stopped and turned to face her. "Yes, Ms. Nicholson?"

Sky took a step forward and looked her directly in the eyes. "Shannon, I am so sorry for your loss."

At this, Shannon's eyes started to fill with tears. She took in a quick, short breath to collect herself. "Thank you," she whispered, turned on her heels, and left the room without making a sound.

Sky sat at the small table set with antique white linen and checked her watch. It was 1:25. She decided to pass the time by taking stock of the table. It had been prepared with the masterful blend of pragmatism and class that Sky had expected—an antique Limoges tea set, 19th-century domestic silver, and water glasses from Crate and Barrel to assure guests that the Hawthornes were really quite down-to-earth.

As she scanned the room, only two things seemed out of place. The first was a small bar cart next to the fireplace, which looked as though it had fallen into a wormhole during the Jazz Age and had appeared just before she arrived. The second was more curious. To the right of the hostess's place setting was a large, sealed envelope with an index card on top of it. Sky had only just noticed this when, from the corner of her eye, she saw Aunt Millie, dressed in black, come down the stairs and into the foyer. Sky leapt to her feet and rushed to greet her.

"Aunt Millie!" she said, "I am so sorry. I don't know what to say." She kissed her on the cheek and gave her a short hug.

"Thank you, dear," Millie said. "Your mother said the same thing. I'm so sorry I was late—I was just paroled from a long phone call with my Board of Directors. Now, please, come sit."

"Board of Directors?" Sky said as they walked into the living room. "That's a bit callous, don't you think?"

Millie Hawthorne walked directly to her late husband's bar cart and laid one hand on a bottle of scotch. "Don't ever forget, dear, whatever your show is, it must go on. That will be what gets you through. Besides, I'm still a bit numb, so it was not as cruel as it might sound." She looked at her hand resting on the scotch. "For example," she said, "look at what I'm doing right now. Did you meet Shannon?"

"I did," Sky said. "She seems wonderful."

"For what I pay her to look after this place," Millie said, "she'd better be." As if on cue, Shannon appeared in the doorway, carrying two cocktails. "Thank you, Shannon," Millie said, "that will do just fine. Leave them on the table."

Shannon set down the drinks, briefly smiled at Sky, and vanished as quickly as she had appeared.

Sky said, "You certainly serve an odd brand of afternoon tea."

"Well," the matriarch said as she took her seat at the table, "a grieving mother gets to choose her own tea. Now, won't you join me?"

"Of course," Sky said. "But to be honest, I'm surprised you're even taking visitors."

"I'm a Dickenson," Millie said. "When life gets hard, we get on with it. When we lost my uncle Marty in the war, my gran told me, 'I left my grief at the graveside, Mildred. Someday, you will have to as well. Get on with it.' And that is what I intend to do."

There was an awkward silence. "Mother sends her love. She would have come herself, but she spent the last week in bed. Migraines again."

"Of course," Millie said quickly. "The poor thing. But when I look at you, dear, I can see her face just as if we were back at Wells. As a matter of fact, just now you reminded me of the wild night we had at the winter formal. Did she ever tell you about that?"

Sky pretended to look surprised. "No, that one never came up."

"I suppose not," Millie said. "Oh, did we ever have fun! I think that was the night I met your father. He was in town from Michigan or somewhere."

"Wisconsin," Sky said. "The University of Wisconsin—in Madison."

Millie wrinkled her nose a bit. "Yes," she said, "of course. I'd tell you more about it, but it's all a blur. We spent years trying to reconstruct the evening from memory, to no avail. I haven't had an old-fashioned since!"

"I don't blame you one bit," Sky replied. They both took another sip, and Sky watched as Millie placed her right hand down on top of the envelope. Shannon arrived and set two more drinks on the table. *Well now*, Sky thought. *It's clear I'm not here just for comfort and support.*

"But enough ancient history about your mother and me," Millie said. "I have had a chance to catch up with your professional accomplishments, Skylar. I have it on good authority that you are quite the reporter—digging for the truth wherever it leads and all that. Clearly, the apple does not fall far from the tree."

Sky's heart sank. She could see why her father was worried. "Well, thank you," she said. "I do enjoy the work."

"That's important," Millie said as she stroked the envelope with her index finger. "Especially when professional setbacks come, as they often do." Millie Hawthorne's eyes were now bearing down on Sky, scanning for evidence of an emotional reaction. "It can be hard to get back on one's feet after something like that, especially when one falls so far from grace. Don't you think?"

Something inside Sky stiffened. *Okay*, she thought, *game on.*

"Skylar, dear," Aunt Millie continued, "I know how hard it can be for a woman to make it in this world. I want to help."

"Thank you," Sky said. "That's generous, but I assure you, I am fine, and my family is fine. We're quite comfortable." Aunt Millie's eyes widened, and Sky knew that her shot had hit its mark.

"Oh, I would never insult you or your mother like that. I am quite aware that your family is well situated when it comes to... all things practical."

"Thank you," Sky said crisply. "And while that is true, it is a point of pride for me that I make my own way."

"I expected no less," Aunt Millie said with a smile, and picked up the envelope.

It was clear to Skylar that Mildred was not going to make whatever she was up to any easier. "I still think I can help my favorite reporter get back on her feet. You'll help me, won't you, dear?"

"That depends," Sky said. "What do you need?" Millie appeared to be on the verge of tears, but Sky's intuition told her they might not be genuine.

"I would have thought," Millie said with a quiver in her voice, "it would be obvious. I need someone to find out who did this to my little boy. Someone I can trust."

"Of course, Aunt Millie," Sky said. "I understand. But I'm a journalist, not a police detective. My job is to tell the world that something horrible like this happened, and let the police figure out the rest. The detectives working on this case are the best in the business. They will find who did this."

Aunt Millie rolled her eyes and set the envelope back on the table. "That," she said, "would mean trusting the government and some Irishman with a badge. We are not going to do that." She pulled the index card off the envelope and set it on the table in front of Sky. "This is the contact information for a private investigator I have on retainer. He is at your disposal and is waiting for your call. In the meantime, I have asked him to look into a few things for me."

"Oh?" Skylar said. She did not like the idea of working with Aunt Millie, much less *for* her, but the reporter inside her needed to know what was in that envelope.

"Did you know," Millie said with a conspiratorial tone, "that we had to have Tyler's car towed from Great Falls? Not a nick on it... but the shift knob was missing. Strange, right? What kind of person would steal a shift knob?"

"That is odd," Sky said. "But it could be a coincidence, or maybe it was already missing."

"Nonsense!" Millie exclaimed and took a long sip of her second drink. "Think bigger, Skylar. Who benefits? They all do. He was in their way. Shouldn't you have a notebook or something to take this all down?"

"Wait," Sky said. "Tyler was in whose way?"

Millie was a bit tipsy by now. She lightly tossed the envelope on the table in front of Sky, then pointed to it. "All of them. They're all in there—the Sierra Club people, Greenpeace, EPA, Soros, Brookings. That's where you start. Just to warn you, until I saw this, I never knew there were so many Jews and Catholics in Washington. Stands to reason."

"Aunt Millie," Sky said in a low whisper. "For shame."

"Don't be so naive," Millie snapped. "It's not a good trait in a reporter." The two women paused their conversation as Shannon arrived again, this time with hot water for tea. Sky tried to catch

Shannon's eye as she poured the water into the antique teapot but failed.

"I'm sorry you had to hear that, Shannon," Millie said, as the woman quickly left the room. "And who, I wonder, was the woman with my son at the restaurant that night? Have you thought about that? You were there. She threw a drink in his face. That has to mean something. Where on earth does someone like that come from?"

Skylar looked at the index card with the private investigator's name on it and realized that Millie Hawthorne might already know the answer to that question.

"Oh, that was Abigayle Sullivan," Sky said. "We were Alpha Chi sisters at UVA. She's from upstate New York—Syracuse, I think. Maybe Utica. Nice girl, but yes, she has a bit of a temper."

Millie's eyes lit up. "Oh, Utica, that would make sense. Was her mother Italian? Sometimes they do the dirty work."

"Millie Hawthorne," Sky exclaimed, "that is quite enough!" But Aunt Millie was no longer listening. She glared at Sky.

"Tell me something, Skylar dear. Why do these people hate us so much? We're the bedrock of this country. Our ancestors—yours and mine—they pulled this country out of the Stone Age! Does anyone appreciate that? No. All they want to do is tear it all down with one hand while picking our pocket with the other. And now even that isn't enough. They're killing our children. Killing *us*! Should anyone be surprised? I don't think so."

"Aunt Millie, that's not true," Sky said as she shook her head. "You know that's not true."

Mille sat back in her chair, undeterred. "And they say it's all about fairness. *Fairness*? Nonsense. It's about envy and greed."

"Aunt Millie," Sky said softly, "I know this has been difficult for you, but—"

"Don't give me that look, young lady," Millie said. "My husband

Gerry understood the value of a dollar, and I'll tell you why. He *earned* every one he had!"

Sky realized that if she was going to leave with the envelope, she needed to let Millie continue. And continue she did.

"Tell me something, Skylar. These people who care so much—about every sapling and everyone's feelings—do they make their own money? No. They're drowning in donations, tax money, and welfare checks. They never had to work for a penny of it. Want money? Try *working* for it, that's what I always say!"

Sky nodded again. Aunt Millie was slurring her words.

"Do you want to know how bad it has become in this country? I pay people *not* to do things—all so that the lights stay on. Yes, you heard me right. I pay people not to do things. Nice work if you can get it."

"Sure is," Sky said softly.

Millie pointed at the envelope. "I'm telling you—now listen to me, Sky—those people would kill each of us for our money before they would work a *single goddamned day*."

Sky took a long sip from her drink.

"Take this museum exhibit business," Millie said. "It's a disaster, from top to bottom. We gave them millions. Free money, Skylar! Money to build an exhibit, and it's a public humiliation waiting to happen. They know how to take the money, sure, but they can't plan a soirée for a few hundred people to open it properly. How is that possible? I'll tell you. No discipline. No work ethic. Always having things handed to you. It's a travesty what has happened to this country."

Shannon suddenly appeared in the doorway. "Mrs. Hawthorne," she said in a calm voice, "your car is ready." This appeared to knock Aunt Millie out of her trance. She rose from her seat.

"Well, I'm afraid I have to run. I'll see you and your mother at the services. As I said, we all must continue to press forward so you can tell me what you've found out at the museum opening. Hunter and Caroline will be there, and I'm sure they would love to see you. It has been too long. Shannon will send you the details." Aunt Millie headed for the door, and Sky got up to give her a farewell peck on the cheek.

"I'll help," she said, "but before I do, I have to ask you one more question. Is there anything Tyler might have been doing—not necessarily the family or the business—that might have given someone reason to do this?" Millie's cold, blue eyes became fierce, and she set her jaw for a moment before answering.

"My son did what he had to do," she said, "and none of it was illegal. That is all you need to know."

CHAPTER 29

Next to Christmas, Thanksgiving week was the worst holiday of the year. After his mom's murder, Jerry had spent holidays with his adopted parents, the Robertsons. They had been kind enough to take him in, but holidays were never as joyous as they were for other folks. Rather, they had always reminded him that he was alone, and that he alone wallowed in the knowledge that he would never receive that warm, motherly embrace children in other families enjoyed on those days.

Congress was out of session for the holiday week, and almost all of his so-called colleagues had scooted to get home to their families, many leaving their mistresses with enough money to shop on black Friday as compensation for abandoning them.

But not Jerry. While he wanted to get back to his truck and maybe do a little deer hunting, it wasn't worth the hassle, and he would be by himself back at Montour Falls. The groundbreaking was coming up soon enough anyway. Jane insisted he come over for a home cooked meal, so he would oblige, but he wasn't terribly excited about the idea. At least there would be football to look forward to for a distraction.

This was going to be a long, excruciating week, and it was only Monday morning. He wasn't expecting any office visitors, any meetings to make himself look busy, or any events to attend to make it appear that he mattered. Jerry sat at his desk in his dungeon of an office and flipped through the weekly calendar he had just printed off, clearly wasting the ink and paper. The most exciting event he'd penciled in was to pick up his dry cleaning at 4 p.m. Friday. He wasn't even sure they were open.

Thanksgiving week was brutal. Jerry was pretty sure the crappy government-issued clock above the doorway was going backward. He stretched his way out of his stiff chair and paced the room a few times, then swung around the doorway into the intern closet. He was surprised he had arrived before his loyal intern. Besides Jane, Chris was his only staff.

After a few spins in a circle like a lonely dog looking to sit down, Jerry plopped into Chris's green chair for a change in scenery.

While there were two other desks for future interns, Chris's desk was purposely closer to the Congressman so that if or when other interns were hired, they would get the message.

Jerry smiled at the not-so-subtle move. *This Chris kid is sharp as a tack.* He settled into Chris's squeaky chair on wheels that almost sent him straight backward. He saw the hot, new government-issued laptop on the desk. *Why the hell does this kid have a souped-up machine that can control the space station while I'm stuck with that old dog?* He thought about it. *Oh, yeah. Chris was the only one doing real work.*

Jerry glanced at the other two desks jammed together, both of which would be shared when he hired more interns. He took a little comfort when he saw the dusty, green-screened desktops as old as time itself. *At least I rank above non-existent interns.*

On Chris's desk, there were files and schedules and a stack of letters written in response to something related to a wealthy home association's concern about black spots on their car roofs throughout their neighborhood. Chris had talked with the EPA and had discovered the spots were insect droppings.

Ha. Figures. Get what they deserve. About time the rich get shit on.

Chris had a couple of pictures of his family set far back on the steel desk, posing with small, crystal clear waves behind them, presumably from vacations to the Caribbean. Jerry unapologetically flipped through a short stack of personal mail, mostly bills of some sort. A gas bill and a cell phone bill didn't total much, but it was likely a fortune to an intern making fifteen bucks an hour.

Jerry opened the drawer to his right. Nothing fun. But a sticky note, taped to the drawer's aluminum side caught his eye. There was a list of passwords.

~~Tndrft13~~

~~SedCls14~~

~~FstCls15~~

~~Star2016~~

~~Life2017~~

Eagle018

They weren't exactly protecting state secrets, but Chris was apparently a little too careless with security. He smiled at his clean-cut assistant's use of scouting ranks. After opening a few more drawers and not really paying attention to their contents, he realized that he was a Congressman who was bored stiff.

Jerry lifted the screen on Chris's laptop, and it hummed to life immediately. He popped in the Eagle018 password, and he was in.

Jesus. This computer is lightning fast.

Chris had the browser open to *The Thread.* The "Gutting on the

Potomac" story only had a few updates, so Jerry checked out the comments. Some were likely from scared college kids worried about walking home at night. Others posted not-so-friendly comments trying to fan police racial profiling, but the author, Ms. Skylar Nicholson, was too clever to take that bait. Jerry took the time to find out more about Nicholson. He found her picture buried on the staff site under the "About" tab. Jerry leaned in. Lipstick girl! The woman at the bar! Interesting.

Jerry returned to the comments with a new sense of purpose. An unusual post he didn't expect caught his eye. He clicked on the post thread and found that an exchange was beginning to take shape that was somewhat buried among the other posts. It was an exchange between two people calling themselves AllKnottedup and Skysthelimit. Jerry assumed Sky had to be the author, Skylar Nicholson. The exchange was focused on the pictures provided in the story. Pictures Skylar Nicholson was claiming had come from those who discovered the body.

AllKnottedup was chatting about the picture details.

AllKnottedup–Long time follower, first time Threading the needle–Skysthelimit–love your picture on the site. Terrific smile. You should scout out the crime scene photos of that poor fellow from the river. There are things that will tie your stories together. You need to do a "cut" check!

Skysthelimit–AllKnottedup–Nice to have a fan out there. Can you be a little less cryptic? I have those pictures up on my screen right now, and I don't see anything the police haven't already focused on. Want to tell me a little about yourself and why you are so interested in this story?

AllKnottedup–Skysthelimit–Well, I may want you to take me out for a beer when you arrive at the real story and remember I helped you get there.

Skysthelimit–AllKnottedup–It would help if you weren't being so cute. If this is how you meet girls, you are going to be lonely this holiday. What the hell are you hinting at?

Jerry did not like the direction these posts were taking. Did this person see something? Or was this person just one of the million nut jobs commenting on local news stories?

CHAPTER 30

A jingle at the door stirred him. "Hey, Jane! You didn't have to come in today. It's going to be slower than molasses."

Jane, in her white blouse and deep burgundy skirt smiled at her charge of over twenty-five years. "Never leave the boss to his own devices." She wasted no time. "Jerry, dear, what are your plans for the holiday?"

Jerry had expected the question, but he would rather not answer truthfully. "Going to watch the game with a few folks and then head over to your place, of course."

Jane could see right through him. "Why don't you come over earlier? I saw Christopher coming down the hall. He will be at the house around noon, then we can cook together and watch the game. You know I love that crazy bearded quarterback. Fitzgerald is so cute. The Bills haven't been the same since Kelly."

If there were ever someone Jerry should love besides his real mother, it might be Jane. But he didn't. He appreciated her but didn't love her. She had stepped in and done her duty as his mother's best friend when he had nowhere to turn, but she wasn't his mom. Deep down, he knew it was all about him. He was sure Jane had felt guilty enough to take him in. He had always thought Jane knew more about his mom's murder than she said. This had eaten at Jerry for a long time, and it was the main reason he remained distant.

"If it isn't a bother, I'll come by just before the game, as long as you agree that I can bring something to support the cause."

Jane's smile said it all.

Jerry returned to his large, spacious desk and slumped into his uncomfortable armchair. Five minutes of library-standard quiet was interrupted by a gentle rap on the door.

Jane peeked in and gave him a gentle look. "Jerry, dear, we have an unannounced visitor. Ms. Skylar Nicholson? She says she is a journalist."

Jerry shot up and stared. He had just seen her picture next to the Hawthorne story. She wasn't just any reporter; she was the lipstick girl from the Good Samaritan. Had she seen him there and now wanted to ask him questions? She had stopped to chat with Mildred. What did that mean? Jerry felt an electric charge sweep across his chest. Did she remember him from the fundraiser? He did his best to keep his cool and nodded to Jane as though this were all routine.

In the steadiest voice possible, Jerry said, "Send her in, and Jane, would you be so kind as to send Chris in as well? I heard him come in a minute ago. Ms. Nicholson may have questions about committee work, and he knows more than the two of us put together."

Jerry rubbed his hands together. He was smart enough to know you never met a reporter without a witness. A lesson he'd begrudgingly learned back when he'd been a county prosecutor. There had been too many entanglements with his least favorite reporter back home.

Jerry checked his red tie in the mirror and regretted not having worn the light blue one that softened his demeanor.

Chris bounded in like a three-month-old golden retriever, eyes all lit up and a smile from ear to ear, tongue sort of hanging out on one side. He had both arms curled around a stack of what had to be twenty fat files.

"Easy now, young man." Jerry always got a kick out of the endless naïveté that shone from Chris's expression. "Just a visit from a reporter—we aren't signing the Declaration of Independence."

"That's funny, sir." Chris couldn't help himself. "Maybe this will get your housing project some attention. It's a big deal for your folks back home!"

"Perhaps, but given her latest story, I would expect public safety to be her top concern." Jerry gave Chris the look that commanded him to tuck himself in the corner while he handled things. *Be ready in case I don't know what the hell I am talking about.*

Chris had learned that look months ago, so he dumped his pile of folders and binders on the table and stood fiddling with his knit tie. His pile of crap slid a bit and almost knocked over the Congressman's shadow box, but Chris caught it in time.

Jane opened the door and with a graceful swing of her arm guided Ms. Nicholson into the office. Jane had made sure their guest was armed with coffee.

Jerry almost chuckled out loud as he surveyed his unexpected visitor. There was no doubt she needed the coffee—maybe a double shot of espresso would be better. The petite reporter looked like she had slept in her rather cheap pantsuit, and the collar of her blouse was a bit off, but he couldn't figure out why. She hadn't taken the time to straighten herself up before coming in. Her hair was up but not straight behind her, cinched a little to her right.

A righty? Or just too much to drink last night? Or had she slept in her car?

Jerry strode up to meet the reporter halfway and provided a slightly over-enthusiastic handshake. "Good morning, Ms. Nicholson.

Congressman Sharpe at your service. This is my trusty right hand, Chris Patterson."

Before Skylar had a chance to return the greeting, Chris leapt at the verbal promotion (he wasn't merely an intern today), and smiled, shook her hand even more vigorously than Sharpe, and perched himself on the edge of his seat somewhat behind the action.

Outside of her initial appearance of rolling out of bed, Jerry was impressed by the journalist. For being younger than most folks working the Hill, Nicholson had a calm, collected way about her. She plopped down in the chair across from his desk without an invitation and placed her coffee dangerously close to the edge.

Jerry guessed this spunky reporter loved arriving unannounced— likely to gain some advantage over less-experienced politicians perhaps. He liked the coffee move. He smiled at the obvious attempt to create unease and watched Chris's eyes bulge at the faux pas. But he wasn't worried about the coffee given the closest thing to important on the desk was his agenda for the day—which didn't offer much other than his lunch and a call to OMB. The story would be how little he had to ruin.

Jerry set out to make it clear he was running the show today. "Ms. Nicholson, what a pleasant surprise. It's nice to see you. Could I have seen you at Chairman Perry's fundraiser?"

"Yes, Congressman, that could be. I was there for a bit. Seemed like everyone and their sister was at the party."

"What an evening. I think that was the year's best event. The food was perfect."

"I appreciate you making time for me without calling ahead."

Jerry knew these meetings didn't last long. Jane was a professional and understood that there was an expected interruption within the first ten minutes. Jerry guessed Skylar Nicholson was likely experienced enough to understand this clock was ticking, so he wanted to get to a few things quickly.

Jerry leaned back, doing his best to look like he had nothing to worry about. "You are always welcome here, Ms. Nicholson. By the way, I saw your coverage of that awful mess with Mr. what's-his-name? Mr. Tyler Hawthorne. Nice work."

"Yes, Congressman, that was a terrible thing that happened. In a way, that is why I popped in today. You were on the City's Special Commission on Safety. I know a meeting hasn't happened in months, but I wanted to get your take on whether the recent increase in city violence might motivate the commission to get back to work."

"Oh, yes, that is an important commission. I haven't heard from the mayor in a bit, but I assume your paper is looking to get things moving?"

Chris almost fell out of his chair. "Congressman, *The Thread* is not a paper. It's one of the most popular news forums in the city. Kind of an interactive thing, sir. Ms. Nicholson is their top reporter." Jerry swung a gentle, knowing eye, maybe even a wink of sorts to his loyal, energetic intern. He knew quite well it wasn't a paper.

The young woman shrugged off the slight and smiled at the intern's compliment at the same time. "Yes, our digital news has really captured a lot of attention lately. And yes, Congressman, there has been a significant increase in violent crime these past few months leading up to the holidays, and more folks are raising concerns about their personal safety. The Hawthorne murder has elevated everyone's anxiety. When will the commission reconvene?"

"I certainly agree with you. Your blog stuff covering the Hawthorne incident was thorough, much better than the *Times*. I liked how you integrated the rather ghastly photos into the story. You must have outstanding sources. Oh, and I referred your story to the mayor right after it broke, but he likely had read it already by that time."

Jerry watched as the young journalist waited patiently for a response to her earlier question. No reaction to the *Times* comment. A bit disappointing.

"Ms. Nicholson, any insight into the police theories on the untimely death of Mr. Hawthorne? You know, any exciting leads?"

"I am sure they are working on it, Congressman. Maybe more effectively than the Safety Commission."

Jerry liked this young, clever reporter. "Ms. Nicholson, do you go to a lot of fundraisers? You are always welcome to come to mine. Chris, would you please give her a business card and be sure to invite her to our upcoming event? It should be fun. I'm holding it at Shelly's. You know the cigar bar?"

The puppy in the back of the room tumbled forward and almost fell over the reporter with a bent business card. Jerry watched Ms. Nicholson lean in to take it, but she placed it on the desk in front of her and reached for her coffee. She took a long draw. "Congressman," she said after swallowing, "I think it might behoove you and others to get the commission back up and running to address the violent crime issues."

"Ms. Nicholson, I noticed at Perry's event that you spent a little time with Abigayle Sullivan. I sort of knew her in my early days upstate. Do you know her well?"

Jerry knew he had hit a nerve this time. He watched as Ms. Nicholson stiffened and took another sip of coffee to gather herself. "Ms. Sullivan and I went to college together, and we have remained friends. Why do you ask?"

Jerry offered, "UVA is a fine school. I have some friends who went to law school there. As for Abigayle, I hadn't seen her in ages. I understand she works for a PR firm now. New World, or Genesis, or something. I was considering using her to help me with the next campaign."

Jerry tried not to release the smirk he felt just below the surface.

He wanted her to know he was paying attention. It was helpful he'd read Skylar's bio on *The Thread.*

After clearly bristling at references to her own personal details, Ms. Nicholson replied, "I will mention your interest next time I see her. Back to my question. Given you last met in April, do you think Mayor Shields and the Commission need to get back to work and take the police head-on to improve safety? Aren't you concerned about the violence?"

Jerry wanted to look like he had juice, and the question was tempting, for sure. He hunted and fished a lot—he knew what bait looked like—but it might be fun to see if she could handle playing this game. "Ms. Nicholson, of course we should be doing more, and I will call the city today to see if I can help get this commission back on its feet. The mayor certainly needs to up his game here, and I am happy to provide you with anything you need."

Another peep from the back of the room. Chris squeaked a friendly amendment to his boss's commitment. "Congressman, please do not forget that Mayor Shields declared the commission over in April or early May and has taken the work in-house."

"Oh, yes. That's right. Thank you, Chris. I am sure Ms. Nicholson knew that already. That's why she's here—to get it restarted, right? Perhaps we should see if we can encourage our mayor to do more publicly, and perhaps given our friend's concerns, reopen the commission. I certainly can't promise anything."

She nodded and jotted down some notes in a small, leatherbound journal.

"Is your interest in the commission about rising crime or is it about what you think might have happened to Mr. Hawthorne?" Jerry watched as the reporter tried to keep her composure. A slight flush, a small cough to clear her throat. Under her chair, she switched her legs, ankles crossed and tucked properly beneath her, as he was sure she had been taught at boarding school—maybe even finishing school.

"No, I'm leaving that to the police for now, but we're getting a lot of leads directly on our site. Did you know Mr. Hawthorne?"

Without missing a beat, Jerry looked her in the eyes with a grim face. "Terrible tragedy, but no. I didn't really know him. I did meet him at the fundraiser, however. He was a charming fellow."

Jerry watched as Ms. Nicholson considered the Congressman and tried to match up his version of Tyler Hawthorne with what she knew of him.

"Anyway, back to Abigayle's PR firm. Maybe you can provide me with a reintroduction of sorts."

Chris piped up again, changing the subject. "Ms. Nicholson, the Congressman was instrumental in bringing affordable housing back to his district. As you know, funding for housing has been knotted up in Congress for years. Congressman Sharpe was a key vote to free up the funding. We are attending a ceremony upstate in a week or so. I think this is a great example of the impact housing investments can have on small-town America, don't you?"

Jerry swung a rather ferocious look at Chris. Knotted up in Congress? Was that a coincidence? But Chris and Nicholson were facing each other, so no one noticed his bewildered look.

Chris must have felt Jerry's eyes boring into him and turned to face his boss, a bit perplexed. "Forgive my pivot, Ms. Nicholson. It's such an important project, I wanted to make sure you were aware of it."

Jerry tried to dismiss the intern's comments and returned his attention to his guest, who was turning up the charm. He was impressed by her ability to manipulate Chris, who was an easier and more appetizing target. He watched as Ms. Nicholson widened her doe-like eyes to drive home a connection. Jerry watched the handsome intern pop out of his own skin with excitement. She didn't say anything at first, but she used the opportunity to deliver the smile Jerry figured was designed to convince young men to buy her drinks. Chris's eyes gave his youth away and darted to anywhere else but to her eyes. "I should take your business card, as well, Christopher." Jerry watched the reporter turn his intern to blubbering mush and provided a knowing smile to her as she returned to the conversation with a slight look of victory on her face.

Jerry was trying to stay focused, but his eyes glanced over her shoulder and fell on the shadow box, the only thing that really made him feel like he had done something worthwhile in his life.

The reporter caught his distraction and turned. "What is that, Congressman?"

Jerry cleared his throat. "That, Ms. Nicholson, is a collection from my days as a Boy Scout. I earned each merit badge and became an Eagle Scout when I was seventeen. The shadow box holds the badges, the eagle scarf and pins, and other things I treasured as a kid. Makes me feel good when I see it. Makes me think of home. Take a look. By the way, our boy here was also an Eagle Scout."

Chris tried not to look directly at Ms. Nicholson at this point, but dutifully handed the shadow box to the reporter. Jerry watched carefully as Skylar lifted the box closer to her face as though she were reading an inscription. She traced the items with her finger as she looked back up.

"Very nice, Congressman. The knife is impressively decorated. I thought shadow boxes were for war veterans, which you are not. I'm pretty sure you never served. Not sure I've seen one for scouts, though." She paused to drive home her point to Jerry. "Perhaps as an Eagle Scout, you might find it important to push the mayor to be more prepared and interact with the folks in the city so they feel like there is something being done to fight this crime wave."

She'd given him a nasty little one-two punch, but he didn't mind.

The week was starting off better than he thought. She didn't have any interest in him or the Hawthorne affair.

The expected rap on the door came, and Jane peeked in.

"Congressman Sharpe, you do have that call at the top of the hour." Jane's eyes connected with Ms. Nicholson, who got the message. Time was up.

"Congressman, would you mind if we get a picture of you in the office so I can post it with my update on the Commission?"

"Of course, Ms. Nicholson." He got up and grabbed his suit jacket off the hanger. He should have worn Armani today.

"Let's get Chris in this one, too. He works hard on behalf of us taxpayers."

Chris quickly glanced down at his knitted tie and khakis. Jerry knew what the poor kid was thinking by the dread in his face. If anyone looked like an intern today, it was him.

They stood by the table with the files piled on it. Jerry knew it would look like there was a lot of work to do.

Ms. Nicholson took a handful of pictures and worked to get Chris's last name spelled right. She snapped a few pictures with the Congressman on his own as well. Jerry was amused to watch his new friend lean in on Chris and gently place her hand on his forearm, melting the poor kid to a steaming puddle. Jerry was enjoying watching this expert develop a source, which he would have to be mindful of going forward.

Jane strode in as though Ms. Nicholson had already left and plopped two binders on the Congressman's desk.

"Jane, please show Ms. Nicholson out. Oh, and please give her the information on our fundraiser. She has promised to stop in." Turning to Nicholson, Jerry said, "And obviously, if we can be of any service, let us know. I would be happy to carve out time in my schedule for you."

Jerry understood Nicholson was in no position to object to her forced departure, and he rather enjoyed her subtly smart-ass smile as they shook hands. Jerry thought for sure she was seriously considering kicking him in the balls. And he wasn't sure he would mind. He watched his guest give Jane a thorough once-over.

"Nice of you to bring your mom to D.C., Congressman Sharpe," Nicholson said.

Jerry felt that one. He wasn't prepared for such a nasty parting shot, but he replied only with a smile. He watched as the door closed behind the two women, then he turned to his intern. Chris's mouth was still open wide enough to catch a frisbee. Jerry thought he might crumble right there.

Chris fumbled about, trying to collect himself as he scooped up files. "Sir, forgive me for my comment and interruption earlier. It won't happen again. What was that all about? She turned kind of mean there in the end, didn't she?"

"Don't worry. She has no interest in housing projects. That, young man, was what you call a fishing expedition. Do you really think that was about the defunct safety commission? I'm pretty sure we were the only people she found swimming in the pond the entire morning. The building is empty, Chris. She wanted to confirm I was at the fundraiser. The commission and the mayor's inaction were just excuses. But to be sure, let's call Shields to give him a heads up."

CHAPTER 31

When Sky came through the kitchen's swinging door with the last bag of groceries, the sight of Abby putting a turkey in the oven brought Thanksgiving to life in her heart. She was dressed in an old Alpha Chi T-shirt, orange sweatpants, and an oversized apron with "KISS THE COOK" printed on the front. The only part of her not marred in flour was her ponytail, which was loosely held in place at the back of her head with a large barrette.

Because Sky's culinary skills were limited to boiling water and paying for takeout, Abby had agreed to do all the cooking, if Sky handled "all the logistics." It was noon, and Sky had already been to the grocery store three times. Abby was frantic.

"Did you get everything?" she said as Sky set the bag down on the kitchen table.

"I think so."

Abby closed the door to the oven, threw the oven mitts on the counter, and made the soft growling noise she used whenever Sky failed to answer a yes-or-no question. "You *think* so?" Abby rifled through the bag. "Really? Is that what I should tell your mother?

'Well, I *think* there's baking powder in these tarts, but I'm not sure. What do you think, Mrs. Nicholson?'"

Sky pulled a small, cylindrical can out of the bag. "Baking powder," she said. "It's all good."

Abby continued to search the bag for what was missing. "It had better be good," she said. "What kind of wine did you buy?" Sky stared at her feet and took a deep breath instead of answering the question.

Abby put both hands on her head. "I can't believe it," she said. "You have to go out *again*? I need your help to get through these dishes by three so we can be ready by four!"

"Don't worry. I'm not going out again," Sky said.

"So I'm supposed to go? Is that it?" Abby said. Her voice was starting to tremble.

"No," Sky said. "We don't need wine. My mother doesn't drink, and having alcohol around is sort of unhelpful. Nicholson family gatherings are dry and have been for about five years."

Abby's mouth fell open. "What?"

"I'm sorry I didn't tell you," Sky said, "but it isn't something that usually comes up in conversation. So keep it to yourself, and pretend it doesn't bother you to drink water."

Abby looked at the four pies cooling on the stovetop, the tart pans waiting for batter, and finally at the turkey baking in the oven. Then she looked back at Sky. "You're telling me we are hosting a Thanksgiving dinner without alcohol."

"That's right," Sky said.

"Thanksgiving," Abby said. "With company. And nothing to take the edge off."

"Yes," Sky said, "and if you had ever seen a Nicholson gathering with alcohol, you would understand why." The two women stared at each other for a moment, and Abby's shoulders fell, as if she had just exhaled, or resigned herself to suffer for the common good.

"I can't thank you enough for all this," Sky said. "I'd be doomed without you. My mother thinks I'm useless in the kitchen, and she's not wrong."

Abby let out a deep sigh. "Oh," she said, "don't mention it. I've always wanted to cook a real Thanksgiving dinner. At my house, Thanksgiving was when we could have pepperoni on our frozen pizza while watching my parents throw things at each other. So this is progress."

"I'm sorry," Sky said.

Abby regained her composure. "Anyway," she said, "I will do this so-called 'dry' Thanksgiving for the sake of the sisterhood. But I might need your parents to sign a waiver. I cannot be held responsible for my actions under these circumstances."

CHAPTER 32

When Abby opened the front door on Thanksgiving Day, she felt as calm and composed as two full days of preparation could make her.

She was immediately overcome by the sight of Sky's mother. Her eyes smiled in tandem with the rest of her face, which, when combined with the way she carried herself, was utterly disarming. She was gorgeous, and to top it all off, she was dressed in a way that honored both the occasion and the neighborhood's bohemian vibe. *My God*, Abby thought, *all this time I thought Grace Kelly was dead. And here she is.*

Next to her stood a tall, thin man holding up a starched button-down, ruffled khakis, and wire-rimmed glasses that were more than two decades old. He was still quite handsome, but he had a formal and somewhat anxious air about him, as if he had lost a blue blazer and was constantly worrying about it. He kept his lips tight in a sort of shy, good-natured smirk while glancing down at a large platter he held in both hands. He was adorable.

Abby's anxiety evaporated. *I don't care what you say, Skylar,* she thought, *but if you don't want them, I'm taking them.* "Well, hello!"

Abby said as she let them into the apartment. "Happy Thanksgiving! I'm Abby. It's so nice to see you again, Mr. and Mrs. Nicholson."

Sky's mother took her hand and looked straight into her eyes. "Oh, please, Abby," she said, "call me Anne. And you remember Arthur from all those parents' weekends in Virginia. What a treat to see you again! You know, it's funny, I was just saying to Art as we came up the stairs, 'Abby will probably come to the door, because God knows Skylar will be plenty busy in the kitchen.'" Anne Nicholson crossed her eyes slightly and made a comic face to underscore her sarcasm. "Didn't I say that, dear?"

"You did, indeed," Art Nicholson replied with a chuckle. Abby grinned.

"I heard that!" Sky said as she came out of the kitchen.

"Oh, you found it!" Abby yelled over her shoulder. "Good. That's called the kitchen, Sky. We are going to need you to go in there later and bring out some food."

***

If Sky's parents felt cheated out of hosting a holiday dinner, they hid it well.

"Well," Anne said. "What a fantastic spread!"

"I'll say," her husband said as he helped himself to some turkey. "Can I make a reservation for next year, or is it too early for that?"

"You are too kind," Abby replied with a smile. "The truth is that my prayers were answered today. I had no idea how any of this would turn out. We're lucky the fire department wasn't involved."

"Nonsense," Anne said. "Clearly, you have a gift. I can't imagine anything that would make it better."

Sweet Jesus, Abby thought, *I can: three glasses of wine.*

"So," Sky said with a mischievous tone in her voice as she

passed the green beans to her father, "what are we going to argue about this year, Dad? There are, after all, traditions to be honored."

Anne let her salad fork drop on her plate just enough to register her displeasure, but not enough to put a chip in it. "I would like to think," she said with a nod to Abby, "that we could drop that so-called 'tradition' once and for all."

"You're no fun," Sky said.

Anne gave Abby a slightly apologetic look. "They do this," she said. "It's like a game for them. I'm lucky you're here this year. Usually I have to sit back and decide which one gets the tranquilizer dart at the end of the night. At least we can have a cup of tea or something once they get started."

Abby laughed. "Of course," she said, "and you can tell me where to get the tranquilizer darts. That sounds quite useful." Sky gave Abby a concerned look as she passed the mashed potatoes to her mother.

"Okay, okay," Art said gently. "We get the point. We are not going to talk about how Sky is turning D.C. upside down with crowd-sourced, R-rated picture collages." Sky's jaw dropped.

"That's right," Anne said, "we don't have to talk about anything like that. Honestly, Arthur—behave yourself. Abby worked hard to make dinner. The last thing we need is a food fight."

"It is not a picture collage," Sky said.

"Never mind," Anne said quickly. "Skylar, I want to hear about your tea with Aunt Millie. How is she doing, the poor thing?"

It was Art Nicholson's turn to set his fork down on his plate for dramatic effect. "Because that isn't controversial at all," he said.

Abby sat back in her chair and smiled. *It would be more entertaining with wine*, she thought, *but I'll still keep them.* She watched as Art tossed the ball of tension across the table to Anne, who promptly ignored it and let it fall to the floor.

"So," she said to Sky, "how was Millie? Your father said I

shouldn't have asked you to go see her, but I explained to him—again—that you are all grown up and can take care of yourself." She wrinkled her nose at her husband, who had his arms folded across his chest.

"Oh, that," Sky said. "She's fine, considering the circumstances. Sends her love. She seems to think that what happened to Tyler has to do with a vast left-wing conspiracy that is trying to take down the family business."

"I'm sure she does," Art said.

"Arthur, please," Anne said with an exasperated look, "we're trying to hear about Skylar's time with Millie. There is no need to editorialize. Go on, dear."

"Well," Sky said, "there's not much more to say. She tried to get me to look into some of her conspiracy theories, and then gave me the name of a private investigator working for her. The whole conversation was odd. Dad gave me some background before I went in, though. That helped."

"Did he, now?" Anne said, turning her gaze to her husband.

"Yes, I did. I had to," Art replied, "and you know damned well why."

"Yes," Anne snapped, "and now Skylar is caught up in one of Millie's little adventures. I hope you're happy."

"I am not caught up in anyone's adventure," Sky protested. Her parents both turned to look at her. "Yes, you are," they said in unison.

There was an awkward silence while Art and Anne slowly turned their gazes back toward one another. "I told you what she knows," Art said to his wife. "Go ahead. If you're so good at this, fix it yourself." His wife gave him a cold, irritated look.

"Fix what?" Sky said. "What are you two talking about?"

Abby was now leaning forward in her chair, putting small forkfuls of mashed potatoes into her mouth as if they were handfuls of popcorn at a movie.

"Enough!" Anne said and turned to Sky. "Darling, did Aunt Millie say anything that surprised you?"

"What do you mean?" Sky said.

"Aunt Millie," Anne said, "never has only one purpose in mind when she does something. In the past, people we've cared about have thought they were doing us a favor by helping Millie but found themselves entangled in something they did not expect and couldn't escape."

"Unless," Art interrupted, "they agreed to do something that would hurt us. That was usually the only way out."

"I was getting to that," Anne said tersely. "Butt out, Arthur." The man returned to his irritated pose on the chair across from her.

"Skylar," she said, "did Millie say anything that surprised you—drop a surprising name or fact, perhaps?"

"Now that you mention it," Sky said, "yes. She asked me about Abby." It was now Abby's turn to drop her fork onto her plate in shock.

"Me?" she said. "She asked about me?"

Anne turned her head back at Abby, then slowly back to Sky. "Why on earth?"

"We were all at the Good Samaritan the night Tyler was murdered—Aunt Millie, Tyler, Abby, and me. She noticed Abby."

"I'm sure she did," Anne said with a smile. "What did she want to know?"

"The usual things," Sky said. "If I knew her, how I knew her, where she was from."

"What did you tell her, Skylar?"

Sky looked at Abby. "That she and I were sorority sisters at UVA. That she's from Syracuse. That's all."

"That's all?" Anne said, as she gave her husband a quick look.

"That's all," Sky said.

"You're sure?" Anne said to Skylar.

"I'm sure."

"I hope your memory is accurate. I really do. Because now you have drawn poor Abby into this and have done so when she's busy trying to get back on her feet. And you don't need that right now, do you, dear?"

"I'm not sure what you mean," Abby said. "I'm not the one who needs...oh." Her face stiffened.

Anne seemed taken aback and returned her gaze to her daughter.

"You don't know what that woman is capable of, Sky," her father said. "That's what I tried to tell you the other day. She'll use anyone, regardless of their circumstances. The woman has no conscience."

The Nicholsons turned to Abby to make an apology for their daughter just in time to see her pick up her plate, walk over to Sky, and scrape the rest of her food into her lap.

"Oh, I'm sorry," Abby said. "I don't know what came over me. It must be all the stress of trying to get back on my feet. I'll just go get the pies. Won't be a second."

"I'm sorry," Sky said. "I deserved that."

Anne Nicholson blushed, looked at her lap, and slowly placed her napkin on her plate.

"You did, Skylar Anne," she said firmly. "You certainly did."

CHAPTER 33

Jane's home was nicer than Jerry's three-room apartment. He had been to Jane's place in D.C. a few times already, had helped her move in, of course, and he had visited her on her birthday, given out candy on Halloween, and dropped her off when she needed a ride late in the evening. She loved animals and had insisted on finding an apartment near the zoo, so she sold her home back upstate just to swing the one-bedroom with a small garden and patio only a few blocks from the national zoo. Jane walked to the zoo almost every day to watch the animals on her way to the office.

Her loyalty to Jerry seemed only rivaled by her love for her favorite animal, the panda. She claimed that she was the one who had submitted "Christopher" as the successful name in the contest last summer.

Jane beamed at Jerry when she answered the door. She was dressed to the nines, with a lovely dark blue dress—one Jerry hadn't seen before. She was wearing a white apron with little yellow flowers, with frills on the shoulders and a small strap that wrapped it tight around the waist. She looked like she had walked off the set of a commercial from the 1950s, advertising some new kitchen appliances from Sears.

Jerry handed over the wine he was to bring and slung a knowing greeting to Chris who was also dressed in a matching apron, chopping up vegetables.

"Our handsome man is overseeing veggies and mashed potatoes tonight. I have the rest under control. Doesn't he look cute in the kitchen?"

Jerry could see the despair on his intern's face. He pulled out his phone and snapped a quick shot, knowing the image of his expression was too good to pass up. Chris raised a knife in protest, sure that a picture of him draped in this woman's apron was going to go viral for all to see.

Jerry winked at him, like Chris was doing his part to hold the fort. "Christopher the sous chef panda. How cute."

Jane did a terrific job on the meal and did more than her fair share of damage to the wine. Jerry could tell Chris was terrified to have alcohol in front of him, so Chris constantly chugged Dr. Pepper, and was frequenting the bathroom by the time a pumpkin pie emerged from the oven.

Jerry was ready for the couch. He loosened his tie and unbuttoned his collar for a little more comfort. He wasn't really interested in the holiday's second game. Detroit was downright awful, but that wasn't much of a surprise, and there was nothing else on.

Then a question from behind him disturbed the tranquility while dishes clanked and continued to be cleaned.

"Mrs. Robertson, what was the Congressman like as a kid? Was he always in charge?"

Jerry sat up straight. While he loved the fact that his intern worshiped him, he didn't like it when people pried into his past.

Jane scooted up to the chair's edge next to Jerry and took a long breath, either taking stock of the man in front of her or steadying herself from the wine. The question brought up a sad memory. She fiddled with the wine glass and tried to adjust how she sat. Her chin was pinned against her neck but she managed to generate a smile for Jerry. A slight sense of pity seemed to come from her as she gazed up into his eyes.

"He was always the most handsome boy in the room. Born to lead. He has always been a hard worker. A go-getter. Much like you are, Christopher."

Chris beamed as he washed a pot with some burnt potato stuck to the bottom. He was assigned that pot given he had forgotten the mashed potatoes when they had sat down.

"Jerry has always been so ambitious. He was able to get scholarships to go to college, and he was always working. He studied hard to be a lawyer and became the county prosecutor quickly. He always looked smashing in his fancy suits."

Jerry considered his college experience as Jane went off on a tangent to lecture Chris on how important college was for him to succeed. Maybe to distract herself from the memories of how he had entered her life.

He was lucky. He had managed to stitch together a wide range of small scholarships to make it all work. And law school wasn't a bank-buster. Buffalo wasn't really attracting the best and brightest. Well, if he didn't count himself. Learning criminal law had helped him understand the mind and heart of a prosecutor's playbook. But Jesus, Buffalo sucked. He couldn't believe the winters were worse than the ones in Montour Falls. Lake effect snow was different in Buffalo. And the football team. Lord.

"Despite that tragic day, we were blessed when he came to us. He was only fifteen, and he had everything he owned in an old, smelly duffel bag. John and I couldn't have children, mind you." Jane paused and cleared her throat. "It was so tough on Jerry. He went through so much as a boy. We were grateful he could come to us and stay. He was such a lovely boy."

Jane reached out her hand and touched Jerry's arm.

Jerry retracted a bit and could see in Christopher's face that he wanted to ask what had been so tragic, and how he had arrived in Mrs. Robertson's care, but he knew better.

Jerry turned and looked over the lines in Jane's face, long imprinted from the daily worry over her inherited charge. Jerry felt the wine's touch, or maybe it was the memory of that wet-dog smelling duffel bag he'd dragged to her house after he'd spent hours in his kitchen slumped on the barstool and watching police and EMTs scurry like mice in and out of his house all afternoon.

On that day, everyone in his house had avoided him, not knowing what to say or do. But he knew he would be safe at the Robertsons' house. Jane was mom's best friend. After grabbing some things, he was driven silently by the sheriff to his new home. The cops didn't know what to say to him either.

The smell of blood, the damp duffel bag. None of that goes away.

Jerry didn't need the reminder of why he hated Thanksgiving. He turned to hide what he was sure was reflected in his eyes.

Jane put her hand to her forehead, clearly feeling the swirl of the chardonnay she had enjoyed too much of that afternoon. She turned a bit so Chris could hear.

Jerry shifted his weight and turned up the TV. He tried to send a subtle message to Jane, but she either ignored him or didn't bother to see the signs, or perhaps the wine was driving the bus at this point.

"He was an Eagle Scout just like you, Christopher! I know that's why he adores you so. He was rather impressive in his uniform too! So handsome. So handsome. I think being outside and hunting had to be your favorite, right, dear?"

Jerry nodded and sent another discouraging look that failed to find its mark.

Jane pointed out the picture on the end table to Chris. He wiped his hands on his apron and scurried over to see what Jane was pointing out.

It was a picture of a deer hanging from a tree. Jerry, who must have been maybe sixteen or seventeen, with a rather round man who hadn't done any of the work. His clothes were spotless. Jerry was wearing a canvas apron soaked in blood, not the frilly thing in which Chris was now adorned. Young Jerry was grinning and holding onto the deer, perhaps to keep it from swaying while the picture was being taken. He had tied the deer's legs and draped it over a large branch to help drain the blood. He was resting his other hand on a leather knife pouch on his belt and beamed into the camera. Chris assumed the man was Mr. Robertson.

Jerry watched Chris examine the picture. "Sir, is that the same knife you have back at the office?"

"Yes, Chris, it is. My mom gave that to me when I started Scouts."

Jerry turned his attention to Jane, who seemed to be aging in front of his eyes. She fiddled with the cuff on her sleeve, searching for the tissues she had tucked underneath. While he wanted to avoid the pity, Jerry didn't withdraw when she reached up to pat his cheek.

"You should not have had to endure so much, dear. It wasn't fair. You were too young. Too young. But you have come so far, haven't you? Your mom would be so proud. John was proud of you too. You will always be my handsome boy."

Jane sniffled and turned away from the two men and whimpered a bit. "Your mom was so beautiful. So beautiful. It should have never happened."

Jerry hated Thanksgiving.

He stood up and placed a gentle hand on her shoulder as he

passed to get a much-needed refill.

"I will always be grateful."

Jerry watched as his fellow Eagle Scout looked down at the picture again. He could tell Chris was trying to look busy and avoid the hard moment.

Jerry's defense mechanisms were kicking in. Chris got a little more information than he'd planned. He was an intelligent young kid. Jerry watched him and wondered if he was admiring the fine ropework in the picture. Was he impressed with the deer? Or was it the knife that had his attention? The kid was quick.

Then Jerry thought what he must have been like when he was Chris's age. He might just be trying not to look at the crying woman in the chair.

CHAPTER 34

Thanksgiving was never as bad as the journey home afterward. There was nothing left there. Mom was long gone; the house was old and empty and had memories that could topple a redwood. And to top it all off, the town was due for one hell of a snowstorm. A typical squall. Lake effect snow was impressive, to say the least.

He needed to do the obligatory groundbreaking in Montour Falls. He delivered on the money and the townsfolk were eager to show off the big investment.

Just to be difficult, Jerry insisted the groundbreaking be held outside. There was nothing else going on in the middle of winter, except for watching kids play hockey on the ponds or maybe hunting deer to cull the herds. He wanted to get the ceremony done as soon as possible so he could get back to D.C. If the event were held in a cozy auditorium, people would linger, and the event would drag on. D.C. was where he knew he was needed. He had important things to figure out, and time was slipping away from him. He needed to prepare. He needed to work out the next move in his chess game with the formidable Mrs. Mildred Hawthorne.

Jerry paused. *Does she even know we're playing chess?*

The Chamber came through and arranged his flight into Syracuse. He brought his faithful sidekick, Chris, to make it look like he had people.

The approach into Syracuse in lake effect snow gales in early December in a plane the size of a Suburban wasn't exactly fun. Jerry had done this miserable flight dozens of times, but this time, he'd gotten a kick out of seeing Chris almost piss himself.

"Uh, you need to hold on, kid. It only gets worse when we try to land."

He enjoyed torturing Chris, who was whiter than the swirling snow tossing the plane up and down on their descent. The pilot managed not to kill the souls on board and planted the Cessna on the runway.

Jerry collected his things and threw on his wool overcoat. "Chris, peel your hands off the armrests. We have to get going."

Jerry smiled, watching the young man gather his thoughts and consider throwing up. The handprints left on the vinyl upholstery were deep. He didn't puke, so that was a bit disappointing, but he did look like shit.

Jerry was already in the car when he watched his intern emerge from the plane. He looked like he was on an arctic expedition, and Jerry half expected to see sled dogs rumble out of the plane with him. He had a brand new, deep yellow winter parka big enough to keep a rhino warm, snow goggles, and mittens that went up to his elbows. Jerry thought they were bigger than his oven mitts.

"Not much snow where you come from?"

"No, sir. Nothing like this!"

"This is a minor storm, so take a deep breath."

The van headed south on 81 toward Cortland. The one-and-a-half-hour ride doubled as the storm gathered strength, picking up tons of moisture over the lakes and dumping truckloads of snow all over the region.

"I have never seen so much snow!" Chris was still tucked deep in his parka as the van rumbled along. Oven mitts were still rubbing together, almost fast enough to start a fire.

"Chris, this is the light stuff. When we get to the Glen, this will look like a flurry." Jerry enjoyed watching the kid mouth to himself, "fuck me."

As the van approached the Glen, it was clear the Congressman knew what he was talking about. Even as the occasional plow charged through the roads, the snow was already piled higher than the van's hood. Mailboxes were buried, and cars were covered. It wouldn't take much to climb into a second-floor window given the snow drifts piling up.

The van made its first stop, dropping Chris at the Falls Motel, which was half buried in snow. The motel was a step up from the Clipper, or maybe two or three. Jerry didn't wait to see if his intern had found his room. He made the driver hit it as soon as Chris had his suitcase out of the trunk. Not his problem.

Jerry's house was only a few minutes away. The driver gratefully took his tip and stayed put in the warm van. Jerry thought he should have had his bag carried in for him given he was a congressman. The simple, white home, which blended nicely into the storm, would go unnoticed from the street, much like the Congressman.

The trip was long, cold, and bumpy from door to door. He slammed the door shut behind him and stood in the darkness for a moment. Jerry flipped the lights on and took a quick glance up the stairs directly in front of him.

He scooted over to the wood stove and was glad he had stacked the wood up the last time he was home. Be prepared. It took him two tries, and the stove was on its way. He knew in the morning he would have a little hot water to start the day.

He flopped onto the couch across from the stove knowing it would be the warmest part of the house. Given the house and its history, he rarely went upstairs. He did take advantage of one luxury, though—the thick down comforter Jane had given him as a gift when he'd won the election. Oh, it was nice, and made all the difference in the world with the wind howling outside.

CHAPTER 35

Monday morning was bitter, even by upstate standards. He was glad to get moving as the couch was not as comfortable as he remembered.

Still wrapped in the comforter, Jerry shuffled to the kitchen window over the sink. The window-mounted thermometer was empty of any red. A closer look, and Jerry could see the minus-five degrees staring back at him, daring him to go outside.

Whose idea was it to have the groundbreaking outside? Oh, yeah.

His mother's house was a simple, aluminum sided, two-bedroom bungalow built sometime in the 1920s. He wished it were better insulated, but it did the job. He was glad he didn't have to show Chris his house. He thought keeping up appearances was difficult enough.

Jerry started poking around the kitchen. He turned and stood in front of the short fridge, pondering the small note taped to the freezer door. It brought him a weak smile, as he touched it gently to ensure it stayed put. She always used pretty, almost frilly, paper—it looked like a doily along the edges:

Sweetie, please pick up some milk and bread on your way home. Love you! — Mom

Jerry loved her beautiful cursive—her penmanship was art-like and was as graceful as she had been. Jerry stood quietly for a moment. The smile dissipated as quickly as it had shown up.

The burning wood almost hid the other smells he remembered from years ago. Almost. After a quick search, Jerry found the only thing consumable this early in the morning—Sanka. It was likely as old as he, but it was always reliable and lasted forever.

Jerry settled onto his barstool at the counter and cradled his coffee in his hands. They were taking a little too long to warm up, but it didn't matter. The house would always be cold to him.

He knew he was on the same barstool. He swiveled to the exact same spot where he'd watched them bring her down. His eyes were magnetically attracted to the stairs. It had been a year since he'd last wandered up there.

The wooden stairs were directly in front of the main door. He had put carpet strips on them long ago, given there had been more than one occasion where he'd taken a tumble as a kid, with the front door stopping him from tumbling into the front yard. Not a pleasant way to stop a fall.

Jerry adjusted his position on the stool. He'd re-lived that horrible day a thousand times, but when he was home, the memories were much more intense.

Junior high was looking good. He started working at the marina when he was twelve, fixing motors and cleaning up boats. He was making decent money for a kid, and he was glad he was helping his mom out with the bills. He knew a nurse didn't make a whole lot upstate. You had to be in the city to make decent money.

He had burst through the door with a sack of milk, bread, and a candy bar for Mom, looking forward to the steak dinner that the two of them had planned earlier in the week.

Mom's car was in the driveway, but the kitchen was quiet. No food was being prepared. She had to be home.

Jerry winced to himself as he remembered the feeling when he'd called out for his mom. The house felt like an ancient cavern, open for the first time in thousands of years. Much like it was now, but at the same time, different.

Jerry could see himself as the young boy standing in the doorway, bag in hand, looking right toward him, perplexed as to why dinner wasn't well underway. He recalled it as clear as day. There, draped on the barstool, was Mom's purse. She was home.

Growing concern bubbled in his stomach. Jerry could feel it now, even twenty-five years later. He left the comforter draped where his mom once hung her purse, walked over to the stairs, and planted himself in the same spot, looking up the stairway.

He remembered his first steps up and began to retrace his movements from that day. He placed the coffee mug on the end table where he had set the brown bag of milk and bread long ago. The smell's intensity seemed to return to Jerry the moment he gazed up the stairway. The silence and the unusual scent told him something was wrong.

Jerry remembered working his way up the stairs. As he climbed, the air was filled with a syrupy, smoky odor. The odor wasn't sweet, but thick, and it didn't really hit him squarely until he was more than halfway up the stairs. He recalled the odd sensation when he had spotted a small waterfall on the top step.

Jerry tried to shake himself free from this cruel memory. Stuffy, uninterrupted air competed for space in his head, but he could still smell it. He was already down the path of the memory, and there was no turning back now.

Jerry arrived at the top of the steps, retracing the same moment over and over again. The landing was the same, except the oval of the blue shag rug was gone. There was no water on the floor. It had a light, bluish-white hue from several layers of dust.

There was a skylight covered in snow, casting the hallway in a soft white tone that reminded him of a museum. It was too late to turn back. Jerry lost himself in the filtered light.

Jerry's mind raced back twenty-five years. He could hear and feel the sloshing under his feet. He thought the toilet had clogged and was spewing water and sewage. The soggy rug was covered with an inch of chocolaty water, and he could almost feel the rug slide under his feet.

As he adjusted his feet at the top of the landing as though the water were still flowing, Jerry took a deep breath as the bathroom doorway came into sight. The door was wide open, and beyond the sink was the claw-footed bathtub, now empty and cold.

Jerry banged up against his memory. He was there again, and he approached the bathroom. She was there, slunk down in the bathtub with one arm sticking up against the wall. A bloody handprint was plastered just above her, and a blue haze of smoke hovering over her.

Her beautiful hands. Such slender, beautiful hands. Graceful. Elegant. Jerry thought she could have been a model. Nursing was just to pay the bills. She was breathtaking. But now her hand was limp with splotches and streaks of blood running and mixing with the water that was flowing over the tub's rounded edges.

Young Jerry sprinted into action and closed in on his mom. He had streaked into the bathroom screaming and plunged into the tub with her. He was covered in her blood, her bathwater, and her vomit.

After two tries, he finally scooped her from the water that looked more like coffee and dragged her limp, naked body into the hall and laid her on that soggy rug. He screamed and tried to revive her, shaking her and howling.

He gathered himself as best he could and desperately began a clumsy version of CPR. He knew he wasn't doing it right, but he did his best. While trying to breathe life into her, his air pushed through her chest and out a hole the size of a quarter. What is that? It bubbled and sputtered blood and blackened water when he blew air into her. Then he knew. He rolled her to her side and could see a much larger gash in her back.

An intense and foul smell of vomit and burnt air pierced his nose and made him dizzy. He turned away to throw up, and then he scooped her up as best he could as he hugged his lifeless mother.

The old wooden floor creaked under him and snapped him back to the quiet, empty hall. Jerry had stopped short of going into the bathroom and just stood where he once had been on his knees, sobbing over his mom. There was no water. No blood-soaked rug. His mom was long gone. Jerry crouched down and touched the floor where she had lain. Nothing.

He stood up and reflected on the sound of water sloshing around. He was able to turn this memory to his recent visit to the Potomac. The night in the river. The night of the storm. The night he began his revenge. He knew Mildred Hawthorne had something to do with this horror. He breathed deeply to regain his sense of self. He knew he had to get back to the city as soon as possible and finish what he began.

CHAPTER 36

The storm had left serious snow on the ground. It looked to be about two feet of fresh powder on what must have been a foot or so from a prior storm. Jerry threw on his overcoat and gloves, stuffed on a wool hat and took the shortest route to the garage, literally plowing his way with his knees.

The International Scout was in pretty good shape. There was a little rust on the panels, and there were a few brush scratches on the fenders. The Scout was beige and featured ugly orange-and-brown plaid upholstery. Jerry reached into the driver's footwell and popped the hood to disconnect the engine block heater and the trickle charger. He knew it would be a few miles on the road before his Harvester had heat. He had locked the hubs before he started it, so he dropped it into low gear and the truck marched out and through the driveway with ease.

He lumbered down to main street and found the town's jewel, the Donut Shop. This was where all the action was in town. The social event before the social event. It was already humming, townsfolk gathering both inside and out, the braver folks leaning on their trucks in this chill, most likely talking about the lousy plowing job Earl and Matty had done—again.

The Donut Shop was built larger than most of their franchises in anticipation of such weather. That was one thing Frankie knew— how to stretch a dollar. When he'd developed this fancy new hangout, he knew it had to tuck a lot of folks in when the weather turned really foul.

There Frankie was, holding court in the corner booth. He clearly spent a lot of time here. His belly and the jelly on his tie told the whole story. It was the same tie he had worn back in D.C.

Jerry recognized faces but didn't remember most names. Some quick introductions and coffee, and he would be able to endure the event. One thing was certain. This place was exclusively for the locals. You would never find any of the summer blue bloods popping in here. They wouldn't be caught eating a Boston Creme, at least not in public.

The blue bloods owned this town in the summer but deserted townsfolk once September came along. They had no problem firing folks or laying them off, because they knew some would come back to work for them again. The Hawthornes summered here, and they had fired and rehired several of Jerry's neighbors over the years.

Locals upstate are tough folks, able to deal with nasty winters, snow piled up through May, and storms from across the lakes that would rival any hurricane in the Atlantic. They were hunters, gatherers, and gritty. Jerry knew that these traits were what made them better. Better than the soft-handed aristocrats. Those blue bloods had never handled a snow shovel, or dug a car out of a snowbank, or worked at the Big M to pay for the heat in their homes. They never split wood in the summer and nursed blisters just to be ready for what was to come.

This could be the only part of coming home that he liked. He liked mixing it up a bit with folks like him, like his mother. People who worked hard and earned their keep. These folks made their own beds in the morning, made the beds of those living in the mansions on the water, and cleaned toilets to get their kids through community college. These were the folks who knew the kids behind the counter serving coffee and donuts. They were their neighbor's kids, their friends, and hard work was always appreciated.

But even with the admiration of his townsfolk, Jerry knew he didn't quite fit in. He never even tried to look the part. He'd been one of them until his mother's murder. Then he was forever that kid who was whispered about, the one everyone shied away from in case death was contagious. And the rumors about what happened to his mom drove him mad.

After an hour of typical town gossip and grand plans to make Watkins Glen the next Sedona, but with a lake as far as the eyes could see, the crowd piled out of the Donut Shop and headed over to the recently plowed housing site, located alongside the not-so-elegant Clipper Inn.

Chris was already there, strutting around in his ridiculous yellow parka covering him from head to toe, while the townsfolk casually milled about in heavy sweaters and thick hats. There was no question who the out-of-towner was.

Jerry surveyed the site and smiled at Chris's work. The sound system was set up, and Chris had managed to erect a tent to cover the speakers to protect the community leaders when they addressed the frozen crowd. There were even two mushroom-shaped heaters flanking the stage. *The kid did his job well.*

Chris was turning into a good advance-man. He even had some hot coffee ready and was directing the Chamber volunteers to get it all set up the way he wanted. Chris greeted Jerry in customary fashion.

"Congressman Sharpe, good morning. A bit chilly, yes?" Chris handed Jerry a few hand warmers. "They are a bitch to open, sir. Maybe someone has scissors?"

Jerry was already on it, whipping his trusty bone-handled knife from his hip, and expertly slicing them open without puncturing the bags. Jerry handed two back to his intern, who was standing there in awe of the Congressman's blade-work, and slipped two others into his gloves.

The handwarmers reminded Jerry how cold it really was. *Jesus, that thermometer must have been lying. Only negative five my ass.*

CHAPTER 37

The program had enough speakers to fill a dump truck. Jerry was one of the first, but he knew that just meant he had to stand there and listen to everyone's crap for the next hour after he'd spoken. Jerry was a little pleased with himself knowing that all the guests at the event would have to suffer the arctic temperatures. He took extra comfort in seeing that there was no sign of Jim, which warmed Jerry's heart a little bit more. He got the message.

Montour Falls was a typical small town in upstate New York. With about 1,700 people, it sat on the southern border of Watkins Glen. The Glen was reasonably famous in comparison given the falls, the racetrack, and of course, the lake. Jerry figured it was cold enough where the waterfalls were frozen over and the town didn't have anything else going on, so a grand opening would be a big deal. The hardy folks of Watkins Glen weren't afraid of a little weather.

Jerry scanned the crowd, a large one by Montour Falls standards. He tried to listen to Frankie read his introduction, which was likely provided by his eager and capable intern. "Folks, our good friend Congressman Sharpe was instrumental in getting the $200 million in funding and housing tax credits for the development of this project to transform our lovely town. Think about all the folks who can move here and stop those hour-long commutes to the hospital! This may be the first time, but it certainly won't be the last time, our local boy brings home the bacon for us!" But the Congressman's mind wandered. He was distracted by the Big M's crappy sign just across the street. The Big M was a convenience store that had one of everything. He had stopped there to pick up milk and bread for his mother that day. He'd even thrown in a Snickers as a surprise for her.

"Congressman? You're up, sir!"

Jerry snapped back to it and gathered himself. He didn't need to relive that again this morning. Once today was enough.

He turned to the reason he was in town. He took a moment at the mike before he got going. He took some pride in the fact that he was able to provide for this working-class town.

"This is why you sent me to Washington. To deliver on the projects and programs others take for granted. Together, we found $200 million for our town!

"Just up the road along the lake, there are empty, warm mansions while our friends here can't find affordable places to raise their families."

Jerry scanned the huddled crowd for affirmation. A few nods.

"I am so grateful all of you took the time to brave this snow flurry today. We may be a small town, but we are mighty! I'm sure our wealthy neighbors are basking in their shorts somewhere in the Caribbean as we get started on building warm homes for our friends." A few generous chuckles from the crowd.

"We know that these winters can be harsh. When the tourists abandon our town during the winter, we are left with our hard work to keep warm, to keep our businesses open, and to make sure we are ready for the spring. We take care of each other."

Jerry smiled to himself. The crowd was eating it up. "I need to thank our 'unofficial' mayor, Frankie. Frankie, thank you for investing in our town and creating much-needed jobs. And thank you to all of you who have supported me. I hope you feel I am delivering on my word."

Jerry left Jim out of the accolades. A congressman could not publicly support a makeshift brothel next door.

"I'd also like to thank Jane." The crowd perked up at the mention of one of their favorite locals. "Jane sends her love to all of you. She misses this place and is looking forward to coming up for a visit soon."

Jerry worked through his prepared remarks with skill. He needed to wrap up before there was a parking lot full of frozen statues in front of him.

"I want to finish my comments by thanking all of you. What makes our town special is all of us. We are all special, like our waitresses, like Susan over there." Jerry threw a wink her way. "And mechanics, like Danny Jr., as well as plumbers and electricians like Lou and Gregg, who will work on this project. We make this town the way it is. We are lucky we get to live in such a wonderful place."

This is where Jerry's authenticity shone through. He was as close as a politician could get to being a local. They knew his mother had worked at the hospital up the road, cleaning other people's shit and doing their linens. She was there for them when they were most in need of help.

He stepped back and waited for the shovels to be handed out. He made sure he was in the middle of the pack but hated the fact that these asses gathered a bit too closely to keep warm. They all took their cue and thrust their golden spray-painted shovels in the dirt that was brought over from the greenhouse connected to the town maintenance facility. The ground was frozen long ago and they would have never made a dent in it otherwise.

Applause. Hot coffee. More hot coffee. Lots of gloved hand shakes and pats on the back. Successful day!

As expected, Jerry spotted the old, grumpy, and always disheveled reporter from the *Review & Express* milling about in the crowd, working his way toward him. The same slug who covered his victory a year ago and put his story with the obituaries. The same guy who covered him when he was a prosecutor, but always managed to make his stories feel like an insult, even when he put the bad guys in jail.

Jerry attempted a smile as he looked over the guy, who was twice his age. He still looked like he had just rolled out of bed and finished his Journalism 101 course online. He was somewhat pear-shaped, and Jerry liked the fact that he towered over the man when he bellied up next to him.

Jerry offered the obligatory handshake and smiled. "How are you holding up in this weather, Polzinetti? Are you going to stick this story next to the weather section on page six?"

"Good. Typical storm these days. This is an exciting initiative. You must be proud. Did you have to punch anyone in the nose to get this done? How can the folks in town reach Chairman Perry to thank him for the project?"

Jerry winced at the combination of cheap shots thrown at him with such malice. They were better than his. Where should he start? "I was a key vote getting the funding passed, so I am sure Perry was appreciative."

Jerry turned to greet some folks looking to get a picture with him but couldn't quite break away in time.

Polzinetti pressed on. "Congressman, it has been an interesting couple of weeks down in D.C. We saw the coverage of Tyler Hawthorne's tragic death. He spent a lot of summers up here. Did you know him?"

CHAPTER 38

Jerry saw the Brick Tavern's hazy lights peek through the now-full snowstorm that was crushing the region. Jerry always thought the Tavern was the only cool hangout in the area. Yes, the lake and waterfalls were nice, but the Tavern had a real history to it. And it was one of the few places that felt cozy to him. At least as cozy as he could feel.

While someone had converted it to a tavern about ten years ago, it was once a stop on the old stagecoach route. It had also once served as a sanatorium in between eras as a rest stop and a place to grab a beer and a good burger. Now that made sense to Jerry.

He ignored the handicapped sign and stuffed his Scout right up against the old stone building. He trotted up to the rather large oak door and quickly swept himself in, slamming the door behind him.

The Tavern was one huge room, like a big ski lodge. The picnic tables were packed in close to each other. Chris was waving him over. He had found a spot to station them as close as possible to the fireplace. Chris's cheeks were rosy, and he clearly could not hide his excitement at being snowed in and having dinner with his boss.

Chris greeted him with a bit more enthusiasm and volume than necessary. "Congressman, it is so good to see you again! Wasn't the event this morning awesome?"

Jerry dumped himself into the spot across from his eager retriever and exchanged nods with folks around the tables who had bothered to see who was being called "Congressman."

The waitress finally made her way over to Jerry and Chris. Jerry smiled to see Chris brighten even more as the waitress leaned in. Chris was no seasoned pro, but he managed to try some familiar tactics. After reading the name tag, Chris took his first shot. "Um, Marie, is it? I think the Congressman and I would like to order a couple of beers before we order dinner."

The waitress, who was likely dealing with too many young guns over the course of the evening, smiled. "Sure, kid. But it's Mary, not Marie. What will you boys have?"

Jerry needed to help the kid out. "Mary, how about a Genesee for me and a Moosehead for my chief of staff here. That work for you, Chris?"

Jerry smiled as the kid restrained himself from jumping over the table to give him a hug.

Mary raised an eyebrow and was now a little more interested in her two new guests. She nodded and threw a more welcoming smile to Chris as she strode off to deliver the order.

Jerry gave his loyal friend a wink. "Thank you for all you did at the event today. I agree, it went well. It was freaking cold, though, even by upstate standards. But we got through it, didn't we?"

The beers were delivered by a much more engaging Mary, and she made sure she bumped into Chris's shoulder and pressed her hip against him while taking the dinner order, even though there was plenty of room to maneuver. Chris couldn't look up at her but kept in contact as well.

"You boys might want to add some potato salad to those burgers. It's the best it's been in a long, long time." Jerry watched her place her hand on Chris's shoulder and give it a squeeze before heading to the kitchen.

He was getting a kick out of this little game of theirs. He could tell Chris wasn't sure which was warmer, the fire at his back or the radiant Mary who was now giving him the attention he desired.

He felt comfortable for the first time in a while. He was enjoying the winter weather, driving his Scout through town and looking forward to a nice cozy meal at the Tavern. Now he was watching his little buddy make real progress with the cutie. Things were looking up.

Then Chris destroyed his good mood. "Congressman, I went to the library this afternoon since it was the only thing open. There was a story from back when you were in the prosecutor's office. Isn't this the place where you punched that guy? The one who owns the Clipper down the road and was in D.C.?"

Jerry sat back and stared at his dinner companion. "That's none of your business, Chris." The scowl should have been enough to make the kid leave town, but Chris didn't catch the nastiness of his response. "All I will tell you is that he got what he deserved. What time is our flight in the morning?"

Chris seemed like he was about to say something. He might have realized that he'd stepped in it. But a chuckle from behind Jerry caught both of their attention.

Jerry recognized the voice. Well, maybe he recognized the chuckle. He was back-to-back with Henrico Polzinetti. Jerry could now smell the heavy swirl of beer from behind him. It seemed like only a minute ago they were at the morning's event, and Jerry hadn't appreciated the cheap shot about Chairman Perry.

"Congressman, I'm pretty sure there was more to that night than you are telling the kid."

Jerry burned hot inside, hotter than the three-foot fire curling around in the stone fireplace behind his intern, who had no idea what he'd just started. But he turned back to his burger, hoping the asshole behind him would shut the fuck up.

Polzinetti continued. "It was in October last year, right, Jerry? You were addressing the Knights that night, trying to raise money for your run when Jefferies was found with a lady of the night. Funny about that fall from grace, don't you think?"

Henrico paused to see if he'd generated a reaction. Seeing none, he continued to press after another swig. "Anyway, Jim was interrupting you and brought up the nasty business about your mother. You know, fraternizing with the enemy or something like that. No one is willing to tell the whole story there, either, but they say you lost it and smashed his nose into bits. Looked like this potato salad here."

Jerry turned and his cold blue eyes burned a gaping hole into Henrico's forehead. He could see the reporter shrink at his intensity. Jerry's entire chest seemed to grow two-fold.

"Hank, it is Hank, isn't it? You don't know shit. If you were such a good reporter, why hasn't the *Times* picked you up? Oh, that's right, you were so smart you had to work your way up from middle school sports to covering the hunting season. You don't know what the fuck you're talking about. Mind your own business, you muckraking dick."

Jerry got up, tossed some cash at Chris and made sure he bumped Hank hard enough to make him spill his beer as he barreled toward the door.

CHAPTER 39

Sky took her seat on the small stage at the Cowboy Café, looked out at the packed bar, and felt slightly sick to her stomach.

Shit, she thought. *This had better work.*

The whole thing had been Abby's idea. Within twenty-four hours of Tyler Hawthorne's death, *The Thread's* coverage of crime in the D.C. area had become must-read content, and within a week of it, #IsDCSafe was a political catch phrase in itself, used to describe a whole basket of the city's problems.

This meant the entire town wanted to staple themselves to the story and the woman who had broken it. *The Thread* had more interview requests for Sky from traditional news outlets than it could handle, and Abby was quick to point out that agreeing to appear on someone else's old-school network was no way to build *The Thread's* particular brand. It was too passive. The solution, she suggested, was to take control of the discussion, "in real life," but in a way *Thread* readers would trust. *The Thread's* publisher agreed, and Is D.C. Safe?: A Listening Session was born.

Sky hated the name but liked the idea. The format was an

unfiltered, live conversation between *Thread* readers, the in-person audience, and representatives from the mayor's office and Congress. It would be live-streamed, and Skylar Nicholson, the name behind the famous hashtag, would moderate the conversation. Abby expected the online audience to outnumber the in-house audience by a hundred to one.

In theory, it was a low-risk proposition—the topic was big enough to notice inside the beltway, and too small for the big media companies to care about. In practice, however, Sky knew that doing it live was a huge risk. Anything could happen, and a disaster would have more reach than a modest success.

After a tense negotiation, the mayor's office grudgingly agreed to send Clarisse Baker-Samuelson, the deputy director for public safety, for what they knew would be a mauling. She knew it, too.

"Hello, Sky," she said as she stepped onto the makeshift stage next to the bar. "Should I have brought my helmet? I keep one in my office."

Sky quickly shook her hand and tried to calm down one of her oldest and most trusted sources. "Hello, Clarisse, thanks so much for coming. Don't worry. It's just a conversation. I won't let it get out of control."

"I know, Sky," she said. "We're good. Just do what you always do. So who on the Hill ended up with the short straw on this one?"

"Congressman Sharpe."

"Who?"

"Jerry Sharpe," Sky said, searching the room for the one puzzle piece that had not yet fallen into place. "23rd district, New York State. Freshman. He was the only guy on the Hill dumb enough to see me about the Hawthorne murder." Clarisse gave Sky a knowing look. Few people on Capitol Hill wanted to take a meeting with Skylar Nicholson.

"Don't worry," she said, "the way this is going for you, they'll be knocking down your door in no time. But I never said that."

"Thanks, Clarisse. I appreciate that. I know this hasn't been easy for you."

"Don't mention it. Anyway, this guy Sharpe. Does he know anything about the problem, or is he just going to come and run his mouth off?"

Sky saw Sharpe walk into the bar's front door and waved to him to come over. Then she turned back to Clarisse.

"I have no idea," she said. "My guess is that he'll run his mouth off. But he strikes me as someone who is full of surprises. So be ready."

Sharpe's staffer Chris appeared at the small stage at the same moment Sky saw his boss enter the Cowboy Café. They were the only people in the place dressed in a suit and tie. The young man had a desperate, rushed, and hopeful expression on his face.

"Good evening, Ms. Nicholson," he said, with more than a little Eddie Haskell in his voice. "The Congressman is here and working the crowd a bit, and I just wanted to assure you that he and I have gone over the format in great detail. Everything is in order."

"Thanks, Chris," Sky said. "I expected no less." The young man blushed and looked at his feet in a futile attempt to hide it. "Also," she said, "I have been thinking about it, and you should grab a microphone during the open forum. If you will check in with Serena over there, she can get you set up. Serena will handle the questions coming in from *The Thread*, and you'll handle the questions from the audience."

Chris's face lit up. He was finally going to be part of the process—part of the *conversation*—and it made him giddy. He had just made it over to Serena's place near the sound equipment when Congressman Sharpe made it to the stage, dressed as though he were headed to work at Goldman Sachs.

"Well, hello," he said in a cheerful voice. "Sorry to cut it a bit close there. This is my first foray to this part of Arlington. I got a bit turned around. It's trickier than it looks."

"Yes," Sky said, "it is. But this is where our readers live when they are not working thirteen-hour days downtown. Thank you for coming, Congressman. This is Clarisse Baker-Samuelson—she is representing the mayor's office tonight."

"My condolences," Sharpe said with a well-timed grimace. It worked. Clarisse smiled.

"Don't worry about me, Congressman," she said. "I'm used to it. Welcome to Washington, by the way."

"Thanks."

The crowd was suddenly silenced by a sharp, loud whistle coming from a young woman with scholarly glasses standing on a chair next to the sound equipment. She pointed at her watch and stared at Sky. Sky got the message and leaned down to a microphone that was set up at her place at the table.

"That was my cue. Thank you, Serena. Ladies and gentlemen, let's hear it for *The Thread's* secret weapon, Ms. Serena Wilson. This is her show." The crowd applauded, and Serena bowed. The panelists took their places at the table. Serena climbed down from the chair, donned a set of headphones, and held one hand into the air for the final countdown. The small crowd at the Cowboy Café caught on and counted with her. *Five, four, three, two, one. And we're live!*

CHAPTER 40

The program's first twenty minutes went smoothly, mostly due to the nature of the venue. The Cowboy Café was a relatively small place—big enough to handle a set of regulars on any given night, but not so big that an evening crowd could become a mob. *This place is perfect*, Sky thought. *Let's just hope the people behave themselves.*

Serena fed Sky a set of testimonials that Thread readers had submitted in advance. The stories were sobering—sexual assaults, muggings, harassment—happening daily around most government buildings after seven o'clock at night. It was not lost on the crowd that these attacks usually happened long after their bosses had gone home to the sleepy suburbs.

Ms. Baker-Samuelson did her best to reassure the uneasy crowd that the mayor's office was aware of the problem and taking it seriously. Congressman Sharpe struck a pose, making sure everyone who could see him on the stage saw how thoughtful he was about the entire situation. And Sky simply did her best to keep the conversation as constructive as possible.

Her ability to do so evaporated as soon as she opened the floor for "an open exchange of ideas." Chris and Serena took turns getting the questions and comments from the audience to the panel. They quickly became more pointed and began to run together until one common, shrill message became obvious: *My friends are getting hurt, I'm afraid I'm next, and what the hell are you doing about this right now?*

There was only so much Sky could do to influence the direction and tone of the questions. The stage was lit in such a way that she couldn't see the audience clearly and therefore couldn't rely on her charm to lower the temperature in the room. And they were quickly seeing that it was impossible to calm the online commenters.

After about ten minutes of pretty vicious questions and comments, Sky decided to get up from her seat and walk to a position where she could see the people in the room. "Okay, folks," she said, "we're all passionate about this. But we are not going to get anywhere with name-calling and ultimatums. These people up here are interested in—" Sky froze as her eyes adjusted to the light and she saw two men she detested in the crowd—Frank Bergeron, her nemesis from the *Times*, and her ex-husband, Chip. *Oh shit*, she thought. *It's an ambush.*

"Interested in your suggestions and ideas," she finished after a pause. "Now let's start again." She saw Chip raise his hand, and the ever-helpful Chris handed him a microphone. *Here we go*, she thought.

"I have a suggestion," he said. "I think the police have a hard enough time without these crimes' gory details posted online. For all we know, some of these guys are getting off on the publicity. Know what I mean?" The crowd issued a low boo, and Sky noticed Chris mouthing Chip's name to Congressman Sharpe.

"I disagree," Sky said. "The more information, the better. Besides, it's about time people got to see how heinous some of these crimes are. Otherwise, it's just words." She saw Bergeron open his notebook.

Chip was going in for the kill.

"Or," Chip said, "it's just click-bait. Does everyone here know the District's crime statistics—what the trend is? It's flat compared to last year at this time, and *down* compared to ten years ago." More boos. Sky stood on the stage, frozen, waiting for the event and her career to disintegrate. Congressman Sharpe watched the scene from his seat and began to scowl.

"But you wouldn't know that," Chip continued, "from a Twitter feed, or a message board, or even *The Thread*."

Sharpe stood up, took four steps forward, and gently took the microphone from Sky's hand. "And you sure wouldn't know about that, or any of what we have been talking about tonight," he said, "by reading *The Washington Post*, would you, Mr. Taylor? Everyone, please meet Mr. Chip Taylor—the man at the *Post* responsible for *not* bringing you the news these past two years. Tell me, Chipster— where the hell have you guys been on this one?"

A round of surprised and enthusiastic applause broke out, with whistles added, and Chip looked like he had been punched in the face. Chris realized at that moment that his boss did read and memorize the reporter bios he had provided him all those months ago. He glowed.

"I—well, what do you mean, exactly, Congressman?"

It was an unwise question to ask Jerry Sharpe ten seconds after he'd decided that he detested you. "What I mean, *Biff*," he said with emphasis, "is that good news coverage comes from whoever is closest to the action. We all know that. That's supposed to be *you*. People expect papers like the *Post* to be all over this sort of thing, but apparently it takes a creative and on-the-ball outfit like *The Thread*, with Ms. Nicholson over here, for you to catch on to the fact that young professionals are dying in Washington and no one in government is paying attention. Go back to sleep."

"Congressman," Chip said, "with all due respect—"

"Are you about to tell me, *Biff*, that if all these people are screwed by the *Post*, that they can always read the *New York Times*?" Sharpe now had his eyes on Bergeron. "Am I supposed to feel better about that?"

"Well, I—"

"Gosh, *Biff*," Sharpe said to what was now a room filled with shocked laughter, "I guess I am just plain dumb. I don't see how a Columbia graduate from Greenwich, Connecticut, who takes the Acela here from New York maybe three times a week can be credible on this story. I must have gone to all the wrong schools. I apologize." Frank Bergeron closed his notebook and looked at his watch.

Chip Taylor's face was bright red, and Sky had regained her composure. Jerry Sharpe handed the microphone back to Sky amid roaring applause.

"Well, thank you, Congressman," she said. "We're ready for the next question."

A medium-sized, pear-shaped man with salt-and-pepper hair gently took the microphone from Chip Taylor. It was now time for Chris to panic. He motioned to the gentleman to hand him the microphone, but the man just smiled and gave him a look that said, *You just try to take it from me.*

"My name is Henrico Polzinetti," he said. "I am from Montour Falls, New York, and I have a question for Jerry Sharpe."

Sharpe stiffened when he heard the voice, and Chris made wild gesticulations at Serena in a vain attempt to have her turn off the microphone.

"Well, welcome, Mr. Polzinetti," Sky said. "You've come a long way. What is your question?"

"I was just wondering," he said, "exactly what the Congressman is doing at the federal level to protect his staff, some from our hometown, and who are clearly at risk. What should I tell the people at home, Jerry? What are *you* doing to keep D.C. safe?"

***

Sky was able to shut the listening session down after ninety grueling minutes. The place cleared out quickly, and the panelists were all gracious as she thanked them for their time. Sharpe seemed positively energized by the experience.

"Thank you again for coming, Congressman," Sky said. "And for your help. I'm sorry about the little surprise at the end. I had no idea anyone would be here from your district."

"No problem," Sharpe said, as he scanned the room for both Chris and the nearest exit. "Hank likes to sneak up on me. But I answered his question. Now, Ms. Nicholson—"

"Please, Congressman, call me Sky."

"Yes. Well, Sky, I hope this went off as well as you hoped it would. I have a lot to think about now. An awful lot. By the way, have you had an opportunity to discuss my business proposition with your friend Ms. Sullivan?" With this, Chris arrived to escort the Congressman quickly into the cold November night.

As soon as she took her eyes off the Congressman, she noticed that the journalist from upstate New York had been watching the two of them from the other side of the room. He walked over to her and extended his hand in greeting.

"Henrico Polzinetti," he said gruffly. "I've noticed your work. Well done. It takes a pretty strong stomach to cover that kind of stuff." He started to walk toward the door.

"Thanks," Sky said. "Have you been covering Sharpe's district for a long time?"

He stopped and turned to face her. "Forever," he said. "Since before you were born, I would guess." His face darkened, and he paused as he chose his next words. "And if you don't mind," he said, "let me give you some free advice."

"I always welcome advice, Henrico. What've you got?"

"I know he helped you out tonight, and sort of saved the day, but don't get too close to Jerry Sharpe. Trust me."

Sky gave Henrico a puzzled look. "Okay," she said, "but why not?"

"I have known Sharpe since he was a Cub Scout. Only two kinds of things happen to the people around him—nothing, and bad things. There is no in between. You seem like a nice lady, so I thought you should know. The odds are not in your favor." He pushed open the door and looked over his shoulder again.

"Stay away from Jerry Sharpe. That's all I have to say."

CHAPTER 41

It was Jerry's turn at the trough. He had been to so many fundraisers in the city over the past month that he had almost forgotten that he got a turn. He had shelled out so much in donations that he was hoping to recover and maybe break even at this point, but he doubted that he could make up the difference.

Jerry wanted to make his fundraiser a bit different from the typical restaurant, but that was increasingly difficult as elected officials were getting creative and slick with their events. He recalled some idiot congresswomen who thought it would be a good idea to have a clown walk around and make balloon animals for folks. Everyone was surprised Bozo made it out alive.

Jerry's fundraisers didn't have the draw given his lack of stature or influence, so he had to pick a smaller venue to make it look full. Plus, he couldn't cover the costs of something like the Good Samaritan. That kind of place was only within reach of the committee chairs and senators, not for a simpleton from upstate New York.

But Jerry would take a crack at it, or Chris would have to. There were a few things that might work in his favor. First, Chris picked a

Monday evening, and a time that might be advantageous. Mondays were usually slow fundraising nights, so there were few to compete with, and this Monday was potentially fruitful because Jerry should be able to draw from a nearby event at the Hamilton.

The flamboyant Congressman Watson from North Carolina was hosting an event at a rather posh restaurant across the street. Jerry not only was able to skip that turd's fifth fundraiser of the year, but he was a bit pleased with himself that he might pull folks from Watson's event. The hobbit-sized southerner was a terrible drunk, and his events quickly turned into a sideshow.

***

"I haven't left yet, Chris. Stay calm."

"Yes, sir. You should know it won't be long before our friend's fundraiser starts to go sour. They should start coming over in about an hour, sir."

"Relax. We knew that was the best shot for us at this point to get a decent crowd. I'll be there soon."

Jerry was modestly confident lobbyists and even perhaps another congressman or two might see his fundraiser as a three-fer for them. They would be able to walk so they didn't have to bother re-parking; they could escape the shitty fundraiser and avoid the roadhouse-like chaos; and they might get a decent smoke out of the deal. An added benefit might be they could check a box by making a junior congressman feel like they cared.

Picking a nearby cigar bar was tactical on Jerry's part. He had frequented it enough to be at least known, and he was able to convince the owner to stay open past eleven on a Monday. Shelly's Back Room was centrally located, only a hop and a skip away from the White House, the pedestrian mall, and City Hall.

Jerry thought the location was ideal, and the short stroll across 14th would help bring folks to the door. But there was nothing like free booze and a couple of cigars to attract a little money. Shelly's was as well-known for its lengthy list of whiskeys as it was for its cigar selection.

But the real reason he was able to convince Shelly O'Brien to host the event and keep his doors open past eleven was his need to improve his bar's rather mixed reputation. Shelly's was not a particularly welcoming place. Known as a local fireman's bar, it was not exactly the place for people of color. If you were Hispanic, it was best you found another spot. The bartenders consistently got pounded on social media for their shitty service to certain clientele.

But Jerry liked the place and the low-key atmosphere. Shelly's wood-lined walls and bar treatments were in some ways reminiscent of pubs upstate, so it felt a little like home. While not a standalone building, Shelly's reminded him a bit of the Brick Tavern back at the Glen. Up to the point when Chris and Polzinetti pissed him off.

Jerry expected to see his fellow Empire State congressmen, and he might even get lucky to pull in his New York Senator, Jonathan Marion, who might pop in for a quick smoke. Chris thought some of his fellow committee members might indulge, but a Monday was tough given the rest of the week was full of fundraisers, charity events, and stupid award ceremonies no one cared about.

Jerry did not expect any whales to show tonight, but he thought it was likely a few Cudas could wander in. The only folks he was sure to see were baitfish. He depended on the young gun lobbyists to show up. They were looking for a place to gain any intel or influence to build their resumes.

Jerry grabbed an Uber even though the location was only a mile from his apartment. He wanted to arrive like he had a driver. He pulled up along F street and hopped out with energy. He was wearing his Armani—a wicked nice red tie with blue stripes that screamed power and influence. He smiled as Chris looked like he was going to puke with anxiety and excitement.

"Evening, Congressman! We have a few early birds already hanging out at the bar. You have time to swing in and say hello before you take your post at the door. Mrs. Robertson is all set up and ready."

"Thanks, Chris. Let's not fuck it up." A quick nod, and Jerry headed to the bar. Shelly gave him a raised eyebrow and a slight head toss toward the far end. Jerry recognized the baitfish since he bumped into them all the time but couldn't remember their names for the life of him.

Chris whispered from somewhere behind him: "Hector and James, from the Sierra Club."

Jerry smiled without turning around, knowing Chris was in his tiny wake as he strode over to the Latino man at the other end of the bar. Jerry thanked these first arrivals for their support, introduced his trusty sidekick and excused himself, as even the younglings knew the ritual of greeting folks as they entered the event.

Jerry strode with confidence toward the front door, patting Jane on the shoulder as he passed. She was dressed like she was going to church, complete with a black, wide-brimmed hat with a black band carrying a rose above her temple. "You look stunning, Jane. Love the hat. These guys will want to kiss you as they hand over their checks."

With a gentle giggle and a gloved hand placed against Jerry's cheek, Jane peered up from under the hat and winked at her charge from upstate.

Jerry was ready.

CHAPTER 42

Folks started to come and greet the good host as he smiled, chuckled, and slapped them on the back, enjoying the attention as people came from across the street. The room was filling quickly, mostly with the baitfish, who donated the minimum of $100 as that was all they could really afford. An occasional bigger check from their PAC later on was always appreciated and acceptable.

A gaggle of college students showed up who were clearly there only to see their friend Chris in action, and Jerry gladly let them in without a donation. They helped make the room look full.

The second wave of folks were coming in as the first hour slipped by. His fellow congressmen from New York, and even one or two from the Garden State, managed to make an appearance. These guys were there primarily to repay the favor of Jerry attending their fundraisers, which was really an easy way to have a little cash flow back and forth between them. Jerry knew that their checks to him would be on the light side, though. They were cheap bastards.

The growing crowd was making Shelly happy down there at the bar. He had both of his barkeeps hustling now, and the diverse crew making a showing would certainly help him shave off some of the criticism he was getting online. More importantly, he was getting paid handsomely by Jerry on an evening he would have otherwise lost money.

Jerry turned to see how Jane was holding up. Perched on her stool and keeping properly organized, she caught his eye and gave him a wry smile. He was about to return the goofy gesture when her eyes lit up.

Jerry snapped back to the door and there was a group of familiar faces from home. Much to Jerry's delight, there was Frankie Dominico leading in a group of homegrown upstaters. Jerry genuinely laughed as the fearless leader from back home beamed at him. Jerry grabbed the man and delivered a bear hug, a bit to Frankie's surprise, and Jerry glowed at this surprise visit.

"Jerry! I brought some of our gang from home to thank you for the great work you did on the housing project!"

Jerry was beside himself. He felt like they knew he mattered. He remembered several folks from the Donut Shop, and others from the groundbreaking event. At least he thought that's where he remembered them from.

Frankie had delivered. He'd brought a dozen folks and they all had checks to hand over to Jane. Of course they all knew her, and each was rewarded with a hug and a kiss as they swept through the door. It felt for a few minutes like folks were coming over for supper rather than a fundraiser. Jerry felt peppy as the troops made their way through the back slaps, hugs, and high fives. This was fun!

As the last of the upstate crew waddled in, Jerry noticed one last person lingering on the sidewalk. Henrico Polzinetti. When their eyes met, Jerry's smile tumbled away as quickly as it had arrived. Did he forget what had happened when they'd run into each other at the Tavern? The bullshit cheap shot at the groundbreaking? The listening session?

Jerry couldn't help himself. "What the fuck are you doing here?"

"Whoa, whoa. Sorry, Congressman. I heard the crew from home was coming, so I had to stop in." Jerry watched as the reporter shifted his weight. Polzinetti offered, "I do apologize for the last time we spoke. A little too much to drink, I'm afraid, and I should have left you be."

Jerry wasn't sure what to do. He knew it would make things worse telling him to take a hike, but did he want to have this clown mingling at his fundraiser?

Jerry was about to ask him to leave when a gloved hand stretched past him to greet Polzinctti. Jane had come to his rescue and offered a curt nod to her hometown reporter. "It's always good to see you, Mr. Polzinetti. Can we hold off on the cheap shots at my boy tonight and make this a nice event?"

CHAPTER 43

As she ran across the street toward Shelly's Cigar Bar, Sky muttered to herself about the insanity of Monday night fundraisers. *I can understand this guy Sharpe trying it,* she thought. *He's brand new and doesn't know the game. But Congressman Watson? The man should know better. He'll end up blowing ten grand so that fifty of the most desperate bottom-feeders in town can each give him a buck. It's not as if this hasn't been tried before. What the hell is he thinking?*

Sky made her way across the street, stared at the heavy oak door which protected Shelly's from the outside world, and hesitated. She owed Congressman Sharpe a favor, but her feelings about this were ambiguous at best. She had ended more than a few evenings at Shelly's with a lit cigar in her mouth—or at least this is what friends had told her later. Those nights were lost to her memory, so it was possible that someone on the other side of that door might know more about those evenings than she did.

To add to this vague sense of discomfort, Shelly's was a safe house of sorts for white members of the D.C. Fire Department. It wasn't explicitly racist in the way some places were, with framed sets of authentic Confederate currency mounted on the walls or prominently placed stars-and-bars in the restrooms. But it was nevertheless working-class and as white as the Wonderbread Shelly O'Brien used to make his sandwiches. This was not a place where a UVA-educated girl from the suburbs would feel welcome, or trusted, whatever the color of her skin.

Sky had only been able to cultivate sources at Shelly's because the owner was an old friend of her boss at the *Times*, and also Ramon's life-long poker buddy—a fact which was both odd and reassuring given the place's reputation. These two facts gave Sky more introductions and tips at Shelly's than she probably deserved. In return for this help, Sky had tried to help Shelly O'Brien understand social media, and why the negative online reviews he was getting from non-white, non-fireman's union people would kill his business. He promised Sky he would fix the problem, but she was not optimistic that he could.

Sky was already late, it was cold, and it was, she thought to herself, *a freaking Monday night*. She made a mental list justifying evasive action. First of all, the event had already started, so Sharpe would probably never hear that she had come. Second, if Shelly was in, he would be immersed in the event's details and unable to catch up. Finally, if she went home to her warm apartment, the drinks there would not cost her the better part of next month's rent.

She had almost made up her mind to go home when the oak door opened, and a man seemingly dressed for a day of deer hunting stood in the doorway. He held the door open as he called back over his shoulder to someone in the darkness.

"Nah, Henrico," he said. "You go ahead. I gotta have a smoke. You're lucky you came down early. You didn't have to be cooped up with those guys for ten hours. Just get me the usual. Yah, and Jane says Sharpe's payin'—how's that for a joke?"

Free drinks, Sky thought. *Dammit. Now I have to go in.*

CHAPTER 44

It was starting to get late, and Jerry figured the crowd in the bar was as big as it would get for the night, which was certainly better now that his hometown supporters managed to surprise him. He was still a bit bitter about Polzinetti showing up, but it was speech time, and he had to pull himself together. He understood to keep it short and sweet, add a touch of humor and remember those who helped get you there.

Jerry poked his head into a few circles of chatter and put his hands on the shoulders as he listened and worked his way to the bar. Shelly had one of the mikes ready, which he usually used when he had the Irish band come on Thursdays, one of Jerry's favorite nights to drop by.

Jerry kept a watchful eye on Polzinetti as he worked the room, looking like a scud missile unsure where to strike. He wished he had someone he really trusted to keep tabs on the man. Why was he here?

Jerry tapped the mike, and the room quickly settled down. He flashed the smile he practiced daily and puffed his chest out to impress the crowd with his fine physique and Armani suit. "What a fantastic crowd we have here tonight! Thank you for coming and for your generosity. Your support means a great deal, and I think I have enough now to fly down to the Keys and stay for the rest of the winter!"

Polite laughing and smiles were enough to prod him along. Jerry took a second to scan the room. He indeed commanded their attention. He was at the center of the moment, and he was energized. Jazzed. Ready to show why he deserved their attention.

When he raised the mike back to his chin, his eyes caught the front door swinging open again. There she was, sliding into the bar, trying to remain anonymous. His new friend, Skylar Nicholson, crack reporter. Or a reporter on crack. He wasn't sure. He was impressed that she had a knack for being in the right place at the right time. While he'd expected her, given his invitation, he needed to keep a watchful eye as she was still chasing the Hawthorne murder. Was she beginning to see a connection? Most reporters didn't bother with a freshman congressman from Nowhere, America. Jerry wondered if she was on to something.

CHAPTER 45

As Sky expected, Shelly was in his element, fretting here and there to make sure the new congressman was pleased with the venue. He waved, and the expression on his face told her that they would have to catch up on another night. This was a load off of her mind and given the fact that he had closed the place to regulars for the night, she felt almost anonymous in one of her old haunts.

She did, however, get more than a wave from the woman behind the bar, whom Sky had pitched to Shelly as his new and proud Latina general manager. Within a minute, she was out from behind the bar with a drink for Sky.

"Brandy old-fashioned, right?" the bartender said. "On the house. I have to keep moving, but I wanted to say thank you again, Sky. Things are going great here. Shelly is a sweetheart."

"Oh," Sky said, "don't mention it. No trouble at all." For the first time in months, her memory failed her and she could not remember the last time she had seen Shelly's newest bartender. *Hm*, she thought. *Maybe it's the place that causes the memory loss, not the drinks.*

She began her time-tested scan of the room and was overwhelmed by the opportunities. There were so many things out of place—so much oddity, so much weirdness—that she wasn't sure where to start.

The oddity in the room surpassing all others was the woman at the door, who was taking money from donors while dressed like Bette Davis in a Hollywood thriller from the forties. Most freshman congressmen hire the hottest twenty-five-year-old they can find to greet all who come to their office or event. Jerry Sharpe, it seemed, had hired his mommy. It was bizarre, eerie, and unsettling.

"Ms. Nicholson?"

The voice came at her in a hoarse whisper and interrupted her analysis of the room. Sky turned to her left and saw Chris Patterson, Sharpe's staffer, standing next to her with an eager, earnest look on his face. He was also standing too close for her liking.

"We're so glad you could come," he whispered. "If you don't mind me saying so, I think this is a great event, don't you? Good turnout, high percentage of likely donors, a few guests from his district, and just enough alcohol flowing to make it fun. Wouldn't you agree?"

"Hello, Chris," she said as she took a small step away from him. "Call me Sky. It's great. Well done. Sorry I'm late. I'd hate to miss any of what Congressman Sharpe has to say. Let's listen a bit, shall we?"

Chris nodded, turned to watch his boss speak, and pretended to forget how much he cared about what Sky Nicholson might think.

CHAPTER 46

"Well, I have some folks I want to thank for putting on such a great evening for all of us. First, I must thank my team. The ever so lovely Ms. Jane Robertson hailing from Montour Falls." The boys from upstate erupted in whoops of affection. "And of course, I cannot forget my trusty Eagle Scout, Chris, without whom I would be lost." A round of applause for someone they didn't see or know but figured was there somewhere. Then a burst of hollers from his little crew huddled in the corner. "Thank you for all you do for me and the community. I also want to thank our host, Shelly O'Brien, who graciously opened his fantastic cigar bar for all of us to enjoy tonight. Isn't this a great place?" Glasses and cigars were raised in appreciation. "Shelly has some great live music on Thursdays, so I encourage you to come out and have a drink, a smoke, a grand time. Right, Shelly?"

A thankful nod from the bar.

"Folks, I must take a second to thank my good friend, our very own Frankie Dominico, who has invested a great deal in our hometown, and he has made a tremendous difference by creating jobs and growing our economy upstate! It is awesome that you and the crew came down tonight!"

Frankie blushed at the recognition, but he clearly appreciated it and gave the Congressman a wink like he was a favorite uncle. Jerry needed Frankie to keep the local donations coming.

"I know many of you go to a lot of these events, but I want to assure you that having you here tonight means a great deal to me. Thank you. As you know, I work hard to support our wonderful district back home, and I spend a lot of my time laboring on behalf of our hard-working folks out there, whether they are taking care of us in the hospitals, repairing our cars, or managing the dairy farms. I am here to work for you!"

A welcoming cheer from the crowd. Jerry watched movement behind the friendly crowd as Polzinetti seemed to be heading in Sky's direction. *What could he possibly want from her?*

Jerry tried not to get distracted and knew he didn't have much time before he annoyed folks with a long-winded speech. "I am also concerned about what is happening with our environment. As you know, I grew up on the lake, fishing and hunting throughout the region. I have a fondness for our wilderness, and I will be working hard to protect it for future generations! I am concerned about the zebra mussel infestation. This invasive species is ruining our beautiful lakes. I will be working to get the EPA moving on this quickly."

The lobbyists from the Sierra Club gave a howl of sorts, as others provided enthusiastic applause.

"Again, thank you for coming tonight, enjoy the evening, make sure you get a nice cigar for the road, and remember to be safe on your way home. I look forward to chatting with you tonight."

CHAPTER 47

Despite the venue's weirdness, the team, and the timing, Sky had to admit that Congressman Sharpe had done well. Not that she had spent much time listening to what he'd actually said—her time and attention were taken up avoiding further conversation with Chris and watching Henrico Polzinetti work the room.

She noticed that he was the only other person at Shelly's who seemed uninterested in what the Congressman had to say. He spent the entire night watching the people who watched Sharpe and chasing them down for comment. After only fifteen minutes, Sky could see that Henrico was a truly gifted reporter, and by the end of the night, she wondered if he might be one of the best she would ever see.

Sharpe bid his loyal crowd a good night and admired the rush to the bar for a last drink. Sky fought for and kept her place at the bar, and after less than a minute found Henrico Polzinetti perched right next to her. She was not surprised by this and decided to play dumb.

"Oh," she said, "Henrico. Hello. I'm sorry, I didn't see you there. Have you been here all night?"

Henrico smirked, looked at his drink, and decided not to play this game. It was getting late and he hadn't eaten since breakfast. No time for nonsense.

"So," he said, "after what I told you the other night, you still want to know more about our host, right?"

Sky smiled. This was someone she could work with. "That's right."

"Figured," Henrico Polzinetti said. "Did you eat yet? I would kill for a sandwich."

CHAPTER 48

"It's not exactly a sandwich place," Sky said, "but every meal comes with a side of pita bread that is to die for. Best in the city. Do you like Middle Eastern food, Henrico?" Her new comrade eyed the menu and the décor with more than a passing interest.

"I used to, yes," he said. "A long time ago, in the Marine Corps, I lived on Lebanese food. Was stationed there for quite a while. But you knew that, didn't you? Wouldn't have been hard to find out."

He winked at her in the same warm, playful way an older uncle would. Sky smiled. "Pretty easy, actually," she said. "We don't have to talk about it if you don't want to."

"Good," Henrico said. "I hope you're hungry."

***

The food came from the kitchen in waves, despite the fact that neither Sky nor Henrico had placed an order. It was divine. With the arrival of each dish, Henrico told the story about where and when he had first tasted it—to the waiter in Arabic, and then to Sky in English.

Sky simply nodded and pretended she believed Henrico when he said he was in the Marine Corps. She let this ride until her curiosity and need to change the subject overwhelmed her.

"So, Henrico," she said. "Did you ever think of going back? You know, to stay?"

This question startled Henrico, and he waited a few seconds to think through his answer. "Well," he said, "what can I say? I fell in love with a real Watkins Glen girl before I left. Been married to her for over thirty years now. Her only two flaws are a fear of leaving New York State and a hatred of exotic food. She's worth it, though. I can't complain."

"I'd bet if you could get her over there, you could change her mind."

"Yeah," he said. "I guess. Look, it's getting late, and here we are just talking about old Henrico. What else can I do for you, other than tell you again to stay away from my Congressman?" Another set of small plates laden with food hit the table.

Something about the personal glimpse she had gotten of Henrico made her want to respond in kind with a secret or some clue about what made her tick. She liked him. Besides, it was clear that this was a man who hated bullshit. So she decided to take an unorthodox approach to their conversation.

"Well," she said, "I do want to make sure I can rely on Sharpe as a source on the D.C. crime story. But that's not the real reason I wanted to talk to you." Henrico stopped eating and looked at Sky, waiting for the next nugget to drop.

"Really?" he said.

"Yeah," Sky replied. "It's just that when I last visited his office, he asked a lot of creepy questions about a friend of mine, totally out of the blue. And, well, given everything else you said, it's on my mind."

Sky gave her new friend a quick recap of her meeting with Sharpe.

"I see," Henrico said. "And this friend. Does this friend have a name?"

Sky looked up. "Abby," she said.

"Well," Henrico said, "then Abby is lucky to have you looking out for her. Because if Jerry Sharpe was asking about a friend of mine like that, I would be concerned." He pushed a bowl toward her. "Here. try some of this. It's roasted eggplant with *banadura harrah*—unbelievable."

"Well, thank you," Sky said. "I thought it was just me. He claims to have met Abby one summer up on Seneca Lake. But she swears she doesn't remember him."

"Uh-oh," Henrico said.

"Really? I was afraid you would say that."

"Sorry."

"Can you please—*please*—tell me again why we should stay away from Jerry Sharpe?" Sky prepared to put a dab of ketchup on the edge of her plate.

"I will," Henrico said quickly, "on one condition."

"What's that?"

"You put that ketchup bottle down and promise me you will never touch it in this restaurant again."

***

"It isn't any one thing," Henrico said as the Turkish coffees arrived. "It's the sum of a lot of smaller things. To his credit, Sharpe worked his ass off to get where he is. He was orphaned as a young boy and had to fight for everything. Eagle Scout. Law degree. Job at the prosecutor's office. Assistant Prosecutor. Prosecutor. Now Congressman."

"He does seem like he hasn't laughed in a while," Sky said.

"That's right. But here's the thing—you never wanted to be the person competing with him for the scholarship or the Klondike Derby trophy. He always had a big chip on his shoulder and could be ruthless at the flip of a switch. The stakes never mattered. If you were competing with him, he would do anything to win. Anything."

"Well," Sky said, "in his defense, most people on the Hill are like that. The job attracts that kind of person."

"I get it," Henrico said. "But they don't snap at odd times the way Sharpe does. Look, we expect our young guys in town to get into a brawl or two as they're coming up. We all did it. But Sharpe never stopped. Twice a year, rain or shine, he'd go from sweetness and light to kicking someone's face in at the local bar. Incredibly vicious stuff. And totally out of the blue."

"Really? He doesn't strike me that way."

"That's what I'm worried about. Now consider this—before anybody in town realizes it, this guy is now Assistant County Prosecutor, right? Nothing comes of his outbursts anymore. He's totally protected. Then comes a huge scandal in the same prosecutor's office. And this guy comes out squeaky clean?"

Sky's face fell. "I see."

"It just never made sense to me how quickly he went from a hard-working townie with a hair-trigger temper to a United States Congressman. And when you look back at it, Jerry Sharpe was always within a stone's throw of every catastrophe that created an opportunity for him. That can't be by chance. It can't be."

"I hear you," Sky said, "but do you have any evidence of this? I mean, again, this town is full of people who are ruthless and climb ladders well."

Henrico held up both of his hands. "Look," he said, "you're right. I don't have fingerprints on this guy or anything. I'm just saying that I'm looking for them. So don't quote me on any of this."

A small entourage of waiters and cooks, led by an old woman who clearly was Mama Fatima, came to the table to ask Henrico's opinion on her cooking. The conversation switched to Arabic. He gushed and motioned to Sky. She made the corresponding faces and silent gestures of wonder and gratitude. Mama Fatima blushed and bowed. Her children explained to Sky in clearer English how grateful their mother was to have an American customer who requested their family's favorite dishes by name. Henrico took out his wallet to pay, but they refused him—three times—and ran back to the kitchen to bring fruit for dessert.

Sky and Henrico managed to escape Mama Fatima's loving embrace three hours (and ten selfies with Mama) after they arrived. Henrico insisted on walking Sky to her car before he hailed a cab.

"Well, Henrico," Sky said as she pulled her keys out of her purse, "thanks for the experience back there. And the advice. If there were some way I could make your wife like babaganoush, I would do it, for your sake."

Henrico smiled. "I'll hold you to that," he said. "Let me know if you come up with a cure. You could liberate half of New York State." He turned to go.

"Henrico?" Sky said. Henrico turned back toward her.

"Yeah?"

"Why did you agree to this?"

"What do you mean?"

"To meet with me. To tell me all this stuff. You're a gentleman and all. I get that, but…"

Henrico looked at Sky for a moment, then at his shoes, and then back at Sky. "Because I can't sleep at night. Here we have this guy who loses his shit two or three times a year, like clockwork. I can't prove it, but I think he's dangerous. And now he's here in D.C., surrounded by an ocean of people who push all of his buttons, and we have heard nothing. Nothing at all. No bar fights. No broken noses in the congressional delegation. Nothing—just sweetness and light. Either someone has paid Jerry Sharpe a million dollars for that chip on his shoulder, or…"

"Or what?" Sky said.

"Or it is only a matter of time before I have to cover a story that's going to shock and embarrass my hometown in a historic way. We don't need that, and I couldn't stand the thought that you might be a part of it. Good night, Sky, and good luck."

CHAPTER 49

When Sky noticed the police cruiser parked just a few spaces down from the entrance to her apartment, she blamed it on Henrico's dire warnings about Jerry Sharpe. Her nonchalance vanished when she unlocked the door to her apartment, took a step inside, and saw Abby on the couch talking to a police officer.

"Who is this?" the officer said as she stood up and spun toward the door.

"It's okay, Officer," Abby said. "That's Skyler Nicholson. She's a friend." The officer lowered her right hand from its position just inches from her service revolver to the side of her thigh.

"What happened?" Sky said.

"Everything's fine," the officer responded, "and I know you. If this is some kind of stunt for your blog, know that it could land you in jail. Please, Miss Sullivan, start again."

"I noticed it as I came across the Key Bridge," Abby began. "It was really nondescript and gray, following about three cars behind me. When I turned left on Wisconsin Avenue, he followed me. I stopped to run an errand at a store along the way—just past the Cathedral—

and when I left ten minutes later, he was still there, three cars behind."

"Can you describe him?"

"Not really. The sun was behind me, so it was hard to see. All I can tell you was that it was one person, seemed like a guy, and he was wearing a hat—like the old ones gangsters used to wear."

"What happened then?" Sky said.

"By the time I got over here to our neighborhood, I freaked out because he was still behind me. And that was when I saw you parked out front. So I pulled up behind you and laid on the horn." Abby started to laugh.

"Yes, you did," the officer said with a grin.

"Sorry."

"Don't apologize—it worked, didn't it?"

This broke the tension in the room and gave Sky the impression she could talk.

"So he left?" Sky said. The officer gave her a look that told her she could speak when given permission.

"Yeah," Abby said. "As soon as he saw you, he took off. I wasn't in the mood to follow him, but I was in the mood to take this conversation indoors." The officer finally turned to Sky.

"And here I was, getting my notebook ready so I could come interview the two people who'd seen Tyler Hawthorne the night he was murdered. Little did I know that we'd have ourselves a stalking case, too. You ladies might want to think about hanging out with a new group of people."

"Yeah," Sky said, as she put her arm around Abby, who all but melted into her embrace.

"Anyway," the officer said as she stood up to go, "I'll come by later to ask more questions. For now, just be vigilant, and let us know if you see this guy again—either of you. And if you think of anything else, here's my card."

CHAPTER 50

Jerry knew Mildred Hawthorne was going to make sure her son Tyler got the royal treatment—a farewell that would rival any prominent politician, including a president. She arranged for the memorial service to be held at Saint John's Church, which is often referred to as the "Church of Presidents."

The historical Episcopal Church, a block from the White House and situated on Lafayette Square, had hosted each president since James Madison. Pew fifty-four was reserved for presidential visits. This would certainly be suitable for a farewell to Mildred's eldest child.

While there was a full obituary in the *Washington Post* as well as many national papers, other news outlets provided a summary:

Tyler Gerald Hawthorne, 43, joined his beloved father, Gerald H. Hawthorne, in eternal life on November 17. The cherished son of Mildred Dickenson Hawthorne and the late Gerald Hunter Hawthorne is survived by his brother Hunter Hawthorne and his sister, Caroline Hawthorne. Tyler was a renowned international business leader and a beloved friend to many, and he often spoke fondly of his brothers at Phi Delta Theta. His generous and kind nature kept him engaged as a board member of the Capital Area Food Bank.

Memorial service on December 4 at 9 a.m. at Saint John's Church, 1525 H St NW, Washington, D.C. 20005. Family and friends are invited to the burial at Oak Hill Cemetery, 3001 R St NW, Washington, D.C. immediately following the memorial service.

Jerry wanted to watch Mildred cry and sob her way down the church's center. He wanted to see her pain. He needed to feel it for himself. He wanted her to feel what he had felt since his mother's murder. He knew she was involved. He just didn't know how. This was what he wanted most on this happy occasion.

Jerry made sure he arrived early, sitting near the President's pew, just in case. He remained closer to the center aisle so he could see the family enter. The pews filled in quickly, and Jerry had to occasionally stand up to let folks in. No presidential presence, but the lack of federal security gave that away. Jerry wasn't surprised to see Chairman Perry enter the church. The big man worked the crowd as he moved down the center aisle. Jerry received an unexpected nod of recognition from Perry as he passed. Perry found a suitable pew right behind where the family was expected to sit.

Feeling at least recognized for being alive, Jerry took a deep breath, puffed out his chest, and scanned the remaining faces in the pews. He sensed that he was swimming in blue blood, recognizing a few huddles of families that had been at some of the more prestigious fundraisers in D.C. He spotted several members of the Brown family he had seen up at the lake playing on the water with their toys. He recalled replacing their jet ski's starter. No tip, of course. They never really bothered with his kind. Commonfolk.

Jerry reminded himself that he was not in his hometown any-more, and there were likely few people in the church who worried about their mortgage or about putting gas in their car in the middle of a winter storm.

The thousand-pound bell that was the work of Paul Revere's son in the early 1820s announced the top of the hour. A hush fell over the room as the doors behind him swung open. Solemn music boomed as the Hawthorne procession entered and made its way down the center aisle.

There were six men carrying Tyler's casket. They were all the same size as their departed friend—broad-shouldered and dressed in suits that didn't quite fit. The pallbearers had arranged to wear the same gray suits and black ties.

Jerry watched the six men do their best not to tip over the casket. He knew that was their greatest fear. They were terrified that they would drop the casket in front of everyone and have a wretched, dis-figured body tumble onto the floor and squish like a dead squid.

Jerry tried to imagine how fun that would be, watching people scatter and scream, and to see Mildred's face as she saw her gutted piece-of-shit son flop out onto the marble. He had to work hard to stifle the smile he could feel creeping up from inside. He bit down on his cheek. The growing taste of blood in his mouth soothed him a bit. His own small-town, working-class blood warmed his mouth, and he tried to take some comfort knowing his blood was red like everyone else in the church.

But he knew deep down that it was not. Not really.

The family emerged and slowly marched in silence behind the ornate casket shouldered by the men. Their dull eyes were somewhat drawn to the tiled, marbled floor below rather than up front and bright.

Jerry tried to make eye contact with Mildred by shifting his weight as she passed, but her eyes never wavered from a point she must have picked out as she entered the church. He let his hand brush up against the bone handle in his pocket. The knife was there with him, keeping him company and focused. It's your turn, Mildred. How does it feel?

Jerry had a bit of trouble hiding his disappointment. Mildred wasn't bawling. Not at all. Given the moment, Mildred was rather composed. She looked put together. Defiant in a way. Jerry had hoped he would see a distraught, crumbling old woman. He wanted to see unabashed pain and suffering in those eyes.

Jerry felt robbed of the image he had played in his head for days. He was disgusted with himself for thinking he had set such high expectations. But the next sight behind Mrs. Hawthorne was worth the trip. Mildred's remaining two children, Tyler's little brother and sister, walked behind her, arm-in-arm and on full display. Caroline was flashing an odd, bright smile like she was on the red carpet in Hollywood. Jerry thought for a moment she was going to wave at some friends on her left as she bent down to peer past some folks blocking her view. Caroline's red dress had small blue-and-green feathers around the waist. It looked like a cocktail number for a masquerade party in the 1970s. And to make whatever point she was shooting for, she sported glossy black boots that went up to her knees, almost goth-like. She had a little pep in her step as she coaxed her brother along for her trip down the center aisle for all to watch.

Caroline's charge on her arm was the complete opposite and may as well have been a member of the Addams Family. Jerry mused that he might be Lurch's little cousin or something. He had dark circles around his eyes, and his skin looked pale and sweaty.

Hunter Hawthorne was certainly not an appropriate name for this weak branch of the family tree. He was decked in a strange black suit, if that's what it was. The lapels were large enough to use as billboards, and he was wearing a white shirt with frills and dangling cuffs. His pirate-like outfit was finished off with a swashbuckler's belt with a silver buckle three sizes too big. To really put a point on the absurdity of the man, the weak, drowned rat of a pirate managed to sport what appeared to be boots that matched his sister's knee-highs.

It was impossible for anyone to think that Hunter and Caroline were twins. Hunter was shorter than his sister. Jerry figured Hunter had likely never grown as the sunlight had always been blocked by his strapping dead brother. Usually, one could spot some common characteristics with fraternal twins, but this was just sad. Jerry was struggling to balance his disappointment that Mildred and her family weren't wailing over the loss of their strapping heir, and his astonishment at how ridiculous the siblings looked as they paraded down the center of the church.

Jerry shook his head. *Who the fuck are these people?*

Now it makes sense why Mildred didn't have these two idiots escort her this morning. Who would? Imagine her disappointment when the two weirdos had emerged.

Jerry imagined what the minister would think when he caught sight of this hot mess and felt sorry for the man. After the spectacle had passed, Jerry needed to regain his focus. He felt a little out of place. The carnival had caught him a little off guard. *What was calming? What was soothing?*

Jerry collected himself by sliding his hand back into his pocket. His urge to laugh was immediately stifled when he felt the knife's cold bone handle. He ran his finger along the carvings and outlined the handle. He picked at the blade, not quite unfolding the knife, but feeling it spring back into the handle.

Jerry caressed and turned his talisman a few times as he contemplated the two clowns trailing their mother into the pew. He felt like he'd regrouped a bit. He began to look forward to the next move in his wicked game. He was already planning to focus on Caroline and then move on to Hunter.

The torture he wanted to inflict had only begun. This was only the first chapter in her worst nightmare.

Millie will be back here soon enough.

CHAPTER 51

Jerry thought there would be a ton more folks filing in as part of the family. But the balance of what was supposed to be a parade of family and friends was scarce. He examined the more appropriately dressed mourners file into the church in two perfect but thin lines like the animals loading into Noah's Ark. These folks were there to support the family, and they looked genuinely sad to be there. Two or three folks looked like they might be the help. They didn't quite match up with the rest of the family and seemed to be carrying things on their behalf.

Jerry was about to turn toward the altar when the last portion of the procession came through the doors. This next group of mourners included some folks he knew, or at least thought he did.

Skylar Nicholson and Abigayle Sullivan were walking together in the procession as if they were part of the Hawthorne family. They certainly looked like they belonged. *But what the fuck were they doing there?* Abigayle's breakup the night of the fundraiser should have kept her away, or at least sitting among the rest of the guests. And Nicholson? She hadn't said anything about a relationship with the Hawthornes! Wait. He did see her chatting with Mildred at the fundraiser, didn't he?

He felt like his mouth was hanging open while he tried not to stare at the women passing by pew 55, and he was flummoxed as he watched them file into two pews behind Mildred and her kids. They sat in front of Chairman Perry. The two women were tucked in against each other, with Abigayle providing whatever comfort she could to her friend.

An older couple settled in on the other side of them, with the gentleman reaching around and comforting both women. The man took a moment and cast a knowing nod to Chairman Perry.

Skylar's folks? Maybe. How are they connected to the Hawthornes? What the hell is going on here? Maybe she has a personal vendetta about all this?

The memorial service began as soon as this last group was seated. Jerry had to look around to get the message that it was time to sit. He was on a roller coaster and felt like he was the only one screaming at the peak of the hill before tumbling down again. Since the church doors had opened, he'd bounced along an emotional ride. Elated to envision the rotting corpse flopping onto the church floor, disappointed in how collected Mildred looked on her worst day, amused and entertained by the modern pirate slithering down the aisle and his ridiculous sister dressed like a clown happy to be out of her hospital ward, then blown away by the two women who didn't belong here. *Or did they?*

Jerry no longer had a sense of what was happening anymore. He thought he was going to see and enjoy some pain and suffering. He thought this morning would help him heal, or maybe envision ideas for the others while watching the Hawthorne family weep. This was not exactly what he had in mind.

Jerry managed to hang with the crowd. He stood up when others did, sat down as instructed, pretended to pray when asked, and dutifully followed directions. This was all he could do at that moment.

The short readings were typical of most funerals, read by some of the men who carried Tyler into the church. He knew they were thankful they hadn't screwed it up and accidentally dumped him onto the floor.

As if the morning hadn't been strange enough, Jerry had to hold his breath as he watched Perry deliver a special speech as part of the service. Perry focused all his time on Mildred and almost forgot to mention Tyler, who was already rotting and stinking up that casket no one wanted to look at during the service.

The priest stood up and thanked the quiet crowd for coming, reminding folks where the cemetery was for those who wished to attend, and noted that Mildred Hawthorne had decided to combine a tribute to her son with the Gerald Hawthorne exhibit grand opening at the Natural History Museum later in the month.

The famous bell rang at ten on the dot as the procession cleared the church, but Jerry didn't notice. Revenge would have to wait. He could barely see as waves of blue blood families flowed out of the church. But he was now on to something. The Natural History Museum. Interesting setting. Interesting opportunity.

CHAPTER 52

Jerry sped ahead of the funeral procession to make sure he had a good view of the carnage he created at Oak Hill Cemetery. For a cemetery located in the heart of D.C., it was rather large—north of twenty acres, with a spaghetti jumble of paths that were perfect for running. He knew where the Hawthorne family plot was—at the interchange of a half-dozen walking paths so passersby would see their fancy stones.

Jerry had stopped on several occasions to look at the gothic head-stone of the late Gerald Hawthorne. There was room for one more right next to him, of course, and that would be only a matter of time.

The grave behind Mr. Gerald Hawthorne was prepped and ready for Tyler. The tent was set up with a dozen or so chairs underneath waiting for the family's arrival. Since he was one of the first to arrive, Jerry settled into a spot so he could enjoy a nice view of the event.

Jerry smiled when he looked over toward the Potomac. It wasn't that long ago they were dragging this pitiful man out of crab-infested water. He hoped this pleasure would warm him, but it was a particularly biting December morning. The bitterness curled around and through him, which was aggravating given he was supposed to be used to this kind of weather. He'd just been back home, and the snow and wind hadn't bothered him then.

Jerry was replaying what he'd seen at the church as he watched folks rolling out of their cars and standing near the hearse. *The crows gather to mourn one of their own.* He assumed Mildred was miserable, but when she clambered out of the black limo, she still didn't look like she was crying. Her freaky kids tumbled out like they were going to an amusement park, and they remained oblivious to what was happening.

He scanned the crowd as it gathered and huddled closer and closer together to ward off the cold. Jerry remembered a documentary he'd seen once where penguins would rotate who was on the huddle's outside so that each bird took a turn staying warm and a turn protecting the rest of the birds and their offspring. Not so with humans. Everyone was responsible for themselves, and the jostling was somewhat amusing.

Jerry watched Mildred and her two strange children huddle together among a dozen or so folks who were provided chairs under the canopy. Blankets were draped over their laps, but they weren't helping stave off the bitter cold. There was a portable heater underneath the canopy, but the wind was carrying the heat away as fast as the propane tank could make it.

Jerry peered into Mildred's eyes as she listened to the minister and nodded in agreement when peace and comfort were offered. She was the only one who didn't show any signs of shivering, but Jerry figured that her heart was made of hard, black coal, which meant she could handle this weather.

Hunter was visibly shivering to the point that his ever-present sister tightened her grip around his arm. She stood out as expected. As if the dress and fuck-me boots weren't enough at the church,

Caroline was now decked out in an alpine white parka that went down to her ankles, and a hood drawn tight around her face with faux fur trimming the edge as well as the cuffs.

Jerry shook a bit after taking this scene in—an old lady keeping a stiff upper lip, a dainty and weak heir to the family fortune shaking like a leaf and likely dying from hypothermia, and the screwball sister who thought she was in some kind of weird, way-off-Broadway play.

Jerry looked over the family plot. Next to dear old dad and the spot where Mildred would be dropped in when the time came, there was enough space to dispose of Tyler and dump the other two kids, whose time was coming sooner than folks knew. Jerry was feeling calmer now that he had been able to get out of the church unscathed. He was formulating another plan in his head. The approaching museum event was cooking inside, tumbling around with possibilities.

Jerry looked over the sullen faces peering into the hole. They were all trying not to imagine their own death or their own kin perishing before their time. Jerry knew that was what was running through their heads. He enjoyed the fact that all these folks had been appalled at the ghastly death Tyler had experienced. But he knew deep inside that the men listening to the comments of peace and rest were really just glad to hear that the Jag was still in one piece. That would have been the real tragedy, and more tears would have been shed.

Jerry grimaced as it occurred to him that the wimpy little brother could inherit his brother's gorgeous Jag. *What a waste.* He found the faces he was searching for among the group of ashen mourners. He spotted Skylar and Abigayle to the right and behind Tyler's frat brothers. *Figures.* Tyler had to be a frat boy. That should have gone without saying.

Jerry turned back to Skylar, who was trying to get warm. She was tucked in tightly with Abigayle and an older couple whom he was pretty sure were Skylar's folks. The older woman had a green mitten wrapped around Sky's right arm. Abigayle was draped in a dark winter parka that went past her knees. He could see the thick wool peeking out from under the collar. That was the coat of a true up-stater. She had an equally warm wool hat stuffed on her head and her oversized sunglasses covered half her face to fight off the wind and the water.

Jerry's new little reporter friend must have borrowed her coat from Abigayle. The coat was way too long but looked equally warm. However, Skylar did not snap it up tight, and she looked to be suffering from penetrating wind that was undeterred by the down in her coat.

The burial ceremony was no fancy affair compared to the memorial service's pomp and circumstance at the church. While the minister was reading another passage, Jerry watched the two women with great interest.

It wasn't that long ago that Skylar Nicholson, today's modern version of Nancy Drew, had been in his office looking for dirt on some stupid commission. But Jerry knew there had to be more to that not-so-coincidental drop-in. Now that he understood there was a relationship with the Hawthornes, he had to be extra careful.

Sky had implied that she barely knew Abigayle—mere acquaintances from way back at UVA. Apparently, that was not the case here. They were leaning on each other for both warmth and comfort. And she didn't let on about any connection to the Hawthornes. She was a sly one who thought she could outmaneuver him.

Jerry tried to shake off the cobwebs that were stretching across his mind, recycling the meeting in his office, watching her work Chris over pretty good, and prying in a way that was likely motivated by her personal connection to the Hawthornes. Jerry tried to recall if he said anything that might point toward himself.

The Hawthornes. That is why I am here. Get it together, Jerry.

Jerry returned his attention to the beautiful casket hovering over its forever hole. The woodwork was certainly worthy of a rich man, and the brass handles were impressive. Jerry assumed a pine box was his own fate.

Jerry closed his eyes to envision what the dearly departed must look like in his box. Disfigured, gutted, and missing body parts given the damage he and the river had done more than two weeks ago. Jerry suppressed another smile as he drew comfort knowing that what was left of the asshole about to be dropped in the dirt had been chewed on by crabs.

The minister's voice picked up a bit and returned Jerry to the present. The minister mercifully got to "ashes to ashes, dust to dust," and they lowered the gutted fish of a man into the ground.

A few roses were tossed, a sob or two came from the crowd tightly pinned together in a failed attempt to generate heat, and it was done. Some tears fell among those watching, but Jerry knew they didn't really care about Tyler. Those tears were likely for their wandering thoughts for those they'd lost themselves, not for Tyler.

As soon as the shoulders in the crowd turned toward their parked cars, Jerry skirted the crowd and made sure he was in front of the makeshift line to deliver his condolences to Mildred. He wanted to see her pain up close and personal.

"Terrible tragedy, Mrs. Hawthorne. I am so sorry for your loss. He is at peace." *In pieces, that is… Ha!*

Mildred was in her own world and clearly in a bit of a haze but was managing to keep herself together. "Thank you, Mr. Sharpe. It was lovely of you to come today. You know, you were likely one of the last people to talk to him that night."

Jerry tried not to look concerned, but he wasn't sure he was pulling it off. "Are these your children?"

"Yes. Hunter and Caroline." Mildred was ready to move on to the next person in line and turned. "May I introduce Mr. Sharpe?"

"Congressman Sharpe."

"Yes. Congressman Sharpe. This is Hunter and Caroline."

Jerry turned to the siblings. Hunter was going through the motions of a funeral. The frail man was acting more like a vampire of sorts, his mouth agape and hugging any willing body that came by, absorbing their warmth so he didn't die in this crappy weather.

Hunter's sidekick looked like she was entertaining an outdoor event—a forced smile, black hair sticking out in different directions from under her hood and a few uncomfortable laughs along the way.

Jerry embraced Hunter and let him take advantage of his warm body for a moment, and at the same time, Jerry offered his gloved hand to baby sister. He tightened down hard to impress on her how dreadful he felt about the whole thing. Caroline's expression switched to pity, eyebrows arched, and eyes widened.

Jerry smiled and let his grip linger before withdrawing.

She is so weird; you must like her. But Hunter? Jesus.

While Jerry wanted to learn more about this odd duo, he felt a bit sullied by Hunter, and the near joyous vibe from sister was over the top. He had to get the hell out of there. Jerry wasn't sure if it was the weather or just the opportunity, but he took broad steps toward the folks huddled by the portable heater that was not really delivering the goods. He cranked up the smile he'd perfected on the campaign trail. He moved in to offer a hug, but Skylar backed into her father.

Awkwardly stepping back, Jerry offered, "Ms. Nicholson, it is good to see you, even on such a difficult occasion. Hello, Abigayle. Good to see you again. Skylar made it sound like you two really didn't know each other or the Hawthornes for that matter. I hope Skylar mentioned our discussion about working on my campaign next year."

Four faces were staring back at Jerry like he'd just stepped on the grave behind him. Come to think of it, he had. The older gentleman behind Skylar came to his senses first and stepped in between them.

"Good morning, Congressman. I am sure Millie appreciates you taking the time to come out for the family today. I am Arthur Nicholson. This is my wife, Anne."

Part of the procession. First-name basis with Mildred. I got the message, Mr. Nicholson. Loud and clear. The blue bloods stick together, don't they?

"Nice to meet you. You must be proud of little Sky here. She has done a marvelous job of regrouping from the *Times* debacle and establishing herself here in D.C. The coverage on Tyler's death was excellent. It was much better than the *Post*, wouldn't you say?" Jerry realized his smile didn't match the nature of the morning's events and tried to tone it down.

Skylar piped up briefly. "Congressman, I didn't realize you knew the Hawthornes so well. I am sure they appreciate you coming today. I recall you saying you met him at the fundraiser?"

Jerry looked at Sky, who was looking through him and toward Mildred behind him. She wasn't really listening to him at all. He wasn't sure if that last part was really an inquiry. Jerry heard Sky whisper to her father. "Dad, let's go see Aunt Millie."

Jerry turned his attention back to Abigayle. "I remember working on your father's boat upstate, Ms. Sullivan. He had that beautiful Motoscafi he imported from Venice. The woodwork on that craft was simply exquisite!"

Abigayle was clearly having a memory lapse, or at least Jerry thought so. He tried to jog her memory again. "We bumped into each other in Watkins Glen a few times when we were young. I certainly remember you!"

Abigayle's eyes darted across her crew who were not able to help her out on this one. "Oh, yes, Congressman, I do recall meeting you one summer. Lovely to see you again. Of course, Sky let me know about your campaign interests. I will follow up with you at a more appropriate time."

Jerry realized what Abigayle really meant.

Leave us the fuck alone so we can grieve with our family. Our family.

Mr. Nicholson took charge of the awkward moment and used his long arms to corral the other two women to follow his daughter to do their duty and shut out this intruder.

Jerry felt like the help, dismissed to his quarters as they pushed past him toward the enemy. The failed attempt at a hug was embarrassing, and he assumed they had all noticed. Jerry watched as Skylar's parents embraced Mildred like the old friends they must be, and Mildred draped her little arm around Sky's waist like she had done it many times before. The misfits-for-siblings huddled around her, as well, with Hunter unapologetically cuddling anyone willing.

Jerry didn't feel the wind's sting anymore. He felt something worse.

CHAPTER 53

Jerry spent the morning getting ready for another big day. He sauntered over to the Natural History Museum on the national mall after a quick appearance at an early committee hearing. He watched as the security guards poked through purses and backpacks in their typical careless manner. He greeted the two massive security guards with a smile and chit-chatted while they let him through without incident. The guards were more interested in discussing the results of basketball games from the past weekend.

Jerry made his way through the familiar museum, past his favorite exhibit, the elephant in the rotunda. He felt that the animal represented power and was the animal kingdom's true leader. Not the lions. The elephant had to work hard to survive, and it had to defend itself from the lions and their constant harassment. The animal kingdom analogy and his "relationship" with the Hawthornes was not lost on Jerry as he made his way toward the area under construction.

The new build-out to finish the Hawthorne Safari Exhibit was well underway to show off Mr. Hawthorne's many adventures, including a range of things he'd collected or killed on his journeys to Africa.

Jerry was focused throughout his recon. He watched the workmen as they erected an exhibit representing a place none of them would ever see in real life.

Lunchtime was perfect. Like clockwork, the union workers cleared out to take advantage of their hour-long break. Jerry surveyed the area to make sure all was quiet. He had been careful to come through security at three different entrances over the past week. This time, he was there to get things prepared.

He looked over the new displays in the primate section. A few were already completed. The gorilla display was finished first, and it was going to serve his needs quite nicely. The display included an observation blind to show how the famous Gerald Hawthorne was able to get close to these creatures without being discovered. He could see the only two security cameras still weren't connected. One last glance around the large room, and Jerry felt comfortable enough to slip in. He uncoiled his parachute cord from his waist and threaded it into the observation blind's side. He had found the right color green, and it blended in nicely along the edges.

Jerry then whisked over to the bathroom across the hall. The empty room was a decent size and was quite old. He pulled a small, tightly wrapped bundle of clothes from under his jacket and stooped under the sink closest to the door. He found the vent he'd discovered on his last visit, slipped the package in, and closed the small door. He was feeling pretty good about how well things were going. He was about to step out of the bathroom when he heard two men chatting and walking through the exhibit room.

"Pascal, I would have just bought you lunch."

"Thanks, but Jenny made an extra sandwich, and I am freaking hungry. I just need a second to grab it."

Jerry was a statue while listening to the two men shuffle about. He didn't breathe. He felt like a deer in a clearing, where every hunter in the region had their sights on him.

The men were quick, and the room fell quiet again. A quick glance at his watch. He had about fifteen minutes before his time was up.

Jerry peeked out of the bathroom to confirm it was clear and attended to the day's last duty. He checked again to confirm the security cameras' height and where they were pointing. There were only two, and they were awkwardly positioned on swivels mounted on the walls given they were temporary cameras with wires dangling about. The room for the exhibit was only being used for the event and would then later be integrated into other parts of the museum. The cheap cameras might be just for show, but they were well within his reach. He scanned to make sure there were no other cameras added. He strode out of the museum with a sense of accomplishment. *Be prepared.*

When he finished at the museum, he scooted back to his office. There was little activity to keep anyone busy, and Jerry was feeling like things were going his way. "Chris, why don't you call it a day?"

"Great! I have to be at the Copycat tonight. Thanks."

Jerry knew the place—a neat little bar that served authentic Chinese food. Jerry gathered that the intern's sprint out the door was to hit a few bars on H street, the newest hot spot for the young and restless of D.C. Jerry realized his favorite golden retriever was enjoying a much more interesting life than his own. He nodded as Chris bolted out the door before he could finish saying *have a good time* or *see you tomorrow*. Jerry understood. *To be honest*, he thought, *if I were you, I would want to get the fuck out of here too. Can I come with you?*

CHAPTER 54

Jerry settled behind his desk, left to his own thoughts. Five was inching closer, but it was taking its time. An evening where there were no events. No fundraisers. Nothing for him to do. Again. He slid written testimony from the morning's hearing into the trash. He knew Chris would save copies, plus, he was never going to read them. He turned to his computer and decided to see what his new friend at *The Thread* was saying about the latest in D.C. and what had turned up since Tyler was discovered.

Jerry lifted the screen, and it hummed to life immediately, much to his surprise given its previous performance issues. The *Gutting on the Potomac* story had really taken off. There were links to related stories and sources of information scattered throughout. It looked to Jerry that a whole staff was now supporting the effort. It covered the funeral and highlighted the famous people in attendance, which did not include him. It was clear from the snippets taken from police reports that Tyler Hawthorne was killed with a knife, which made Jerry smile as he looked at the shadow box across the room. Assuming Nicholson was thorough, he saw no forensic evidence offered at this point.

The comments section had ballooned, and there were hundreds and hundreds of crazy theories of why he was murdered, including his favorite theory about Putin being involved. The Putin comment stirred something in him. He had forgotten to follow up on the messages that had caught his attention earlier. He played with the filter and found the first one again and saw that the exchange had continued:

AllKnottedup–Long time follower, first time Threading the needle. Skysthelimit–love your picture on the site. Terrific smile. You should scout out the crime scene photos of that poor fellow from the river. There are things that will tie your stories together. You need to do a "cut" check!

Skysthelimit–AllKnottedup–Nice to have a fan out there. Can you be a little less cryptic? I have those pictures up on my screen right now, and I don't see anything the police haven't already focused on. Want to tell me a little about yourself and why you are so interested in this story?

AllKnottedup–Skysthelimit–Well, I may want you to take me out for a beer when you arrive at the real story and remember I helped you get there.

Skysthelimit–AllKnottedup–It would help if you weren't being so cute. If this is how you meet girls, you are going to be lonely this holiday. And what the hell are you hinting at?

AllKnottedup–Skysthelimit–It's clear the perpetrator knows how to gut a fish and take care of his cutlery. The man you are searching for knows his way around the woods, doesn't he? But this guy is likely to be a thorn in your side for some time.

Skysthelimit–AllKnottedup–Okay. Enough. If you have something to say, how about I buy you that beer?

There were other comments, and it was becoming increasingly concerning.

AllKnottedup–Skysthelimit–You have met me before! In fact, I was almost in one of your recent stories, but I ended up on the cutting floor!

Skysthelimit–AllKnottedup–I'll buy you that beer tonight. Will text you time and place.

Jerry checked the date the message was posted and bolted upright. *Today's* tonight? He leapt from his chair and started to pace. Nicholson must have thought enough of the lead to get on it. This was no whack job hanging around political websites and throwing out conspiracy theories. He worked his way around the room at a quickening pace, knocking over a few files on the side table.

Someone knew a little more about the murder than he'd thought. Had someone witnessed him that night? Who was this person? Jerry looked over the comments again. He looked over the pictures in the story that were being referred to by the exchange.

This is stupid. The exchange was juvenile. Like a teenager trying to pick up an older woman at a bar.

Jerry tried to gather his thoughts. He found himself wandering into the intern's room. He flicked the lights on and stuffed himself into Chris's wobbly chair, almost losing his balance when he dumped himself into it. As he righted himself, he scanned the room looking for something to anchor himself to think. He must have missed something. Why would Nicholson care about some person on the web?

They are all nuts, right?

Jerry carefully leaned back in the chair to make sure he didn't topple over again. He tried to calm himself. He closed his eyes and counted to ten. His breathing steadied and he opened them, calmer than expected. His eyes focused on the display on the wall right above Chris's desk. It was a scouting display showing four rows of labeled knots. He recognized the bowline, square, and taut line. Scouts were required to learn these knots. Jerry had made a board like that when he was a scout about twenty years ago.

Jerry understood the exchange's innuendo he had just read. *Scout. Tie things together. Knows his way around the woods.* The writer had to be a scout or a hunter himself and recognized how Tyler had been killed.

AllKnottedup. He thought about the comments left on *The Thread.* Looked up at the board. He knew all the knots. He learned them all a long time ago. Contemplated the posts again. "You have met me before! In fact, I was almost in one of your recent stories, but I ended up on the cutting floor." He thought about when Skylar was in the office.

Jesus! Chris? Did he figure out the killer was a scout? Does he suspect me? AllKnottedup? He knows I was a scout. How could he? Goddamnit. He used those same phrases in our discussion with Nicholson. "Congress was all knotted up…"

Jerry regretted the Thanksgiving discussion about his hunting expertise. And the knife. *Was that why he'd been lingering on the knife? He saw the picture of me and that deer at Jane's house. Did he put it together?*

What could he know? If he did, why would he mess around? He would go to the police, right? Where did he say he was going tonight?

CHAPTER 55

Sky opened the door to the restaurant and headed for the bar, wondering if meeting Chris Patterson at a Chinese restaurant for drinks was the most cynical move of her career, the most desperate, or both. It didn't matter. She needed an answer to a nagging question: Congressman Jerry Sharpe was either a young, up-and-coming political force for good, or a ticking time bomb set to explode. Which one was it? The only person left to ask was Patterson, the staffer who had spent five minutes in Sharpe's office trying to look down her blouse. Sky would never trade sex for a story, but she was not above using a man's ambitions to get him to talk, so she had invited Chris for drinks and let the nature of their meeting—business or pleasure—remain ambiguous.

"Sky?"

Chris was at the bar waiting for her, and Sky soon found herself in an awkward, half-hearted hug, complete with an obligatory (and unwelcome) peck on her cheek. The junior staffer smelled of Jäger-meister and breath mints.

"Hi, Chris," she said. "Thanks for meeting me on such short

notice."

"It's my pleasure," he said in as deep a voice as he could muster. "Please—our table is right this way." He beamed at her. Then, as if catching himself in a mistake, put on what he thought was a more mature and confident face.

"Well, thank you, Chris," Sky said as they passed empty tables littered with plastic beer pitchers and abandoned plates. "You certainly know how to treat a lady. I haven't had a CopyCat scorpion shot for the *longest* time. Do they still come in the little plastic cups?"

Chris's face turned pink, and Sky knew she was on her way.

***

By the time Chris realized that this former sorority girl debutante could drink him under the table, it was too late to do anything about it but pray. She threw everything she had at him—a round of shots, work questions, a beautiful smile to encourage him, another round of shots, and more questions. It wasn't a fair fight.

"But what I can't understand," Sky said, "is how quickly your boss made it to Congress. I mean, I can see why you wanted to work for him, but you must have seen the same things in his background that I did. There were lots of convenient accidents and weird machinations up there. Doesn't that make you wonder—even a bit?"

"The fight at the Tavern?" Chris managed to say. "Only what I read. He isn't one to talk about such things. Did you know he's an Eagle Scout? The Congressman, I mean."

"Yes, I did. Do you think that helped?"

"For sure," Chris said with an exaggerated nod. "Oh, yeah. I'm an Eagle Scout, too."

"Really?" Sky said. "That's impressive." Chris nodded in agreement, then leaned over his plate of lo mein to let her in on a deep, dark secret. Sky leaned in closer so she wouldn't miss whatever might be coming—but not too close.

"It is impressive," he said. "And do you know what else is impressive?"

"I don't," Sky said sweetly. "Tell me." She could see Chris take a deep breath. He was struggling to concentrate at this point.

"I kind of know how he thinks. *That* is how I'm always one step ahead of him. He decides he wants to go someplace, or do something, and once he starts on it, I'm already there. I *see* how he thinks, Sky—what he's going to do next. It's an Eagle Scout thing. Sounds stupid, but *that's* my secret. *That's* how I do it." He winked.

Sky knew she wasn't getting anywhere and adding more booze to the situation seemed like a bad idea. *It's sad*, she thought. *Don't they teach kids how to drink in college anymore?*

"Aha!" Sky said. "That's why you're 'AllKnottedup,' right?" She smiled. He nodded and started to blush.

"That's right," he said. "I'm in his head."

Sky thought about knives, knots, and *AllKnottedup*. Something inside her shifted.

"Is it a safe place?" she asked.

"Where?" Chris replied.

"His head. You know—all that experience with knives and tying things up." Sky smiled, tilting her head as if she had made a joke, but watching Chris for any sign of distress. His face turned bright red.

"Oh, yes," Chris gushed. "Quite safe. The Congressman is—well, an *outstanding* man and a *great* boss."

Just stop, Sky thought, *you answered the question before you opened your mouth.*

"Of course," Sky said. "Hey—here's some free advice from an old lady. Have a few more noodles. They'll soak up the alcohol." Chris started to laugh.

"Old lady," he said. "You? An old lady?" There was something funny about this that only Chris understood, and he came down with a case of tequila-induced giggles.

Sky tried not to roll her eyes and asked a passing waitress to bring Chris a glass of water for the hiccups that would come next. *What an amazing waste of time*, she thought. *He doesn't know any more about Jerry Sharpe than I do, and it doesn't bother him at all.*

Sky had just begun to ponder this question when Chris answered it—by spilling the glass of water the waitress brought and insisting on cleaning it up himself. *No, wait*, she thought. *Look at him. He's clueless. Harmless. Starry-eyed. If Sharpe wanted to keep something in his past frozen forever in the snow banks of New York State, he couldn't do better than to hire Chris Patterson.*

The queasy feeling this thought put in her stomach made her flag down the waitress and ask for the check. Playtime was over.

"Are you sure you are okay?" Sky said as she took the check from their waitress.

"Oh, yeah," Chris said, "I'm…fine, I'm *totally* fine. Here, let me get that."

"Not a chance. You're not driving, are you?"

Chris winced again. "I told you—I'm okay. Besides, I live not too far from here. It's a short walk... I can show you." He let the sentence hang in the air, unassisted, both because he had not intended to say anything suggestive and because, even if it had been his intention, he had no idea how to close the deal.

I guess we're there, Sky thought. *Time to lower the boom.* "That's okay," she said as she picked up her phone, "I prefer to be by myself."

Chris tried to hide his disappointment behind a beltway smile. He still liked her and—this was Washington—might need her help someday. So he did his best to stand up without incident as she left.

"Well, Sky," he said. "Thanks for the drinks. Let me know if I can help you with anything from Congressman Sharpe's office."

Sky smiled. "Thanks," she said, "I hope I won't need it."

"I don't think you will. Is there anything else I can do for you?"

Sky paused as she considered whether what she needed to say came from pure intuition or rational, logical thought. After a split second, she decided that it didn't matter.

"Yes," she said. "Do me a favor. Keep an eye on your boss, and watch your back. I know you think he walks on water, but if he did, he would be the first Congressman in our country's history to do so."

"I don't understand," Chris said. "Congressman Sharpe is a—"

Sky held her hands out in front of her to silence the staffer. "I get it," she said. "He's awesome, and you have to say he's awesome. I'm just saying keep your eyes open, in case he turns out to be like the rest of his peers. And if that happens, I'd love to be the first to hear about it. You know, because I was the old lady who bought you shots and gave you some free advice. Agreed?" Chris Patterson smiled, and managed a sloppy, short, self-effacing bow. "Yes, ma'am," he said. "Agreed."

CHAPTER 56

Jerry positioned himself across the street from the CopyCat. He saw Chris waltz into the bar and find a spot by the window. Then about twenty minutes later, there she was. Jerry watched the reporter jump out of an Uber and scan the street. It felt like she lingered when she looked in his direction. He took a slow step backward, deeper into the shadow of the night.

This was a major problem. Jerry almost shit his pants as he watched her search the room and brighten as she greeted Chris with a friendly hug and a pat on the shoulder.

Chris was awkward standing up like an old school gentleman, and it was clear he had the same look he'd had back at the Tavern in New York. He was looking for a little action.

Jerry didn't know what to do. The rain was dumping gallons of water on him, even though a few steps behind him was an awning that would have kept him dry. He was too stunned to notice.

Jerry felt his chest tighten under his coat. He stumbled into the lamppost and tried to gather himself. He gasped as he stood there and watched the two of them huddle together and order drinks. They were shoulder-to-shoulder in a way that was all too friendly. This was not what he expected to be seeing tonight.

Jerry spoke out loud to himself. "Fucking traitor! Are you dropping a dime on me for a piece of ass?"

Jerry started to pace like the lion stuck on the other side of the moat at the National Zoo.

The rain was really picking up. The puddles on the sidewalk were overflowing into the street. Jerry felt like time began to speed up as the streets quickly flooded with Ubers and cabs zooming in to pick up stranded bar-hoppers.

He didn't know what to do. He backed under the awning, hoping it would help shield him from being spotted, but he was steaming, boiling inside, and his body language was enough to keep anyone from parking under the same cover. A few yuppie types pretended not to see him and looked for other shelter.

Jerry's imagination grew wilder and wilder.

Has Chris been spying on me this whole time? Had they known each other before she'd come to the office? They'd talked at Shelly's. They were friendly.

Was this going on all this time? What does he know? How could he suspect anything at all? If he did, why not go to the police?

There were several quick rounds of alcohol. Then, as quickly as it began, this clandestine meeting of his once-loyal sidekick and this reporter was over.

Nicholson stood up and was offering to pay the bill. A hug, and a kiss on the cheek, maybe promising something more, then she strolled out of the restaurant, clutching her oversized bag tighter on her shoulder.

Jerry wrestled with what to do next. Follow the reporter or deal with the traitor about to emerge from the bar?

She looked at her cell phone at the top of the steps, and then seemed to look across the street right at him. He stiffened and wondered if the darkness shielded him. A moment later, she waved down a cab and got lucky given the nasty weather. She sprinted out from under the doorway, dodging rain and diving into the red cab, disappearing as quickly as she'd arrived.

Jerry wasn't sure what was happening.

Fuck! I can't follow her now! What is this? How on earth could these two be connected?

His bulging eyes could burn a hole in Chris's chest as his stare barreled at the intern getting up from his table across the street.

Jerry banged his hands against the wall behind him as he hid in the shadows. He needed to settle down. *Focus. Can't take care of Nicholson just now. She will be on alert at this point. But her time will come quickly enough. Focus on the prick with the Nationals hat.*

Jerry knew he had to move quickly now. He needed to finish his task with the Hawthornes and not let this development derail him. Tomorrow night is his night.

Jerry came to the conclusion fast. He couldn't afford to take any chances. Chris knew something.

How could that little bastard figure this out when the cops were baffled? Had he made the connection with his boss? Or was he just being a helpful little nerd to bag Skylar?

In his head, Jerry replayed the last couple of weeks like he was rewinding an old VCR tape. There was nothing unusual that would have tipped off the kid. The night of Tyler's well-deserved death was of little interest. Chris didn't even come with him to the fundraiser.

Jerry was growing increasingly anxious about what his intern was doing, or maybe he was growing more anxious about what he knew he had to do. He needed to put a plan together. Now.

The door swung open, and Chris tumbled down the steps. The alcohol had a good grip on him as he stopped at the bottom to right himself. He appeared to be contemplating his next move. Should he chase down his friends and admit defeat, or head home and crash?

Jerry was getting impatient. He needed to act. He reached into his pocket and stared at his phone. The facial ID didn't work. Not even his phone recognized him. He tapped his four digits in and punched Chris's number. He watched Chris pat himself down in search of his vibrating phone. He answered immediately.

"Chris, it's Jerry. Chairman Perry called and wanted to meet for breakfast. He wants to talk to me about the budget. I need a few intelligent things to say, so can you shoot me some key points? I wouldn't ask if it wasn't important."

Chris immediately straightened up at the call. If he was wearing a tie, he would have tightened it up. "Congressman, of course! I will get something to you in about an hour or so. Need to stop back at my place. I have some of those files at home."

From the tone, it sounded like Chris didn't miss a beat and didn't suspect a thing. But he'd just met with Nicholson and didn't say anything about it. He was purposely hiding this meeting. *She is sniffing around, and Chris doesn't need to be sharing anything he knows.*

This was not part of the plan. Jerry didn't want to think about what needed to be done. He was going off script. He was one night away from step two in his plan with the Hawthornes. This was a major diversion and would make time his enemy. He would not be able to deal with Nicholson tonight.

How would he take care of that loose end? Would he need to?

Chris came from a working-class family. The first to go to college. He was making it. But he'd crossed the line. He had to go.

Jerry shook rain from his shoulders, turned, and watched Chris head home.

He skirted across the street, tracking his prey, considering his options. Time was slipping through his fingers. He still had things to do. This detour would put everything in jeopardy, but it had to be done.

His pace quickened and he made up ground as the crowds started to thin. His treasonous intern was heading in the opposite direction of the bar scene.

As he watched his target waddle home, Jerry began to think about how he needed to deal with Nicholson. It was going to be trickier to deal with a reporter, even one that had dropped to the bottom of the totem pole. Once she disappeared, there would be a serious manhunt. Abigayle would be all over it. Wait. Would Skylar confide in her about what she knew? Was that another problem? Taking care of Skylar, or maybe both, would be difficult and would get a lot of attention very quickly. He needed a plan, and soon. And it couldn't interfere with his primary goal—Hawthorne.

CHAPTER 57

Jerry was careful but not worried about following Chris. Chris was heavy on the drink as he stumbled a few times and caught his breath. Two more blocks, and the young man entered the right-hand door of a triple-decker squeezed in between a dive bar and another triple-decker.

The first two floors' windows were black and quiet. No activity. Jerry watched from below as hallway lights flipped on and off, then the third floor lit up like a Christmas tree, but the shades were down, and only vague shadows bounced around.

Jerry had to move swiftly. The bar was the only thing that seemed somewhat alive on the entire block. Well, maybe the bar was on life support. It was clearly not a popular place, with only one or two folks standing around having a smoke.

Jerry strode along the street and scooted across out of sight of the smokers. He made his way back, pried the door open, and quietly snapped it shut behind him. He stood in the dark hallway and listened while he peered up. There were wet footprints making their way up the stairs. The stairwell made one turn on the second-floor landing and then up to the top. While needing paint, the stairs were in good shape, and Jerry was fortunate not to make much noise as he began to inch his way up. The music from the neighboring bar also helped cover his footsteps as he made his way to the third floor. No one seemed to be home, or else they were asleep.

He leaned against the wood trim outlining the door and collected himself. This was not what he wanted. He appreciated the kid. But the little investigator must have figured things out. He could hear Chris shuffling around, and Jerry didn't want to waste any more time. He couldn't risk a major disruption. He only needed a few more days to finish his quest. His gloved hand gripped the knob, opened the door, and slipped in once it was wide enough. He gently closed it behind him.

Jerry stood quietly in the hallway, assessing the space. He panned the apartment. There was a bathroom on his right and a tiny kitchen on his left, which was painted a rather ghastly yellow with old countertops that reminded Jerry a little bit of Jane's old kitchen back upstate.

Jane. What would Jane think of what he was about to do?

He could see Chris sitting with his back to him at a small desk facing the window that looked down at the street. He knew this was his opportunity. The desk lamp was casting a gentle glow on the kid. If Jerry wasn't so furious, he might have thought the lamp cast an angelic hue on the young man pecking away at his laptop.

Jerry's prey was oblivious to what was about to happen. Chris was knocking out the useless talking points in fine fashion, flipping through some documents, then rapping on the keyboard.

Jerry had hunted a lot of different game in his time, and this was no different. In some ways a bit easier. Chris was not concerned or worried sitting in his own home.

Jerry moved swiftly so his intern wouldn't see it coming. He worried he might be seen in the window reflection as he approached. He slipped up behind Chris in one coordinated move. He was not distracted by Chris's eyes rising in surprise to see his boss behind him. Jerry grabbed the boy's forehead and ripped the blade across his throat. A stream of hot blood spurted across the window and onto the laptop. A cough of sorts. The arms never grabbed or flailed. They just fell to his sides.

Jerry was pleased with his speed. Chris didn't even have time to grab at him.

Jerry slammed his intern backward and out of the chair, cracking his head against the wood floor that quickly pooled with deep red blood. He watched Chris's eyes. They darted and linked with Jerry's for a moment. A gurgle. Another gurgle, with some bubbles from his mouth and nose. Then there was the gaze. He was gone. Forever.

Jerry hovered for a moment, his heart bursting in his chest, then took a few steps back and sank into the ripped easy chair against the wall. He started to calm as more blood drained from his former intern. The pool engulfed much of Chris's body and was spreading across the hardwood. Jerry took a deep breath. Chris wasn't going anywhere.

Jerry knew this was not in the original plan. He needed to buy some time so he could get to what he had set out to do. He looked down at the corpse in front of him. While necessary, it didn't give him the joy he'd experienced in the river. That was a carefully planned hunt for a Hawthorne. Tonight he felt betrayed and angry. He tried to reach into his own gut to generate the feelings he had when he disposed of Tyler. He couldn't recreate them.

Jerry shook himself to get moving. He looked at the empty eyes staring up at him and muttered, "You brought this on yourself, AllKnottedup. Stupid fucking alias. Just had to stick your nose in it, didn't you? Or maybe it was your girlfriend, Ms. Nicholson. She's next, kiddo."

Jerry looked around the apartment that would have to be cleaned out by Chris's devastated family. Maybe he could do them a favor. Hanging on the door to the bedroom was that ridiculous yellow parka he'd worn upstate. The kid must have spent two weeks' salary on that thing. He grabbed the parka and tossed it on top of the boy. He gathered what he could find. Newspapers, paper from the printer. Anything that would burn and piled them up unceremoniously on top of Chris.

He stepped around to make sure he didn't walk in the blood seeping across the floor and looked over the desk. He grabbed the laptop and tossed it onto the pile.

The kid's blood had streaked across the desk and splattered onto two photos. He had seen the first one before—it was Chris and his little brother leaning against a small broken-down boat that was grounded on the beach. The second picture was of a young woman about Chris's age. It took him a second, then he remembered the face. Marcy. No, Mary. Marie? From the Tavern. *Who cares? Now that is just too bad. She was cute. She'll have to find a local boy now.*

He lit the girl's senior picture and tossed it onto the pile covering his late intern to get things going.

CHAPTER 58

Sky ran down the steep, narrow staircase to *The Thread's* office, unlocked the front door, and gave Henrico no time for niceties.

"Quick," she said, "follow me. Abby's ready."

Henrico made sure to only breathe through his mouth so that the stench of mildew rising from the stairway carpet would not kill him by the time he reached the top of the stairs.

"Well," he said, "this takes me back. Early morning meetings about secret subjects held at some hole-in-the-wall downtown. I have to give you credit, Sky—people say that Millennials have a hard-on for authenticity, and here we are. I can even smell the beer and vomit from closing time last night. I must be special. Is that it, Sky? Am I special, or are you in a ton of trouble?"

"You're special," Sky said. "And the walls here don't have ears."

"Well now," Henrico said as Sky led him up the stairs, "that is special. And a good thing, too. I left all my spy-catching gadgets back at the hotel."

The two walked up the stairs into the cramped, glorious closet of *The Thread's* offices. The windows were covered in heavy drapes.

In the center of a large, shared working area, Abby was setting up two small screens on a rickety card table for Sky's upcoming demonstration. When she looked up to greet them, Henrico temporarily lost the ability to breathe. Sky's friend was, he realized, the most beautiful woman he had ever seen. He looked intensely at Sky for a quick moment, then back at Abby, and extended his hand to her.

"So," he said, "you must be the lady Skylar Nicholson was so worried about the other night. She wouldn't stop talking about you, and if you don't mind me saying so, I can understand why. I'm Henrico. Nice to meet you."

For the first time in over a decade, Abby Sullivan blushed from a man's compliment. "Well," she said, "I'm not sure what Sky told you about me, but I can assure you I'm just fine." She reached out to shake Henrico's hand. "I'm Abby. I hope you're here to talk some sense into Sky. As you are about to see, sometimes she suffers from journalistic hallucinations." Then she winked at him.

Henrico laughed and smiled. For a moment, he was not sure he was going to be able to stop staring at Abby, so he set his briefcase down on the table and pretended to look for a new notebook. The room fell silent.

Much to both Sky's and Henrico's surprise, Abby spoke first. "Sky thinks Congressman Sharpe might have already popped. Just weeks ago, Hawthorne got cut up and left in the—"

Sky cut her off. "He didn't flinch!" she said. "Did you see that? You just said—out loud—that Jerry Sharpe murdered and mutilated a human being, and a guy who has known him all his life didn't even blink."

"That's right," she said, and looked at Henrico with an intrigued stare. "Why doesn't that surprise you, Henrico? Most people would at least seem surprised."

Henrico saw the game immediately—Sky would feed Abby questions, and then Abby would ask them while batting her eyes. He didn't mind.

"Well, look, I told Sky most of what I know the other night. I've been covering this guy in our local paper for years. It never made sense to me—who he is, what he's good at, and especially how he climbed so high so quickly. I mean, he came home from school one day and found his mother's body covered in blood. Brutally murdered. He had no family. He spent the rest of his childhood being raised by family friends."

Abby covered her face with her hands. "My God," she said. "I didn't know that."

Henrico continued. "Who comes back from that kind of experience as a kid, you know? Seems to me only two kinds of people—those who get the right kind of help, and psychopaths. Most of the town thinks he's the first type, but I've always wondered whether he was the second. But killing people? I don't know about that."

"Do you see that?" Abby said, looking over at Sky. "That there is what you call restraint."

Sky rolled her eyes.

"That's funny," Henrico said, "unless you're me. Whenever something happens in this guy's life, good or bad, his next move is made possible by somebody else's corpse. And nobody asks questions. I'm the coyote trying to catch the roadrunner."

"And you said he flies off the handle," Sky interjected, "right? You told me you were worried that once he'd gotten to D.C., he would snap. And here we are."

Henrico went quiet, took a deep breath, and suddenly put his hands together as if calling a time-out on a football field. "Stop right there," he said, turning to Sky. "Why am I answering all the questions here? You called me and said you had something I could use. Don't get me wrong—you are fine company—but we all have things to do today. What have you got?"

CHAPTER 59

Henrico put on his reading glasses and leaned over until his face was an inch from one of the monitor screens. He was inspecting the cuts in Tyler Hawthorne's torso. "I can see how these could have been done by someone who knew what he was doing. A surgeon maybe," he said, "but a scout? Yes, Sharpe was an Eagle Scout. But I still don't see how that means he did the deed."

Sky threw her hands down on the table. "Yes, but we told you about how the Hawthornes summered up on the lake. You know how Sharpe feels about—"

"I know," Henrico said. "About city people, rich people, the 'blue bloods.' I know all about those families trekking to our town with their money and shitting all over it. I get it. The problem is that a lot of people where I come from agree with Sharpe on this. If deer season ever overlapped with the summer lake season in Watkins Glen, a lot of rich people wouldn't make it home alive. You can quote me on that."

"Henrico," Abby said, "why didn't Sharpe live with his father after his mother was killed?"

Sky shot Abby a look which suggested the team did not need another lead detective on this case. Henrico picked up on this and found it mildly entertaining.

"He died when Jerry was quite young. That's what I heard, anyway."

Sky spun to face Abby. A line had been crossed.

"What does that have to do with anything?"

Abby's eyes narrowed. "You want to understand this guy. You want to understand what makes him tick."

"Yes," Sky snapped, "I do. What I don't understand is why you are so interested in him all of a sudden."

Henrico began to chuckle, looked at his feet, then silenced himself. "None of my business," he said, "but I thought it was a fair question." When he raised his head again, he saw Abby Sullivan in full attack mode.

"I'm interested," she said to Sky in a low voice, "because he keeps calling my office insisting to meet me in person. Because Ramon says he saw Sharpe and Tyler together at the bar. Because your *Thread* source suggested that he might fit the profile. Because I don't want anyone else to get sliced up—especially me!"

"Whoa," Henrico said. "Wait—what? Who is Ramon, and who saw Sharpe with this guy who got killed?"

"Oh," Sky said to Abby with a roll of her eyes. "And I *want* that? Is that what you think? That I want you sliced up?"

Abby was not amused by Sky's sarcastic outburst. Her voice rose. "And how do you know," she continued, "that Jerry Sharpe isn't going to be at this little soirée tonight with your Aunt Millie, the mother of our murder victim? I mean, he came to the funeral *and* the burial, didn't he? Have you thought about how you might get to ask him a few questions on behalf of *The Thread*? Or is that just the air-headed PR chick in me talking?"

"LADIES!" Henrico shouted. The two women snapped out of their spat and turned to him as if he were the one causing a scene.

"Excuse me, but we don't have all day. Who is Ramon?"

"A friend," Sky said.

"Who works at the Good Samaritan," Abby continued. "At the front door. He saw Jerry Sharpe and Tyler Hawthorne leave together the night he was killed."

Henrico leaned back in his chair and took in a deep breath. "Jeeeeesus," he said as he exhaled. "That's not good. Do the cops know?"

"Ramon spent twenty-five years with the D.C. police," Sky said. "They know. So I'm not sure what we can do with all of this."

"Henrico," Abby said, "can you have someone back home get us the basics about Sharpe and his family—birth and death certificates, that sort of thing?"

"You don't have to," Sky said. "It's just a hunch."

Henrico looked at Abby and smiled. "Good hunch," he said. "If you don't mind me saying so, you should listen more carefully to your PR consultant." Abby returned his smile.

"My niece works at the courthouse," he said. "She should be able to pull files."

The two women stared at Henrico, silent for about five seconds, until his face became twisted into a shocked and incredulous look. "*Now?* On Sunday, right before the Bills game? I'd be shot the day I got back into town." The stares continued. Henrico groaned. "Okay," he said as he took his phone out of his pocket. "Give me a minute."

CHAPTER 60

Sky and Abby continued their argument in the relative privacy of her editor's office.

"It's basic research," Abby said. "You're getting your file together on this guy. It's due diligence you'd have to do at some point. That's all I'm saying."

"No, it isn't," Sky said. "It's your intuition on overdrive. And your vanity. Trust me—if you hadn't batted your eyes at him, he wouldn't be doing any of this. I realize you haven't been on a date in a few days, but now is not the time."

Abby decided it was time to defuse the spat. "Can we keep the outbursts outside of the workplace, please? Company policy." It worked. Sky exhaled.

"We need to focus," she said.

"Yes," Abby said, "and you're not helping. What was Sharpe's motive, Sky? Why would a kid from Watkins Glen, New York, care so much about the Hawthorne family in the first place? Were they going to level the race track? Close the Donut Shop?"

Sky's face lit up. "The Hawthornes summered there every year.

He probably knew them. Maybe something happened with Tyler, and he never forgot it."

"Really?" Abby said. "I worked two summers on Seneca Lake. Hundreds of families summer there. There's no way to know whether they knew each other. Besides, even if they did, knowing and disliking him isn't the same as waiting decades to murder him."

"That's true," Sky said. "It would have to be something—" Sky's voice faded to a whisper.

"What?" Abby said. "What is it?"

Sky turned to Abby with her jaw wide open.

"What is it, Sky?"

"I just remembered something Dad told me."

***

Henrico burst into Eric Zimmerman's office, cell phone still pressed against one ear, and started to wave his free hand in a way that told Sky and Abby that his pen had run out of ink. A cartoonish scene followed as the children of the digital age were temporarily unable to find a pen in a newsroom. Henrico finished his scribbles with a new pen and ended his call.

"It's blank," he said.

"What?" Sky said. "What's blank? What are you talking about?"

"The father on Sharpe's birth certificate. It's blank. There's no father listed on it."

Abby turned quickly to Sky. "Don't you start jumping to conclusions. Don't you dare. A single mother, or a grieving wife... None of those people would be forced to list a father on the birth certificate if they didn't want to."

"That's not the problem," Henrico said. "Apparently, it's pretty common for a birth certificate to list the father as 'unknown' or 'n/a,' or something."

"So?" Abby said.

"The only thing it can't be," Henrico said, "is blank. It can't be blank."

Sky stood up from the table. "It's my turn to be confused. I don't get it."

"Falsifying a birth certificate isn't just sloppy, or fishy," Henrico explained. "It's a crime. What's more, there have only been three clerks doing that job in town over the past sixty years. If someone broke the law like that, and it was exposed later, there would be no doubt about who did it. Which means that whoever did this was taking a huge risk."

"And I would bet," Abby said, "a risk that only made sense if one were paid a significant amount of money."

"Yeah," Henrico said. "I don't like it, but yeah."

"Henrico," Sky said, "what's the month on Sharpe's birth certificate?"

"May," he said. "Why do you ask?" Sky stared at him as he did the math.

"Which means he would have been conceived in…"

"Holy shit," Henrico said as he stared at his notebook. "August."

***

Sky stood on the street in front of *The Thread's* offices trying to sort it all out. The timelines, knives, murder. A few feet away, Abby and Henrico were whispering about what to do next. Sky turned to face Henrico on the sidewalk.

"There isn't enough, and you know it." Henrico started. "This isn't about printing a story that might ruffle a few feathers. If we're wrong here, an innocent man could go to jail. A United States

Congressman. Not something you would want on your resumé!"

"It's also about a killer on the loose, Henrico. That same United States Congressman."

"Maybe," Henrico said. "Okay, probably. But Sky, we've only been working on this theory for a few hours. Besides, the cops will send a small fleet of cruisers over to the Hawthorne place once we tell them our theory. The old woman will be fine."

"It's not just a theory, and that won't work. Aunt Millie hates cops. She'll make a well-placed phone call and have them sent away," Sky said.

Sky picked up her phone and prepared to make a call, but Abby put a hand on her arm.

"What?" Sky said. "I have to warn Aunt Millie."

"Sky, stop it," Abby said. "You're a reporter. You're supposed to be calm and objective."

"I don't care."

"You're forgetting one thing," Henrico said. Sky turned to him and glared.

"What's that?"

"Sharpe is really careful. If you're right, and he is the killer, he will lay low and gloat for a while. Take some time to clear your head. Let the cops get their game on. In the meantime, I'll see if I can make any sense of this birth certificate business."

Sky scowled. "And," she said, "be the first to report on all of this. Is that what this waiting around is about—the scoop?"

Henrico's face turned bright red. "Listen, *Buffy*," he said. "You can have the scoop. You can get to be prom queen, or valedictorian, or class president, or whatever it is you're trying to add to your resumé this week, okay? I don't give a shit. I just want to be right. Now if you'll excuse me, I should probably catch a cab before I commit a crime of my own."

With this, Henrico turned and stomped away. Abby followed him for a while, urging him to come back, but gave up and came back to Sky. The two women stood together, alone and cold on the sidewalk.

"That was not helpful," Abby said, "or necessary."

"He was an asshole," Sky said. "Besides, we don't even know if—"

"Listen to me," Abby said. "I believe you. I think Sharpe is no good. But we don't know that for sure yet. And if you start stirring the pot—all by yourself, again—he'll notice. He'll know someone is on to him. Then he'll use all his power to cover his tracks. He'll walk, Sky, just like they all do. Just like Senator Roll—"

Sky raised her hands to shush her best friend. "I got it. You don't have to say it."

"Good. Now let's go home and start getting ready for this party—*Buffy*."

CHAPTER 61

The President had just performed the annual lighting ceremony for the National Christmas Tree, which seemed to dwarf everything else around it. Of course, half of Congress had to attend to demonstrate solidarity, but most were not sticking around for the caroling or the obligatory Santa visit.

Jerry came to the White House alone and would be leaving alone. He just needed to be around long enough to say he was there. The real action tonight was at the Natural History Museum, where his good friend Mildred Hawthorne will be dedicating an exhibit in honor of her late husband and hosting another wake for her son. Jerry needed to be there for that. What was left of her litter would be there. There were things to do tonight.

Jerry found himself lost in thought as he wandered around the monster tree. Chris would never see another Christmas, but he got what he deserved. Jerry began to reflect on the lifeless intern laid out in a pool of his blood before he'd torched the place. That boy should still be kicking, but he chose to deceive his boss. Yes, his family wouldn't be able to have a happy holiday ever again, but was that his problem? Jerry pictured the boy in the apron on Thanksgiving. The sunny smile he cast from the kitchen. Was he faking it then too? Was he prying Jane for information then?

He swatted the thoughts of his traitor aside and watched the boisterous Santa entertaining rich people's kids and giving away the official White House ornament to each spoiled brat as they bounced off his knee.

Those kids are getting ripped off. Couldn't they give them a G.I. Joe or a Barbie? Cheap bastards. What kid wants an ornament?

Seeing kids get robbed of a decent gift soured Jerry's mood, so he made his way outside to set out for his next destination. He was getting used to the dreary clouds that seemed to perpetually follow him throughout the city. The whipping rain and sleet forced him to button the top of his overcoat, but it didn't really help much. He tightened down his fedora for extra coverage.

The whole week was riddled with rain and sleet showers. Storms, really. Jerry thought they might as well have been hurricanes. Wind off the water was painfully relentless and found its way between the buttons of the standard-issue trench coats one sees overwhelming Constitution Avenue. It was strange that it felt worse than the weather off the Seneca Lake upstate. Maybe he was used to different kinds of wind.

The lousy weather was cold enough to be miserable, but not enough to snow. He missed the snow. A snowstorm in D.C. was a couple of inches. Drivers would lose their minds, crashing into historic trees or each other, snarling up traffic for hours. Amateurs. A squall would stir up stupidity.

But back in Watkins Glen, a few inches would be called a gentle flurry and would not require sand, salt or the use of a plow. You would need at least six or seven inches before folks were thinking it was time to shovel. A typical storm off Seneca Lake was a real winter storm. If the icy wind flying all over the place wasn't enough, throw in a few feet of lake effect snow, and you have yourself a nice plow-breaking dump that piles up, and then piles up some more. No rain to melt it. The sides of the roads would have six, seven feet of grimy, blackened snow from storm after storm.

But from October through March, you dressed for the nasty weather. You needed real boots like his Timberlands. Sweaters, parkas, thick gloves, and a hat that heated up your head so much you could melt the ice caps.

But the D.C. rain. Jesus. Who the hell thought it was a good idea to build the nation's capital on a swamp? Disgusting in the summer, relentless in the winter.

The city of cement would boil from May through August, and folks jumped or scurried from AC taxi to AC office to AC homes. But the winters. They were as wet as the everglades and just cold enough to suck. *No wonder Virginia and Maryland had been so eager to give this land up to the Feds.*

Jerry pressed on and felt like he had to part the curtains of rain to see how far he had to go. Before heading up the street toward the museum, he glanced down the opposite way toward the Lincoln Memorial. *Bet Mr. Lincoln doesn't mind the weather given he's made of granite.*

He couldn't make out the Potomac from where he stood, but he knew it was there. He wished he was standing by the river and watching Tyler's body bob on by. That would have been fun. He thought about what Arlington Cemetery might be like on a night like tonight. Hundreds of thousands of souls like his were alone and soaked to the bone—a bit more literally for them, he guessed.

The only sign of life in Arlington would be the soldiers of the Old Guard, who served as the volunteer elite sentinels who patrol the Tomb of the Unknown Soldier twenty-four seven, three hundred sixty-five days a year. Real men. Those tough bastards refused to leave their posts even in weather like this. He wanted to be like them but knew he didn't have the chops. Plus, he had other things to attend to tonight.

Jerry hunched his shoulders and pushed ahead through the rain to demonstrate he was as tough as those guys. Well, almost as tough.

CHAPTER 62

The museum's line was longer than expected, but that was good for Jerry. Security would want to move things along. Jerry stepped forward to skirt the metal detector, but as he expected and planned for, a familiar security officer the size of Mount Rushmore stopped him and reminded him to go through the metal detector.

What happened to the privilege of being a congressman? Chris could arrange safe passage at an event like this. Oh yeah, he's dead.

Jerry had already planned to be searched, but his sliver of hope to bypass the process was dashed. His ego felt a bit bruised, and more concerning, would his plan to get through undetected work?

Jerry lingered and let the water run off his coat a bit more to make a show of his dire need to get inside. He took a moment to catch his breath, then briskly and with a look of "I have nothing to hide," he passed through the detector. The machine immediately beeped, and rather than backing up, he strode to the other side, and dug into his pockets.

He handed the officer his keys and a cheap one-inch red Swiss army knife attached to his keychain.

"Oh, boy. I keep forgetting I have that thing on me. Sorry. I'm in a rush, so you can just toss the damn thing?"

The security guard scoffed at the puny pocket knife that his eight-year-old might use for an elementary school art project. Jerry watched him smile as he rolled the weak-ass excuse for a knife around in his monster-sized hands and looked over the drenched congressman. Jerry assumed he wanted to make a crack about its lack of, well, size. The officer glanced at the growing line of folks, many of whom were standing out in the rain.

Jerry held his breath. The moment of truth. Was he going to get searched again? Made to pass through the detector again? Or as the line of people massed on the other side, would he get the wave to move on?

Heart pounding but not trying to give himself away, he shook his shoulders to throw off some rain and watched the guard consider sending him through again, but he saw the same thing Jerry was counting on. The other exasperated guard tossed a knowing nod to his twin manning the machine and waved the congressman on.

With a feeble smile and a nod of gratitude for not embarrassing him, Jerry collected his bent pocket umbrella and scooted down the hall.

Jerry had counted on the guards' laziness and mentally checked the next box on the list he was carrying in his head. The Swiss army knife concealed his bone-handled friend strapped to the inside of thigh. He patted himself to confirm his only reliable friend was still with him.

There must have been 600 interns working the event, and Jerry got the pock-marked twenty-two-year-old dork who literally took two wrong turns up and down staircases to find the reception area just off the rotunda displaying the African elephant since who-knows-when.

How the hell did this kid not know how to get to the main freaking part of the museum?

Jerry hung up his coat and umbrella at the temporary coat rack tucked behind a huge column, realizing he might be the only one with suit pants soaked below the knees, dripping and leaving a trail. Most of the guests had likely arrived by limo, so they had avoided the rain. A quick squeeze, or more like a wring, and he was comfortable enough to engage the crowd.

CHAPTER 63

The rotunda was full of dark suits and dresses jammed together. This made sense to Jerry given it was the opening of an exhibit and sort of a wake at the same time. It was an event that must have taken a year to plan. Hawthorne had apparently done several safaris in his day, and brought back trophies, maps, and pictures of his adventures. There were well-worn trunks propped open displaying binoculars, hip boots, and bed rolls. These were likely not for the permanent exhibit but were intended to demonstrate the worldly experience of the money bag who had made this day happen.

Gerald wanted to be remembered as a rich man's Indiana Jones.

Before entering the fray, Jerry scanned the crowd huddled together in the rotunda under the massive pachyderm. The elephant commanded respect from visitors to his favorite museum in D.C. It was handsome and dominated the museum's atrium. It represented independence, power, and perseverance. No other animal on the planet could take on such a beast, except for a human. Perhaps Mr. Hawthorne wanted to be equated to this stunning animal. That would be a legacy for a man, but Jerry was certain he had fallen short of that goal.

Whoever had done the planning for the Hawthorne Primate Exhibit dedication did a terrific job. They managed to use Christmas decorations as a way to outline the event's boundaries without making it feel like a stable, and the lights were set up to guide guests down one corridor to the actual exhibit in the African mammal section.

There were a handful of cocktail tables scattered about, but not enough to make it easy for people to park and take up space. The layout was designed to keep the crowd circulating with no real destination until they were herded down the corridor.

A small crowd was gathered beneath the elephant, dwarfed by its size. Jerry did love that elephant. He had a hard time taking his eyes off it. He had seen so many TV programs on elephants, he thought of himself as somewhat of an expert. No one paid attention to this beautiful beast, awaiting the guests of honor to pay homage to the family and their respects for the recent loss of Tyler.

At the mouth blocking the path to the actual exhibit stood a podium, and slightly to the right were a few wooden chairs for special guests. To the left was a larger-than-life portrait of Sir Gerald Hawthorne. Yes, Sir. He'd been knighted by the Queen, just like Sir Anthony Hopkins. Made him sound more aristocratic than he already was. Both were apparently actors.

The portrait was impressive. The rather dark-toned painting represented a giant of a man, clearly well over six feet. His broad shoulders filled a terrific gray suit featuring subtle pinstripes, and he was posed next to a mantle with a smoldering fire. There were towering bookshelves lining the walls on each side of the enormous fireplace, stuffed with leather bound tomes. Maybe first editions? A person could stand inside the fireplace. Little Mildred certainly could. The fireplace was adorned with beautiful tiles, with rich chocolaty woodwork trim that spoke to enormous wealth.

Sir Hawthorne had a stern yet handsome face, weathered by his time in the sun. He offered a square-shaped chin and jaw. Jerry thought he looked a lot like President Eisenhower. Folks would focus on the crooked, knowing smile and his deep blue eyes, not the graying, balding head.

Jerry liked the portrait. It was a well-balanced piece of art with a man who looked important. Jerry guessed Sir Hawthorne would have been pleased with it. And of course, the classic and quiet blue tie pulled it all together. If only he could stop hating the man.

After taking a few minutes to quietly admire and despise the dead guest of honor, Jerry dove further into the crowd, spreading the typical niceties around to look like he belonged. But he didn't.

The faces and groups were the crème de la crème of the blue bloods. They were a strange mixture of beautiful people and their relatives who had clearly married their cousins. Jerry thought they would fit in just fine along the Shenandoah Valley if it weren't for their expensive wardrobes and aristocratic accents.

Those gathering to pay their respects were dressed in the drab colors of a wake, with some men trying to brighten the mood with a colorful hankie inserted into the breast pocket, but they didn't match the ties, so they looked silly.

He already knew the men were wearing suits they had owned since they'd gotten married, except for the young whales who were in the latest Tom Ford suits. Jerry recognized the style of one that he had taken a liking to only a few weeks ago. It was a shame he ruined it.

What was so special about Ford suits anyway? Oh, that's right. The bargains went for eight thousand dollars.

The women looked like they were grown on the same farm, wearing black, proper dresses and white pearls, respectable shoes, and a handbag that could hold a cell phone. Maybe a small one. Did they all shop at the same boutique in the city?

A receiving line of sorts was taking shape, and Jerry parked himself among a group of young businessmen. They were friendly enough, but he mainly shuffled along the line in silence with an occasional nod to a lobbyist he recognized from fundraisers. Jerry was slightly impressed that they had dared to sneak into the event.

Jerry couldn't see her, but Mildred Hawthorne was at the podium, greeting her friends and accepting congratulations for her husband's accomplishments and sympathies for her late son who was found bloated and gutted like a perch only weeks ago.

No one spoke of how he died. No one dared.

He was getting closer, and he was beginning to get a little uncomfortable for the first time that evening. She was so close yet seemed so far away. Mildred had her twins with her at the end of this receiving line.

He had already seen enough of those two clowns. Their time was coming. Soon.

There, Hunter slouched, looking like an afterthought, hunched behind the tiny head of the family. He was clearly her bitch. The feeble Hunter dutifully listened to her introductions of people he clearly didn't know or care to.

Hunter didn't live up to his name and didn't look anything like the late guest of honor. Gerald was a towering man, and so had been his son who was now in a hole not too far from the museum. Hunter sure was a wimpy looking guy, like an accountant you would find in the bowels of the OMB putting spreadsheets together for someone three rungs up the food chain.

Jerry looked the little man over. Hunter might have disappeared if he had turned sideways. His ill-fitted suit crumpled over his ankles and scraped the floor. The suit looked like it needed a few trips to the dry cleaners and was a funny brown that didn't fit the occasion. It might not have been his suit. Maybe it was a last-minute deal. At least he abandoned the goth-pirate thing he was going for the day of his brother's funeral.

Jerry pondered the fact that, with all that cash, Hunter should be able to get a decent suit on the spot. Maybe even a Tom Ford. And the tie. Jesus. It was a clown-sized width of roses that clashed with the brown suit. Terrible. He had either picked that piece of shit out on his own or grabbed it off a bum on the way in tonight.

But there was no question about one thing. Hunter was definitely Mildred's kid. He had the same height, same slight build, and he had her narrow eyes and pointy nose. No mistaking the shallow gene pool there.

Then there was his little buddy, Caroline. The forgotten kid. Well, at least until now. She was slightly more important to the family given their recent loss. She'd moved up in the chain of command by default. She didn't have a care in the world, though, and Jerry got a real kick out of her—again.

Caroline was a younger but prettier version of her mother, but two things set her apart and made Jerry smile for the first time that night. That crazy black hair with wisps of silver was literally all over the place. She looked like she'd stuck her head in a blender. But it looked kind of cool. Artsy. Made a statement of sorts—*I'm here, and the rest of you can fuck off.*

She didn't look like the stuffy blue bloods shuffling around the room. She looked more like that crazy relative you only see at weddings and funerals. She was the eccentric relative who sent you handmade crap as gifts for birthdays.

Caroline wore a gray pantsuit instead of a wild dress like she had at the funeral, but the pantsuit was another touch of badass in the world of conservative, black dresses and suits. Her shoulders were wrapped in a wild paisley scarf or cape. Jerry wasn't quite sure, but that made up for no feathers or leather.

Then there were the piercing blue eyes. *She has her dad's eyes.*

Those pools filled the big, wide orbs with flecks of gray swimming about, and they leapt out at you as if they were going to grab you and shake you. While he recalled them from the memorial service, they were glorious tonight.

Jerry swept back to the portrait. The artist didn't do Sir Hawthorne's eyes justice if they were like the daughter's.

She was stroking her brother's arm like a kitten and exchanging pleasantries as required. The two were inseparable. Weird. Twins are strange. The tabloid coverage had them together all the time. They were seen together when skiing, swimming, and lounging at some Ritz here or there. Mutt and Geoff. Tom and Jerry.

CHAPTER 64

The makeshift receiving line was moving in fits and starts, and Jerry was approaching his turn faster than he thought. He just had time to straighten his tie, and then he entered the witch's lair.

"Good evening, Mrs. Hawthorne. Congratulations on the exhibit. I'm sure it is marvelous. I'm certain Mr. Hawthorne would have been pleased."

"Yes, thank you, Congressman Harp. Oh, forgive me, Sharpe, right? from Upstate? The one with the Impressionist fetish if I recall."

"Yes, ma'am." He ignored the two swats across the face. "I was grateful for your advice weeks ago. We did include the funding in the bill. I'm sure they will take other artists in mind when rounding off their exhibit."

Jerry smiled and watched her take a breath and consider the tall, athletic man towering over her. He could see it in her eyes. She thought him handsome. That he was young and offered a twinkle in his eye. He caught her gaze on his lapel where he wore his school pin of crimson. "Mr. Sharpe, did you grow up in Ithaca, and how did you like Cornell?"

Ignoring the Cornell portion of the question, Jerry leaned in. "Close, Mrs. Hawthorne. I grew up near Watkins Glen, a much smaller town, but I know you and your family summered nearby over the years. But it is a small, uninteresting town, so I'm glad to be here in the Capital City where big things happen."

Mrs. Hawthorne seemed to have a bit of distaste for what he said. She took a tiny step backward. Jerry watched as this quick exchange had clearly struck her. As he'd expected, she was reflecting on the cut of his jib, and Jerry could tell she liked his blue-gray eyes, but a bit of a frown crept onto her lips.

A firm handshake also helped, but he knew Mildred was sensing there was more to the man in front of her, but she wasn't quite sure what to make of him.

"I hope you enjoy the evening, Mr. Sharpe. You remember my son Hunter and my daughter Caroline."

"I was fortunate to meet them briefly at Tyler's memorial service."

While Mildred lingered a bit as she handed off the Congressman, Lurch extended his limp-ass hand. Jerry recalled how Hunter had tried to suck all his body warmth away at the funeral. Hunter's girly handshake was better than being molested for his body heat.

Jerry kept a watchful eye on Mildred as he began to woo the two weirdos. Mildred wasn't paying attention to the businessmen doting over her. He could see her watching him out of the corner of her eye. Jerry took full advantage of his size and towered over Mildred's tiny son who looked like a teenager shaking his hand. The congressman was built like a track star, and he knew his light gray suit fit him nicely.

Jerry smiled at Caroline and stepped closer to say hello. There was barely enough room between them to offer a hand. She remembered him from Tyler's services. Jerry was hoping that she was attracted to him and might even consider him her new plaything.

"C, you remember the good congressman from the funeral, yes?"

Jerry nodded and before turning to Caroline, made quick work of the son. Jerry praised the father and his legacy and lavished his admiration for how they could stick together for the opening in such difficult times. "I am impressed, Mr. Hawthorne. You have all managed to stay put together tonight. And you, Ms. Hawthorne, how is your work at Teach for America going? I am sure your father would be proud of you."

Maybe it was the tone, or perhaps the fact that the congressman wasn't pressing for support of a project, or asking straight up for money, or maybe it was because he wasn't kissing their asses so much that they were chafing, but they were warming to him.

Jerry observed the two smile at each other and mentally connect that they were on the same team on this one. They looked like two ducks in water, or maybe in their case, more like two young killer whales circling their prey. He wasn't quite sure.

Caroline spoke words other than "thank you" and "I appreciate you coming" for the first time that night: "Mr. Sharpe, excuse me, Congressman Sharpe, I appreciate that you came to the funeral. That was thoughtful of you. I am on some leave given recent, um, events, then in February I am expected back at the reservation. I think it's somewhat in your neck of the woods if I recall, yes?" Her blue eyes widened with interest and lit up the room. Combined with the crazy hair, her eyes made her appear more like a character from an Anime comic book. Jerry noticed she was not one who needed makeup and fancy touches to radiate her beauty. He still got a kick out of the wild hair. It swirled and curled, almost on its own, and it made a statement in the room, perhaps even competing with the elephant behind him.

Well, not really. She had to go.

"Please, Ms. Hawthorne, call me Jerry. And the work you are doing for the Onondaga Nation is impressive. They have suffered too long in poverty. Thank you for your service. I have a number of

Onondaga friends who speak highly of the Teach for America program."

Jerry put a gentle hand on her forearm while leaning into her brother to impose his size. As expected, it caught their attention, and they both drew in a fresh breath in unison. Caroline didn't pull back from the advance, and Jerry knew his charm would move the plan along. He caught her approving look to her brother. She knew the line behind him would get backed up but didn't care. And Jerry's new friend, Hunter, was soaking up the attention from Jerry, breathing a bit of life into him.

Jerry was banking on the idea that treating them like normal people would pay off. He wanted them to trust him.

"Jerry, thank you for spending time with us. I would like to connect with you once all this nonsense is over tonight. We are hosting a private reception afterward, and we can talk more then, perhaps more privately. Just find me at the exhibit around nine. That's when we are to retire to the room."

"That is generous of you. I look forward to seeing you then. Again, your father would be most impressed with how you have both handled things, and he certainly would be pleased with the exhibit."

Jerry's steel blues connected again with hers, then he watched Hunter smirk at her in playful approval as he provided a quick nod.

"C, we have other guests to attend to. You can play later."

They liked him. He'd certainly caught their attention. Especially hers.

CHAPTER 65

Thank God the speeches and presentations exalting the escapades of Gerald Hawthorne were almost over. Last to speak was, of course, Mrs. Mildred Hawthorne. The imposing portrait to her right as she faced the crowd made her look somewhat dwarf-like. Her sharp nose peeked over the podium as she began to deliver what would surely be an impressive rendition of her late husband's exploits.

She rolled on with Gerald's love for Africa, the outdoors, and fishing, especially upstate. Jerry listened as Mildred cackled some lame jokes to the crowd about her husband's adventures and mishaps, failing to deliver on the authenticity of her husband and downplaying their wealth.

Jerry lost focus and wandered a bit. His thoughts drifted back to the book on crows again as the stocky and stout woman dressed in black still looked the part. He understood better now that a murder of crows was aggressive, even to their own kind, and should never be underestimated. This snapped him back to the speech with no content.

Jerry watched as she missed a beat in her speech when she reflected on upstate. She was clearly searching the crowd in front of her. Something distracted her.

Jerry was a little taken aback when Mildred lifted her beady eyes and connected with him. The two locked eyes and for a moment the air fell away in the room. Jerry felt that they were sharing some anger. The guests in the audience seemed to disappear, the lights dimmed and the background noise quieted like a cold moment on an ice-covered lake. Lifeless. Bitter. Cold. Like an upstate winter gale.

Jerry began to feel that they were in a staring contest that could last for days, and the one who lost was forever doomed. Had she sensed something about why he was there? He tried to stay with her and keep his emotions in check. He could feel her eyes working past the crowd in front of him and reaching into his soul. Jerry felt like a searchlight was peering through him. He knew she was focused on him, but her eyes seemed to be working on something new, something that seemed to take her breath away.

What was she looking for? What did she find? What made her lose her place?

Jerry was a patient man, but even Mildred's pauses were getting to him. He was certain they were locked in quiet combat, and that she kept returning to focus on him. He was glad to see her gather herself a bit to crank through the boring remarks. The balance of the speech was hurried, and others could tell she was off her game.

Jerry could not help feeling like she was looking through him. *Who are you kidding, Sharpe? She wouldn't give you a second thought. You're the help, for crying out loud. You are a speck in her world—a lesser bloodline, born out of poverty and therefore without history. Did you really think she would look at you? What would her friends think?*

Maybe she was just leaning on tricks for public speaking when she lost her place. He had to do that when he was speaking to crowds. But she looked a little angry, like she was working on a puzzle that was missing pieces. *Maybe. She is a smart little Devil Dog. Hopefully she hasn't picked up on anything that makes me stand out. Not yet.*

The crowd's applause brought Jerry back into the moment, then the guests were herded down the corridor with the Christmas lights draped along the walls. There was an intern for almost every bulb on the wall directing oncoming traffic. *Where is that little troll who needed a map to find the rotunda? Or his own ass for that matter?*

While the crowd was moving toward the new exhibit, Jerry gazed toward the museum's gorgeous ceiling and tried to find some peace in the breathtaking view. He knew few folks bothered to admire the architecture and the detail in the walls and the arches above.

Jerry loved this museum. He felt there were few places where he felt relaxed and somewhat connected in D.C. He liked the concept of bringing in the outdoors and showcasing all the wildlife around the world. He didn't feel like he was among the fat lemmings now bustling down the corridor to pretend they cared about the late Sir Hawthorne's adventures. While he knew what was to come next, and that would bring him pleasure, he realized this was likely the last time he would be here.

Jerry emerged from the crowded hallway and took in the spectacle. He had watched the exhibit get built over the past couple of weeks. The dedicated room and its so-called artifacts represented the trophies of a man who took what he wanted, when he wanted.

Jerry soured as he scanned the room. The final exhibit was ghastly. He had watched the exhibits begin to take shape, but the final decorations looked fake and cheap. The Hawthorne family had sullied his beloved museum with their Christmas-like exhibit. Yes, the Gerald Hawthorne exhibit included several dozen stuffed animals set in a range of poses and in their little fake worlds. He envisioned Hawthorne sneaking up on these poor creatures while they were asleep and then insisting the taxidermist present them in more interesting and ferocious poses.

Some of the displays began to remind him of the way he felt every day. Out of place, away from home, and in a display that quite frankly, in a few weeks, no one will bother to look at. All the kids want to see the massive dinosaurs, the slithery reptiles, and the stunning gems. Not gorillas and monkeys.

The crowd graciously pretended to show real interest in the displays, the artistry of the taxidermy, and the history of Sir Gerald Hawthorne. The hum was only disturbed by a waiter who dropped a tray full of glasses. At least the blue bloods have style. Those were not plastic champagne glasses. Glass shattered across the floor, but of course, the blue bloods ignored the accident and just expected the help to clean it without further interrupting their evening.

While most of the displays were artificial, attempting to bring Africa to D.C., the last portion of the exhibit was impressive. It was the large glassed-in exhibit of a troop of gorillas working their way along the jungle floor that Jerry had watched get built over the past few weeks. It reminded him of the Korean War Memorial on the National Mall. He smiled knowing that he had already been inside the exhibit to prepare.

Jerry figured that the late Mr. Hawthorne focused his donated exhibit with this display in mind. Perhaps the silverback was to be a symbol representing the man himself. Jerry was sure Gerald fathomed himself as king of his jungle. The ceilings were still unfinished, and while there was wiring strewn above, only the two security cameras were mounted on the walls. Jerry began to embrace his plan for the night. The river wouldn't be good enough now. The king of the jungle! Perfect. There it was, right in front of him.

Jerry started to examine the glass walls and the infrastructure supporting the gorillas. He found the crease in the glass with hinges above and below the sight line. Nothing had changed since his last visit. The door was tucked into the diorama's rear. The workmen had added another trio of large fake trees by the blind since his last visit. That was even better than he imagined!

Jerry swiftly reached up and pulled the two wires connecting the cameras. Now he had more room for his plan.

He stepped closer and pressed his nose against the glass. He was no longer admiring the posed taxidermy sprawled throughout the display. He was admiring Caroline and Hunter working the room.

He was entertained by their offbeat style of networking. The brother-sister duo engaged folks without any real effort, and seemed like old hands, even like an old married couple hosting a small dinner in their backyard. This freestyle was more their comfort zone than a receiving line. He watched Caroline guide her brother along, using her free hand to gingerly twirl a small strand of that crazy hair.

Jerry needed to get to work. He made sure he worked the room enough to be seen, but not so much as to be remembered. He scoffed at himself because not being remembered was his area of expertise. He made his way to his two new friends. Caroline with her art-deco style stood out a bit—well, maybe her hair did.

She was engaged in a debate over Native American rights or something of that matter. Jerry admired her style while she debated. She talked over her lesser, less-informed opponent and positioned herself like a third baseman to make her point. Her forcefulness was amplified by her feeble brother slouching next to her, listening intently and giving supportive nods when she squeezed his arm.

Jerry politely interrupted and hung in there for a while, offering the insight that all folks are unwelcome immigrants except for the Native Americans, and we all are responsible for brutally taking their land and sticking them in undesirable areas to keep them quiet. Or something along those lines. He really didn't care that much.

But Caroline was on board, and she was further taken by her new congressman toy. He began to separate her from her brother, which he'd assumed would be difficult. But she broke away easily enough and began to chat him up, ignoring the guests. Jerry gently put his arm on Caroline's left shoulder like an old friend, someone trusted and secure. He knew she was getting the vibe. Hunter got the message and didn't want to disrupt his sister, so he took others with him toward the stairs.

The evening was starting to get stale. You can only look at stuffed monkeys and trinkets for so long before you feel like you are on a school field trip. The museum officials and interns were tasked with pushing folks through so they could exit the exhibition room and leave the museum. They implied that they had some real cleaning to do for tomorrow's events, but Jerry knew they just wanted to go home.

Jerry watched Mildred climb a few steps to stand above the dwindling crowd and announce that those who were invited could come to the African Room upstairs for a late private reception. As blue bloods would, she made sure others knew they weren't invited.

"Thank you all for coming. The private reception will start in a few moments. Those invited, and you know who you are, please head up the stairs to your right and the room will be only a few feet to your left!"

The exhibit quickly parsed into the haves and those who wished they had. Hunter dutifully waved at his sister and hustled up the stairs after his mother gave him a stern look requiring obedience.

Jerry saw Mildred lead the charge up the remaining stairs, and for a second, he thought he should take advantage and rub elbows with the blue blood tribe. Jerry thought about it. These are the same "tribes" that got wealthy on those Native Americans displaced across the country. But he had other matters to attend to this evening.

CHAPTER 66

Sky and Abby had agreed in advance how they would handle the museum reception. Abby would work the left-hand side of the room, playing dumb about Tyler's death in case a useful rumor or opinion emerged. Sky would head to the right, reconnect with a few family friends, and learn as much about Tyler's D.C. activities as she could. Both would keep a watchful eye for Sharpe. In an hour, they would meet at the far end of the room, thank Aunt Millie for the invitation, and leave before she could cause them any trouble.

The VIP reception was vintage Millie Hawthorne—intimate without being too familiar, and formal without a whiff of pretentious-ness. Her guests knew that at one of Millie's soirées they would not need to impress or be impressed, and therefore could enjoy the closest thing to friendship Washington had to offer. It was a time to catch up, inquire about grandchildren, and reminisce. Nothing more, nothing less.

They reached the top of the stairs and headed down a short hall-way toward the reception. As they got closer to the open set of double doors, Abby slowed down a bit. Sky put a hand on the small of her back and prodded her forward. "Hey," she whispered in her ear. "You'll be fine. Just smile a lot and save the profanity for later."

CHAPTER 67

Guests had done their duty, admired Sir Hawthorne's monkey legacy, given their condolences to Mildred, and were now scooting as quickly as they could to slip out as soon as possible. Escape routes were taken advantage of, and the exhibit was quickly losing its admirers.

The intern infestation scattered like little uniformed cockroaches when the flooring was lifted. Mildred's rather rude announcement was like a starting gun to escape. Jerry was impressed at the speed with which folks fled. Ejecting from political fundraisers was an art more than a science, but folks at this event made it look like a well-practiced tradition.

With the have-nots scurrying out first, Jerry had to hand it to the Hawthorne matriarch. With pursed lips and an approving nod to himself, Jerry almost said what he was thinking: *The firm use of power to parse the crowd, insult some and endear herself to others at the same time, was an interesting flex of her muscles. That is true power.*

The room became quiet faster than he expected. The blue bloods hurried up the stairs to get the real party started, and the folks who had been hoping to get attached to them tried to outrun the interns and museum staff to the exits. The lights dimmed, and the room grew quiet.

However, Jerry knew the room wasn't completely empty with glass-eyed primates remaining to keep him company. As expected, a gentle hand slipped into his. Jerry smiled to himself as his new friend caressed his skin. Jerry turned to greet his new blue blood girl. As expected, the drink was deep in Caroline's gut, and she steadied herself from an evening of indulgence against his arm.

It was amusing to see that within the last hour, Caroline's hair had taken on another life of its own, swirling around her head, half of it remaining fluffy and the other half sort of slicked back like she had been working hard. It almost looked like she'd gotten honey stuck in half of her hair and had failed to tease it out.

"Did you see their faces?" Caroline was waving at the two or three people lingering at the top of the steps with her third or fourth champagne glass. While they may have been disappointed that they were not part of the real family and friends crew, perhaps they were secretly thrilled they were going home. "Mother certainly has a way with the common folk, doesn't she?"

"Yes, Caroline, she certainly does." He was now on a first-name basis with the artsy woman.

"You can call me C. Hunter likes to call me that. Mother hates it. So yes, you can call me C."

He leaned down to be closer to the eye-level of his prey and placed a gentle kiss on her lips. "Yes, C. I like that." *So this is what it feels like to face one of the Sirens?*

He now had a better understanding of Odysseus's perverted challenge to escape the Siren's trappings. But Jerry felt that he likely faced less attractive adversaries than Homer's hero. Where was his own Circe to advise him on his quest? But he always understood he was on this adventure alone. He's been alone since his mother was killed.

Jerry considered the evening's circumstances and his own role in tonight's story. While Mildred's daughter might think the opposite given the family's hubris, he might be the siren. He was the one luring her into a dark cavern that was sure to ruin her on the shores of death.

"How about we hang back a bit?" Jerry wanted to move quickly. He snatched a freshly opened bottle of what he assumed was top grade champagne. It had to be French, otherwise it's just sparkling wine. The folks upstate know the difference since their vineyards are not permitted to call it champagne. He poured and poured until her glass overflowed onto the floor in excess like everything else that night.

"It's amazing how fast the room emptied. Your mother certainly has a way with folks. I think we had a little moment back there, don't you?"

Jerry made a show of what was to come next, removing his pressed gray suit coat and draping it on a nearby chair. He pushed a plate and two half-empty glasses to the side, and expertly swept off the tablecloth and folded it in his arms, making the clear suggestion it had a different purpose for the two of them this evening.

Caroline was getting anxious, and she was licking her lips so much they were likely to crack within the hour. She slid her hand in and gently stroked Jerry behind the shoulders. "Yes, I think we did, and the night is still young. Maybe, well maybe, we can be a little late to the boring party upstairs?" Caroline's lustful eyes could not hide the fact that champagne was hitting the spot.

Jerry knew this was getting easier by the minute but didn't want any interruptions from lollygaggers. Interns tend to show up at the most inconvenient times. When they do, they end up dead. He took advantage of his size and managed to steer his new friend back toward the gorilla diorama. The field blind was set up in the back. The plastic green-leafed shield caught Caroline's eyes as well, and she downed the last full glass before she used her pointy little nose to direct Jerry as if it were her idea.

"Oh, yes. Oh, yes indeed!"

Just as Caroline tossed her now empty champagne glass to the side, Jerry took the initiative and pried the glass door open with his backside. Just as it swung open, someone turned the lights off in the halls, leaving only the looped Christmas lights to shine a low and gentle hue, which made for a much more subdued room.

The two froze like rabbits in the snow. For having downed such a large amount of alcohol, Caroline stood remarkably still, as though she were listening to the sounds of the forest. Satisfied there was no one hunting her, she scooted in first without reservation. Jerry managed to slip in behind her and ease the door closed without his hands.

There was no question Caroline was bombed, but she beamed with excitement and enthusiasm. She was on all fours and pretended to crawl to the field blind, on the prowl, a cougar or something, purring and arching her back as she made her way toward the blind. Jerry enjoyed watching Caroline turn to face her new lover. She leaned against him while on her knees to plant kisses on his neck while running her tiny, slender hands down his crotch. She clenched down hard on him. She looked up at Jerry with those cartoon eyes and he watched her smirk in approval.

She made sure to rub up against him as she positioned herself to duck into the blind's privacy. Jerry moved swiftly around the fake trees to behind the blind with his newfound friend.

Caroline had already unbuttoned her blouse and turned to Jerry with a cat-like snarl, making a show of her breasts. She hadn't worn a bra, perhaps in anticipation of some fun for the night or she had managed to slip it off earlier. Jerry didn't know or care. She stretched backward and dug her foot into Jerry's crotch and curled her toes into him.

Jerry was certainly aroused and amused at the same time. Her bizarre frolic certainly added to the jungle image, but Jerry only smiled and followed her.

It was like the field blind was put there just for him.

Caroline was still jazzed and stripped faster than she had downed her last drink. She wrapped her hands tightly around his waist. Having a little fun was a bonus.

After a few minutes, Jerry was good to go. He didn't wait for any more so-called pleasantries.

CHAPTER 68

Jerry looked up at the clock above the fire extinguisher. *Twenty minutes.* That was quicker than he expected. He examined his handiwork in the life-sized diorama to make sure he didn't forget anything. He was glad to know there had been so many people in this room, it would be difficult to narrow things down.

The tablecloth was a mess, so he left it as part of the display among the gorillas. He had set it up almost like a bloody flag to surrender.

He was careful not to touch anything or leave a mark, but he wiped things down thoroughly. He was trying to remember the lessons he'd learned upstate about what others carelessly left behind when they committed such crimes.

He turned to head to the bathroom when he heard someone stumbling down the stairway. It was dark, and the intruder was barely able to hold himself up.

Jerry stiffened and pressed up against the wall next to the stairs. He flipped the blade out again, still hot and slick from his earlier deed.

Did someone hear him? Had someone come looking for her?

Jerry watched as the dark figure straightened itself up from the floor, rubbing its neck from the graceless entrance into the room. It reeked of alcohol, and it almost had a mist of vapor around it. A hand went up to the eyes as if blocking the Christmas bulb lights on the far wall would help see in the dark room. A whisper.

"C? Are you still down here? C?" A little louder: "Caroline? Where the hell are you?"

Jerry could now easily see the small man's outline standing only feet in front of him, slowly taking frightened steps into the room.

Jerry held his breath. He recognized the hunched figure in the shadows. He watched as his eyes began to fix on the gorilla display. He began to see what Jerry had left for others. His hand slid from above his eyes to his mouth that was open to scream but couldn't find the right sound. A whimper and a half step forward. Hunter's hand briefly reached forward toward the brutal scene in front of him.

Jerry could not believe his luck. He smiled to himself and slipped behind the frail man and in one synchronized motion, wrapped his massive hands around his prey and drove his trusty knife through the chest of the boy-sized man. He struck with such force that he almost drove his knife clean through, but the tip must have struck the spinal cord. Steaming blood pumped into the hall as he giddily tossed the dead man onto the sticky floor.

Jerry stood there, heart pounding and his voice fighting to burst up into the dark void. He wanted to scream in the victory of his slaughter but stopped himself and gazed upon his handiwork. Jerry hovered over Hunter and watched him twitch a few times on the floor.

Sometimes, luck smiles upon those in the right place, at the right time. For others, like the piece of shit on the floor, luck lands on you like a fucking piano.

He marched into the bathroom to clean himself up. He dumped all his clothes in a plastic bag from the garbage and scrubbed as deeply and swiftly as he could. He reached under the counter and found his stash. Three minutes later, he looked at himself. The mirror could lie of course, but he was cleaner than he thought he should be given the spectacle he had just left behind.

Jerry smiled as his eyes met in the mirror. They went down like sheep. He was both prepared and lucky. Jerry slipped his favorite tool into his pocket and buttoned up the jacket. Overall, he was pleased with the night. He'd done a lot more than shear these two lambs.

Jerry pushed the bathroom door open with a piece of paper towel and scanned the room. Quiet. A little too quiet. He could hear the party's muffled sound from upstairs fill in the background a bit, but nothing else. The Christmas lights made the entire area look gentle. It reminded Jerry of a light snow at midnight with only a few street lamps on.

He took a second to admire his Gorillas in the Mist diorama one last time. He basked in his work. The low light reflected in the beast's glass eyes, including in the one he had just added for others to admire. His contribution to the display would catch folks' attention.

Keeping his cool, he scooped up his bag of bloodied clothes and worked around Hunter's heap, careful not to step near any of the blood. He was tempted to give the sticky mess that was once the heir of the Hawthorne riches one last kick, but he stopped himself and scurried toward the exit. He grabbed his coat and broken umbrella and made a quick exit through the service doors down the hall as planned.

Jerry didn't want to look like he was in too much of a hurry or attract any attention, but he was starting to lose his shit. The night had been so perfect. His artistry and butchery were on full display for those blue blood bitches to find. And Mildred would fold like a deck of cards. One more to go. Wait. He still had to find Skylar. One problem he didn't have a plan to solve. Did he have time?

Jerry found his way out quickly and was on the street fending off the rain. He managed to keep away from the puddled curbs in search of a cab. A black SUV swerved a bit toward a puddle in front of him, trying to give him a nice splash. A quick sidestep, and he stayed just out of reach.

Jerry knew he only had to go a block or two to see an ocean of red and yellow cars. He could avoid those asses trying to get him.

Just before he reached the first intersection, he sucked in a gasp as he approached an unmarked car parked near the corner, wipers occasionally clearing the screen. His blood rushed through his entire body, but he did his best to keep his cool and didn't change his pace.

Jerry pulled his fedora tight on his head as the wind was picking up. He didn't look up, but he managed to throw a little salute to the faceless cop in the driver's seat, acknowledging the tough duty the guy had drawn that night. He got a bleep and a flicker of lights as a thank you, and he continued on his way.

As he approached the intersection, he thanked the gods that there were cabbies pulling in left and right from the corner, and he quickly chased one down.

Jerry settled into the wet cloth seats, which were soaked from all the soggy passengers that evening. He didn't care.

Off to the Cannon Building. The cabbie had no concerns about dropping his charge at the freight entrance. It was his last run of the night.

CHAPTER 69

Sky was ready to leave the reception ten minutes after she had arrived—Aunt Millie's gift for gossip had seen to that. Mrs. Ariana Driesen, heiress and Sky's one-time Girl Scout leader, wanted to commiserate over the terms of her divorce before offering Sky a job in talk-radio. Sky managed to politely decline, but only after distracting her would-be patroness with a dry comment about Aunt Millie's offer to defenestrate Chip from his position at the *Post*.

"Don't worry," Mrs. Driesen said. "There's still time. My son Daniel has several eligible friends. When you're ready, give me a call."

After downing her second flute of champagne, Sky thanked Mrs. Driesen and looked across the ballroom at Abby, who had attracted her usual circle of fans. Abby caught her gaze and gave her a wink. *You're right, Mrs. D.*, Sky thought, *I have plenty of time. As long as I stop coming to events like this.* Mrs. Driesen was in the middle of a story about one of her grandchildren when Sky felt the phone in her small purse vibrate twice. Staring at a phone at such a gathering would cause a small scandal, so Sky excused herself to the ladies' room, stood in a stall, and pulled out her phone. The message was from her editor.

Arlington fire declared arson. Chris Patterson, staffer on Hill, died in the fire. Right up your alley... #IsDCSafe

Sky gasped. Her hands shook as she re-read the text. For once, she could not conjure up a smartass response to her boss. Even though she had spent the last two weeks curating the stories of heinous, violent crimes committed against people like Chris, this was a blow. Chris was young, decent, enthusiastic, and excited about working for a congressman in Washington.

And what was his reward for coming to Washington to serve his country? Sky thought to herself.

Sky leapt up and bolted out of the ladies' room and collided with Millie Hawthorne only feet from the door.

"Oh, Skylar—good," Millie said quickly, as she looked over her shoulder. "I was hoping we could have a word, dear. Do you have a minute?"

Sky's eyes darted across the room, searching for Abby over Millie's shoulders. Her eyes then dropped to Millie's. She did her best to hide her despair and her shock at Millie's sudden appearance. "Of course, Aunt Millie. Such a wonderful reception..."

"I only have a minute, dear," she said, "and this is important. They are onto us. Be careful."

"I'm sorry," Sky replied, "but who is onto us?"

Aunt Millie's whisper began to sound like a hiss. "The people who did this to Tyler—the people you are investigating. *The ones who want to do us in!* Come on, dear. Pay attention."

"Oh," Skylar said. "Yes, that is unfortunate. Are you sure?"

Aunt Millie loosened her grip on Sky's elbow and laid it softly on her forearm. "Quite sure, my dear," she said. "You may not have thought it necessary to know my private investigator, but I thought it necessary that he knew you."

"What? I don't understand," Sky said.

A man's voice from the banquet hall called out for Millie. She took two measured steps back into the line of sight of her guests and gave the poor man a look which would buy her some time.

"And," Millie said, "I only have a minute. My PI called me and said someone was following you yesterday." It was Skylar's turn to gasp.

"Are you sure?"

"Of course I'm sure!" Millie hissed. "I pay for certainty! Whoever it was followed you halfway across town, then sat across the street from your apartment for at least an hour after you got home."

"My God," Sky said. "That's creepy."

Millie's tone softened. "I don't mean to alarm you," she said, "and I am quite confident in your ability to take care of yourself, given what you do for a living. That said, do be careful. We have had enough misfortune lately, as you know."

With her insinuations still hanging in the air, Millie put a smile back on her face and turned to return to the reception.

"Aunt Millie, I know you need to go, but did Congressman Sharpe come to the event tonight?"

"Yes, dear, he was kind enough to stop by, but I think he left earlier. Now, if you'll excuse me, I need to catch up with Senator Mitchell before he listens to any of those people over there. Oh, dear." Her conspiratorial scowl melted into a hostess's smile as she swept back into the reception hall.

Sky stood just outside the entrance to the ladies' room and tried to digest what she had just heard. *The poor woman*, she thought. *She's crazy. Why would anyone be following me? If anything is creepy here, it's that Millie hired a private investigator to spy on me. Let it go, Skylar. Let it go. See if Sharpe is here, come back up to get Abby, and go home. Simple as that.*

CHAPTER 70

Sky took the main stairs into the rotunda in search of the congressman. It took a moment for Sky's senses to adjust to the silent darkness. The rotunda was empty, save for a few tables and chairs and, of course, the massive elephant dominating the middle of the room. She walked through the rotunda and thought she saw Congressman Sharpe in the ape exhibit's entrance out of the corner of her eye.

"Congressman Sharpe?" she said. "Jerry?" No response.

She walked toward the new exhibit. Instead of the congressman, she found the portrait of Sir Gerry Hawthorne staring back at her from its new position in the exhibit hall which bore his name.

The pristine silence was broken by a single, soft, wet sound that ricocheted against the marble floors and walls.

Thwap.

Sky blinked and shook her head. Something about the sound was odd, as well as the nauseous feeling that arrived with it. Something was terribly out of place.

Thwap. Thwap-thwap.

Sky turned to her left and looked up to see if the ceiling had a leak and was letting drops of rainwater into the ten-million-dollar ape exhibit. Nothing.

Thwap.

She looked at the floor for any evidence of water. Nothing.

Thwap-thwap.

A dark, cold feeling came over Sky as she realized there was only one other place to look for the sound's source. She raised her gaze from the floor and looked directly into the Hawthorne gorilla exhibit.

CHAPTER 71

Sky blinked three times as her brain strained to make sense of the scene in front of her. Caroline Hawthorne's naked corpse was standing upright, her face pressed against the glass. The stuffed silverback gorilla had been moved into position behind her, holding her body against the glass and appearing to violate her from behind. The two were lashed together with some kind of cord. Caroline's mouth hung wide open, and various extremities twitched.

Skylar fell slightly backward as she took it all in. Blood ran down Caroline's collar bones onto the front of her chest, and now dripped slowly onto the floor.

Thwap. Thwap-thwap.

Sky felt like she had grabbed a high-tension wire with both hands as her central nervous system was straining to process the load. Caroline had been gutted as Tyler had been, and the contents of her bodily cavities were arranged in a neat pile on the floor.

Thwap. Thwap-thwap. Thwap.

Skylar raised both hands to her head and dry-heaved, trying to scream. The weak sound of her voice barely echoing in the museum hall startled her, and she realized she held her phone in her left hand. *This is a crime scene*, she thought. *There should be pictures.*

The stench of Caroline's intestines began to fill the hall, and waves of horror ran through Sky as she lifted her phone and filmed the scene. She sobbed for the girl she had once played with at the lake, for Millie, and for those who were going to have to see this. Sky backed away, out of both a sense of horror and a journalistic desire to cover the whole crime scene with her pictures. Her right heel hit something and she tripped backward, falling not on the hard exhibit floor as she expected, but on an event table that had not yet been cleared away. Something on the table jabbed Sky in the back and forced her to her hands and knees on the floor. She looked up and screamed again.

There, not four inches from her face, were the shocked eyes of Hunter Hawthorne. He was lying on his stomach in a pool of blood, his head twisted toward her like a doll. Sky started to hyperventilate, scrambled for her phone, and rose to her feet. *Tyler, Hunter, Caroline,* she thought. *I played with them. I knew them. It's almost as if—*

She looked over her shoulder into the rotunda. Then she turned back toward Hunter's body dumped on the floor. She spun around again. *He could still be in here*, she thought—*after all of us, ready to kill us all, just like Aunt Millie said.* Sky took two more steps backward, then stopped.

Is this how it ends? Sky thought. *Slashed and gutted at the Smithsonian? They'll have to catch me first.*

CHAPTER 72

Sky kicked her high heels onto the marble floor and sprinted out of the ape exhibit. At the far end of the rotunda, a line of security guards guided the last of the guests from the after-party down the stairs, along a short passageway, and out into the street.

None of the security guards expected Chantilly High's star soccer forward to come at them from behind, or with such speed. But Sky had caught sight of Abby coming down the stairs. The guards never knew what hit them.

"Hey, whoa!" one said, as he managed to catch her by the arm. "Where are you going in such a hurry? Hey Pete, give me a hand here."

Sky looked over her shoulder. "No," she said, "let me go. He— he did it *again*. It was *him*. And *them*..." Her voice faded into a whisper.

The first guard let go of Sky just as a younger one grabbed her forearm, saw the phone in her hand, and lifted it in front of his face.

"And what," he said, "is this? There's no photography in here, miss. Especially after hours. What were you doing back there? And don't lie to me—we have cameras watching every corner of this place."

In a single, fluid motion, Sky moved her weight from her front foot to her back foot, rotated her hips, and ripped her forearm out of the guard's hand with such force that his nails tore five deep scratches in her arm. The guard pulled his hand back in shock, and blood from Sky's forearm began to trickle down toward her elbow. She pointed at the phone with her other hand.

"This," she hissed, "is *mine*."

The two guards took a step toward Sky, just as Abby got to the bottom of the stairs. "She's with me," Abby yelled. "Please, she's with me. She's okay." The guards turned to look at Abby as she ran toward them.

"Skylar?" Abby said as she finally reached her. "What's wrong? Skylar—look at me." But Sky was still glaring at the security guard who had dared touch her. Her whole body was trembling. Blood dripped off her elbow onto the floor. One of the guards reached for his radio just as it started to scream at him.

"All units—we have a 536-b in 134. I repeat, 536-b. Secure the area and await backup. Secure the area immediately." An alarm bell sounded in the hall.

"Holy shit," the younger guard said. "That's the ape exhibit."

The older guard nodded. "Focus, kid—*focus*. 536-b. This whole area is now a crime scene. That means no one leaves. I'm going to seal off 134. You stay with these two until the police arrive. Got it?"

"Got it," the young guard said.

Sky turned her head slowly, trying to get her bearings, then looked at the guard with a blank stare.

"Home," she said.

The guard looked at Sky's face. She was now shaking so much that she could barely stand. His expression softened into one of concern, and then firm resolve. The man turned, put his arm around them both, and started to help Abby move Sky down the hallway toward the exit. He radiated calm.

"What's your name, Miss?" he said to Sky.

"I want to go home," she said.

"Her name is Skylar," Abby said.

"Hi, Skylar," the guard said calmly as they walked. "My name's Pete. You're going home, for sure. But first, we're going outside and sit down for a bit. You need some air. Besides, there are some people coming who are going to want to talk to you."

The sound of sirens, usually only part of the background noise of the city, grew louder as the first wave of police and ambulances arrived.

"Abby?" Sky said. The guard looked at Abby, and his eyes lit up with recognition.

"Yes, Abby too," he said. "She's right here."

"Let's go," Sky said. "Abby." Her steps were stronger now.

"Indeed," the guard said. "Not much farther now. Just through that door."

"Okay," Sky said.

They managed to get Sky out the door and onto the sidewalk. The early evening's heavy rain had tapered into a soft, misty drizzle as a swarm of police officers cordoned off most of the museum in yellow tape.

The guard flagged down an EMT, who threw a blanket around Sky's shoulders and helped her to a nearby bench. Sky sat down, put her head between her knees, and began to vomit on the sidewalk. A tall, muscular police officer reached them just as she began her first set of dry heaves.

"She's in shock," the officer said. Abby thought he was talking to her but realized that he was barking orders at the EMT. "Keep her hydrated and warm. Watch her blood pressure. Once she is stable, take her to—" A smile broke out across the young EMT's face, and the officer stopped himself. "I'm sorry," he said.

"That's okay," she said. "I can take it from here, soldier." The policeman grimaced and looked down at his boots.

"I apologize," he said. "Old habits die hard."

"Tell me about it," she said as she took Sky's pulse. "Army Medical Corps. Two tours in Iraq, one in Afghanistan. Never a dull moment."

"I know," he said with a smile, and looked back at the Museum.

Abby reached out from her seat on the bench and touched the officer on the elbow. "Thank you," she said. He nodded, stared at Sky for a moment, then turned back to Abby.

"Listen," he said, "as soon as she comes out of this, one of our detectives is going to want to talk to her about what she saw in there."

He tried to offer his business card, but before it was out of its holder, Abby had extended hers to him.

"Nicholson. Skylar Nicholson. She lives in Adams Morgan. Sky doesn't carry business cards anymore, but call me when you need to talk to her, and I'll make sure she answers any questions you have." The man held back a grin. "Is that so?" he said. "Well, in that case, I would say she is lucky to have you around."

"She is," Abby replied.

"One more thing, Miss Sullivan."

"Yes?"

The officer broke eye contact with Abby and appeared to be looking past her into the distance. "If she saw something bad tonight and can't stop seeing it, make sure she talks to somebody, okay? A professional."

Abby nodded as the man's radio screeched. Both the EMT and the officer understood what the dispatcher had said. Abby didn't understand a word.

"It sounds like you had better get back in there," the EMT said. "Whatever it is, I want you to deal with it. You wouldn't believe who they let carry a gun and a badge in this country. Am I right?"

The officer smiled, nodded, and ran back into the museum.

The EMT handed Sky a paper cup filled with orange juice and began to wrap a bandage around her bloody forearm. "She's definitely in shock," the woman said to Abby. "Best to send her to the ER. Can you stay with her until then?"

"Yes," Abby said, "of course."

"Good. They'll probably want to keep her overnight as a precaution. Understand?"

"I'm sorry," Abby said as she shook her head, "but I don't understand. What could have done this to her? We were at a cocktail reception, she left for a while, and the next thing I knew the party was over and everyone was leaving. I caught up with her ten yards from the door, and she's like this."

"Look," the EMT said, "I don't have many details. We got a call for a homicide in the museum. Based on the number of people running around here with guns, they are trying to secure the place in case the perpetrators are still inside."

Abby gasped and looked at Sky. "Oh my god," she said. "What did you see in there?"

Sky looked up at the EMT. "I'm okay," she said. "I just want to go home."

"We will, hon," Abby said. "Just one stop first."

Sky lowered her head again to stare at the sidewalk. She wanted to tell them what she had seen but began to wonder if any of it was true. *Did I really see that*, she thought to herself, *or not? Maybe it was different from what I remember. Maybe I saw it wrong. I need to be sure.*

She closed her eyes and could see Caroline's face as she had seen it in the exhibit—ashen, ghoul-like, her mouth wide open and lips twitching. She opened her eyes, took a drink of the orange juice, and slowly closed them again. Her face was still there.

How can I not be sure? Sky thought. *Why don't I feel sure?*

"Skylar," Abby said softly, "Talk to me. What happened?"

Sky squinted, banished Caroline's face from her mind's eye, and tried to sort through what she could say.

CHAPTER 73

Abby wasn't expecting the ER nurse to come check on Sky so quickly—this meant that she was both surprised by her arrival and a little embarrassed to be caught leaning in a doorway finishing a text to Sky's mother:

Sky and I are both fine. Don't watch the news. Talk soon.

"So how is she doing?" the nurse asked. "Still asleep?"

"Oh. Yes," Abby replied. "I was just texting her mother."

The nurse smiled. "She'll be fine," the older woman said. "We'll just keep an eye on her for a while."

Abby looked at the only person who had ever cared about her—who had ever bothered to actually *help* her—fast asleep on an emergency room cot, still wearing the dress she had refused to take off when they arrived. The nurse put a hand on Abby's arm.

"You should go get some sleep, too, honey. We'll watch her and call you when she's up."

"I don't think you know what that woman is capable of," Abby said with a tired grin as she pulled her keys out of her purse.

"Perhaps," the nurse said, "but remember. Once we release her, she's all yours. If she is as much of a handful as you say, you're going to need your beauty sleep."

Abby laughed softly as she turned to leave.

"Just call me when she's up, okay?"

"Of course."

CHAPTER 74

Mildred Hawthorne was having the toughest evening of her life-time. Her beloved Gerald was gone one year ago almost to the day. Over the past month, she had lost all three of her kids to horrible, violent acts. The Hawthornes were being systematically annihilated and she was the last one standing.

And if that didn't have Mildred out of her mind, she had just thrown out the useless pykies some people call the police. They had no clue what was going on. If they couldn't keep her children safe, what could they do for her?

Mildred gazed into the smoldering fire and reflected on her old-est son, her handsome Tyler, found lifeless and tossed in the Potomac like a piece of trash. Then her sweet Hunter and Caroline, both hor-rifically murdered. She vomited when the image of her baby posed in such a humiliating way crashed into her mind.

Mildred poured another drink and sank into the chair. Someone had wiped out her family.

"Mrs. Hawthorne, can I get you anything?" Shannon stammered as she closed the front door behind her.

Mildred turned in her chair just enough to reveal fire in her eyes. "What do you think? Are you just going to gawk at me all night? Go pack my bags. We are leaving tonight!"

Shannon whimpered and scurried away like a mouse under chase.

Winter had yet to release its grip on the Capital City, and it certainly was tightening around Mildred's neck with death and humiliation. Her bloodline had ended. So far, she was defiant and resolved to fight the good fight. But she was feeling it in her gut.

She quickly forgot about her faithful maid and turned back to gaze into the fireplace. The same fireplace Gerald had posed next to for the portrait that now hung in that dreadful museum. She would never see it again. That portrait was supposed to come home with her. Not now. She looked over to the dinner plate-sized picture of her and her late husband resting on the oak table at her side. *That will have to do.*

She was into her third or perhaps fourth bourbon. She wasn't sure now. The smell outweighed the fire's smoky finish as it spit and crackled away in front of her.

When one was having a bitch of an evening like this, one was required to grab something stiff, but the bourbon wasn't quite getting the job done. Mildred could not shake the past's ashes, watching limb after limb of the Hawthorne family tree being torn off. Right in front of her, no less.

She pretended Gerald was listening. "Why? Who would want to hurt us so badly, so brutally? Who would be capable of such things? We have never stepped over that line, have we?" Maybe once, but she had deserved it. And that was 25 years ago. *And you are to blame for that. Not my children.*

The fourth, or maybe it was a fifth bourbon, hit a spot that stirred her. Yes, 25 years ago. She stiffened in her high-back that made her look elf-like with her feet dangling, scratching the wood floor if she stretched a bit.

Jesus. Is that what we, I mean I, am dealing with? Why now?

The liquor had fueled her like a NASCAR pit stop in Watkins Glen. *Yes, Watkins Glen.*

She managed to regain her focus and temporarily wipe away the fog to make her way up the staircase to her bedroom. It was once an elegant private sanctuary that was left hollow and cold a year ago when Gerald failed to come home. She avoided it much of the time, sleeping in the family room next to the fire. It was a comfort to hear the pops and whiffs of the fire.

Mildred hadn't the nerve to go into Gerald's closet up until now, but it was time. The man's private world would have to be cracked open, even just for a little bit. She felt like an intruder in her own home. While the lights in the room brightened the lifeless chamber, she soon lost her warmth as she opened the great wooden door to her husband's private closet.

It was paneled in rich, dark Bocate, a beautiful wood that Gerald had used when he rebuilt the boat up on the lake. As expected, it had darkened over the years. The exotic grain screamed wealth and retained the supple feel of the old world, when kings and queens demanded only the best from their land. Mildred ran her tiny hands along the panel to her right as she stepped into the dark room.

She scanned the enormous closet, breathing in the smells of her man. This surprised her a bit. She could still smell his cigar as she stroked the suits' fine wools that he filled so nicely. They were hung with precision, as Gerald took pride in being organized and in how he looked. Most of the suits were hand made in Italy, and they all were a variant of gray.

Mildred whimpered a bit, knowing that these gray suits brought those tremendous blue-gray eyes to life.

Oh, he was a handsome man. Those steely eyes.

Mildred admired Gerald's well-polished collection of Italian and

British shoes. All were black. Gerald did not like the latest fashion where younger men donned brown shoes with gray and blue suits. "Uncouth," he would say when he was greeted with beaming browns under the subtle class of gray. He was a man bred in the world of classics. Those shoes spoke volumes on the spirit of a man.

The shoes. The shoes. I remember the shoes.

The closet was bigger than she remembered, at least from afar given she never dared to intrude until tonight, but it was closing in on her a bit, or maybe the drink was just taking hold of her a bit more. Or was it the realization that her family was just butchered? She drew up enough courage and pushed through to the back of the room.

She took a moment to take in the gun rack that was the closet's centerpiece. She didn't count, but there were at least five or six antique rifles or such behind the glass casing. They weren't there for protection. They were part of his personal collection. They were the guns he used on his safaris back in the day.

But she was not looking for antique rifles. She was looking for his trunk. The heavy, well-worn locker he lugged around most of his life. It was tucked below his gun rack, nestled between two pillars in the closet, almost like it was built to be tucked in there just right. The brass edges and the lock hinges were worn since he first took it overseas in 1963, but the bones of the glorified crate in front of her were strong. The leather straps were fastened, but the buckles were showing their age.

Gerald had quite an affinity for it, taking it on his travels to Africa and his trip down under. The travel-inflicted scratches and dents described a man on the go, a man who explored places that others only wished or dreamed they could. He always said the true wealth of a man was reflected in what he did with his time.

If there were any secrets to be found, they would be here.

CHAPTER 75

The bourbon was starting to dominate her. She was tired, and the room was blurry. Or was it the fear welling up as she wondered what she would find?

She crunched the lock with a brass doorstop, opened the heavy lid and propped it open. She knelt there, gazing into a trove of things only meant for her husband's eyes. There were three boxes that seemed to fit snugly side-by-side. Mildred didn't know where to start. She looked at the three smaller boxes, and the situation reminded her of a game show.

Where is the prize?

She started with the middle box. It slid out a lot more smoothly than she thought it might. It was slightly bigger than a shoe box. She snapped the cover off and dumped the contents onto the closet floor.

The box was filled with postcards and letters she had written to him over the years, and she could still catch the scent of her perfume as she flipped through them. Paris, Rome, Naples. She remembered that trip. She had taken Tyler. It was just the two of them then… While she was pleased to see he saved her letters, the thought of Tyler upset her, and she dug around to see what else was in this buried treasure. She was not seeing what she was looking for in the pile. A few photos of them together and some ticket stubs from the Eurail.

She yanked the second box which was heavier and had a different way about it. Mildred immediately felt like she shouldn't manhandle it and calmed herself down. She stood and walked out of the closet with more regard, using both hands to carry the box. The smell from the box was from something familiar, but she couldn't place it. Propped back in her blue chair, she began a staring contest with the box. Mildred was well into it now. She turned the top off and peered inside, where two smaller boxes lay within.

Tumbling down the rabbit hole.

She opened the narrow brown cardboard box and watched two beautifully carved pocket knives tumble out between her feet. She picked each up. Both handles looked like they were carved from bone. The first one had a mountain range embedded in the handle, the other a deer, or antelope or something like that. She set them aside, and stared at the other box, more the size of a large book.

The black leather box looked familiar. It resembled the trunk that it was buried in. It had metal corners and a small keyhole, like the one that would be found on a briefcase. The label on the box confirmed what she had seen once before:

Smith & Wesson

Model 36—Chiefs Special

I thought this was at the bottom of the lake.

She pulled on the tab, and it opened effortlessly. A thick, rich, oily smell immediately attacked her senses. A cotton towel was wrapped loosely around a gun. She eased the box out, cradling it in both hands. The revolver's weight felt familiar. Its dark brown handle was almost the same color as the paneling in the closet. She shook; she thought she would never see this ghastly thing again.

Why would Gerald keep this?

She took a moment and placed it on the towel draped on the coffee table. She contemplated the gun like it was someone she met on the street lifetimes ago. She watched it like it was supposed to do something on its own. It felt strange. It felt like she was doing something illegal and violent just having it sit there.

Baffled, Mildred got up and struck a more determined line back to the closet for the last box. She walked carefully around the table to be sure to keep an arm's distance from her adversary. She snatched the last box and brought it to the bed so she was far enough away from the gun but still close enough to keep an eye on it.

This box clearly didn't have much in it. It was lighter than the other two. Mildred popped the top off and took a gander. Was she feeling more lucid? The gun seemed to shake her and wake her up. Either way, she didn't care. She was in full detective mode now.

There was a letter on delicate paper, two polaroid pictures and a handkerchief. It was Gerald's hankie, given he always had two on him like all proper men should.

As calmly as she could, she picked up the picture on top first. It was a bit faded in color and grainy, but the image was clear enough. There Gerald was, standing on the beach in his blue bathing trunks with a red stripe down one thigh. There she was, standing next to him, leaning on his shoulder and smiling meekly at the camera. Her thick brown hair was tied into a bunch stacked up high to keep dry. Her dark oversized sunglasses were propped up on her forehead and her slim silhouette was covered in a one piece that looked like it was still wet. She really didn't notice, but behind them was the family boat they had up at the lake.

She knew where they were. And she knew who the woman was.

Mildred could tell it was at their place on Sunset Shores. She was there. She slowly put the picture down, and tried to gather herself, but it wasn't working. After almost thirty years of trying to forget what she'd done, this woman was right there staring back at her. The two lovers stood in front of her boat. She took up the old hankie and wiped her eyes and nose.

After a few minutes of crying, Mildred managed to collect herself enough to look at the rest of the box's contents. She picked up the second picture, which was facing down in the box.

Bourbon came up. She threw up a bit before she could catch herself. The hankie helped catch some of the hot liquid.

He was only a few years old, and he had a round, happy face. But she saw them. Those piercing blue gray eyes. They were staring right back at her. She knew those eyes. She knew. She had always known. Well, maybe. But was she really surprised? Trembling hands, her heart dancing and leaping in her chest, she unfolded the only piece of paper in the box, which was doily-like in texture, almost like something a teenager would use to write a note at a party.

No going back now.

In elegant cursive, the note tumbled at her.

Mildred couldn't help herself anymore. She drove her face into the comforter, trying to silence the screams. The smoking gun had been right there in front of her for weeks. Not the one she'd handled all those years ago glaring at her on the table, but the one she had seen staring back at her, shaking her hand, consoling her, watching her, and butchering her children.

CHAPTER 76

Eric smiled at Serena and motioned for her to come into his office at *The Thread*.

"I'm sorry, Eric," she said, "but there was a man here to see Sky. He was on his way to the airport and said she needed to see this right away. It's a copy of some legal filings, faxed from upper New York State to a hotel in the district."

"That's odd," he said, and pointed to a chair so that his protégé could sit and have her next lesson in investigative journalism.

"It is," Serena replied. "And there was a note attached to it. Check it out." She handed it to him, and he saw immediately that the handwriting was born in a Catholic school, honed in the military, and refined in hundreds of steno notebooks over the past thirty years. He hadn't seen anything like it since his first job out of college. He read the note out loud:

Buffy—

Here's your scoop. It's amazing what you can find when you're not looking on the internet.

You're right about the boy. Warn your fairy godmother.

Call me if you want and I'll explain.

Henrico

"My first question was," Serena said, "who is 'Buffy,' and what does she have to do with this?"

Eric started to laugh. "I think I know who Buffy is," he said. "It's Sky. And Henrico is her source on this guy Jerry Sharpe. He's been following this guy for years."

Eric flipped through the stack of documents, covered with arrows, asterisks, and circles of Henrico's design. Then he looked up at Serena. He knew her well enough to know that she had perused enough of the file to have an opinion. It was his job to teach her that she should trust it.

"What do you see here?"

"It's the deed and tax records for a house in someplace called Montour Falls, New York. The current owner is this guy Jerry Sharpe."

"That makes sense," Eric said. "He's Sky's latest obsession. But what do you think it means? Is there something odd about the documents—anything strange?" Serena took a half step back toward the door, as if such a direct question had knocked her off balance.

"I don't know, Eric, I'm not a lawyer or anything."

"Think about it," Eric said. "Trust your instincts. People don't send perfectly normal property deeds to reporters, right? Especially not to Sky Nicholson. Something is out of place. Something's odd, and you caught it. I know you did."

Serena hesitated a second as she flipped through the deed.

"Well," she said, "there was one thing." Eric slapped the desk in front of him.

"I knew it. Hit me."

"Well, it's a residential house. It should have only been bought and sold between people, right?"

"Right," Eric said.

"It was once owned by a woman named Elizabeth Sharpe. Was that Jerry's mother?"

"Probably." Serena flipped to a new page.

"Well, thirty years ago she sold it for $200,000 to a company called Big Game Enterprises, LLC."

"Wow," Eric said, and shot a look at Serena. "$200,000 is a lot of money even now, but back then it would have been a fortune. The house wasn't worth a fraction of that back then."

"I know," Serena said. "And that's not the weirdest thing."

"Really?" Eric braced himself as Serena turned the page.

"Yeah. Look here—Big Game Enterprises sold it back to her the next day. For a dollar." Eric Zimmerman's demeanor changed. He sat up in his chair.

"Holy shit," he said. "Let me see that." Serena handed the pages back to Eric and he saw it. All of it.

"My God," she said, "She was right. It makes sense. His birthday. The attitude. The anger. Everything." Serena stared at her editor.

"Right about what?"

"Keep going. What else did this guy Henrico give us?"

"Okay," she said. "So at the time, Big Game Enterprises was owned by another company called GHH Holdings, LLC."

"Which," Eric said, wincing, "was, in turn, owned by…"

"Gerald H. Hawthorne," Serena said.

"Who, as our star reporter has been trying to tell us," Eric said, "*is Jerry's biological father*. He bought out his mistress to provide for his illegitimate son and make sure his secret was safe. This proves it." Serena dropped the file on Eric's desk and instinctively took two steps away from it and all it might mean.

Eric covered his face in his hands. "And now, the illegitimate son is tracking down his half-family and wiping them out, one by one. It's right out of Shakespeare."

CHAPTER 77

Mildred straightened herself to regroup. She needed to act. Mildred gathered the pictures, the letter, and the gun and carefully navigated the stairs back to the fireplace. She laid them out on the tablecloth strewn across the coffee table and watched them like they were supposed to do something. Perform. Tell a story. But the gun just sat there. The faces in the pictures just stared back at her. The letter lay there like it hadn't inflicted any harm on her.

The son of bitch butchered my babies. It's your turn, Jerry!

She threw a fierce glance at the ornate clock propped up next to the stairs. Just shy of midnight. She snatched her bottle of bourbon from the cart. It was still taking the edge off her pain, but she could do with one more to steady herself.

Mildred slowly paced the room, passing the fire a dozen times. The flame was dying and receding into embers. She was about to call out for Shannon, but remembered she was getting her things ready. Shannon would be two floors up and likely couldn't hear her anyway.

After taking on the work of common folk by tossing a couple of logs on, Mildred settled into her chair. Her mind was cooking a lot hotter than the fire in front of her.

He is coming for me. I am the only one left. He will be coming through the door to finish me off. Has to be tonight. Has to be. There is no going back now. I will hurt him like he did me. I will break that bastard's heart, and I will watch him cower and crumble and cry like the little bastard he is. How dare he attack us!

Her bourbon coursed through her chest, warming her insides like slow-moving Vermont syrup. It was making her start to doze a bit. She adjusted herself in the chair and looked up at the fireplace mantle.

Gerald's portrait at the Museum was supposed to go there. But how could she ever look at him again? *His selfishness destroyed this family. This was his fault, not mine. How dare he lay with that cheap tramp. How could he sleep with that white trash and then be careless enough to father a child?*

Mildred peered into her empty glass. That would be the last one. No. Another should do the trick. She tried to fend off that dozing feeling, but it was a struggle.

She turned to the small picture of Gerald propped up on the end table next to her. No more longing, no more grief. She hadn't been this angry since she'd come face-to-face with that...that girl, twenty, no, nearly thirty something years ago!

Gerald and that goddamn boat. Laying with that whore…

CHAPTER 78

She had just arrived at the summer house when the gardener came rushing in to tell her that Gerald had been in an accident, and he was to drive her down to the hospital. She hadn't even unpacked.

Mildred leapt into action and clambered into the town car, and Mr. Morales drove as fast as he could along the shoreline to get his charge to the hospital. She couldn't get any details. Morales had taken the call, but his English was shit, so she was left to her own thoughts.

He dropped her right at the Emergency Entrance, and she dashed in. She was met immediately by the station nurse, who was doing all she could to calm her down.

"Mrs. Hawthorne, take a breath. Your husband is going to be okay. He is already out of surgery and is recovering. His leg had multiple compound fractures, which required surgery and a lot of stitches, and he has a concussion, but he is going to be fine. When the doctor comes out, we will bring you back to see him."

Mrs. Hawthorne made a stink of things, but this nurse was not budging. She was a young, tough Irish woman.

Who is this dirty wench to boss me around?

Disgruntled, Mildred settled into a plastic chair connected to five others like she was in an airport waiting to fly commercial. Or at least that's what she imagined flying like that would feel like. She tried to calm herself and scanned the emergency room. There were quite a few nurses running around. It looked like something big had happened. She didn't really care, but she worried the doctors would be distracted and not take care of her man.

After forty-five minutes that felt like three days, a young doctor approached her, and he was making a show of little concern. "Mrs. Hawthorne, thank you for your patience. Your husband is resting and will be okay. He was in a boating accident just north of here. He collided with a tour boat. He is lucky to be alive. There were others hurt, but none seriously. I think he likely took the brunt of it. I have been told your boat was pretty much destroyed."

"Do you think I care about the goddamn boat? I want to see Gerald right away."

The doctor did his part. He waved to the nurse at the desk, and she was quick to arrive on the scene. "Mrs. Robertson, please escort Mrs. Hawthorne to Room ED-3"

The young nurse escorted Mildred down the hall. The private room was small, but the noise died down as soon as the door closed. She was alone with him. He was sound asleep, his head was wrapped tightly, and his leg was splinted and wrapped as well. Wires and hoses were crisscrossed over his chest, and only the occasional beep of monitors broke the silence. She didn't dare touch him other than a gentle peck on his cheek.

She was exhausted. The flight into Rochester had been enough, but the stress from streaking to the hospital put her over the top. She quickly fell asleep in the corner chair, which was slightly more comfortable than the plastic ones in the waiting room.

A few hours passed, and Mildred sensed there was someone in

the room. It was dark, and only the low light from the monitors was keeping her from feeling like she was in a cave. A nurse was standing over her husband, taking his vitals and recording her findings on a clipboard.

The nurse paid no attention to Mildred. She didn't even know she was in the corner. Or else she thought she was asleep.

Mildred felt some comfort watching the kindness she was witnessing as the nurse tended to her ailing husband. Then she saw them. Those blazing blue eyes. She smiled. She was about to open her mouth to greet him when the nurse bent over and kissed him. Not a peck on the cheek or a reassuring kiss on the forehead. No. It was a loving, gentle kiss on the lips, and she could see his crooked smile curl next to hers.

"What the hell was that?" Mildred nearly shouted.

The nurse leapt back in horror and let out a scream that would curl your toes. Gerald's eyes grew cold and terrified, seeing his red-hot wife erupt from the back of the room. The nurse panicked and tried to escape, but Mildred leaped from her seat, blocked the door, and grabbed the first thing she could lay her hands on. The bedpan flew like a Yankees fastball and crashed above the nurse's head, spewing runny shit and piss all over her and Gerald. Mildred went in for the attack, flailing her arms at this intruder, tearing at her hair and clothes. The nurse buckled, and Gerald lay helpless watching his scorned wife scream and grab and snatch at the nurse.

A doctor came hurling in and grabbed Mildred to pull her off, but she spat in fury at the doctor and did her best to inflect her rage on him. "Liz! Get out of here now!"

"Millie! Millie!" Gerald shouted. "Calm down, please. She meant no harm, I swear!"

Mildred whirled to her husband, her hair tossed about, her blouse torn, and her makeup destroyed. She delivered a hefty swing onto his broken leg, which made Gerald howl in agony. "You bastard! I saw what I saw, and you can die right here, right now, you son of a bitch!"

Without further assistance from the bewildered doctor, Mildred stormed through the emergency room, knocking over a little girl with an icepack on her head.

Mildred shook the cobwebs from her tired brain as she woke herself from a quick nap. How could she not have seen the connection before? Ms. Sharpe? She eased herself to the edge of the high back and looked down at the coffee table. The letter and pictures were still strewn across, awaiting their final opportunity to inflict real pain. She slipped the knife into her pocket, picked up the gun, and waited.

CHAPTER 79

Jerry had leapt over the edge. There was no turning back now. He knew that he had left two bodies in his wake tonight. He needed to move fast if he was going to finish this. He could taste the anguish he was inflicting and wanted to see Millie wallow in her pain first-hand. He had destroyed her family and humiliated her. Now he could reveal himself to her and watch her whimper and beg for mercy.

He assumed Mildred's own friends had immediately turned away from the scandal of her daughter. Seeing or hearing about her naked and bound to the gorilla in such a raw, sexual act had to be too much for the chandelier set. The blue bloods usually circled the wagons when it came to public humiliation of this sort, but this was over the top.

He knew she was home. She had to be. And there were no cars in her drive. It was time. He took a deep breath and thrust his weight against the door, smashing the lock and splintering the door jamb. He leapt through into the hall.

To his surprise, a calm but stern voice immediately filled his ears. "The door was open, Gerald. There was no need for violence. I have been waiting for you to come home."

Gerald? Home?

Jerry's adrenaline drained. She was expecting him. He scanned the room and saw the fireplace he had seen in Mr. Hawthorne's portrait, with two high-backed chairs facing each other in front, with Mildred in the one facing him, leveling a gun at him as he tried to right himself in the hall.

With the nose of the gun, Mildred motioned to Jerry to settle into the twin chair across from her.

He was dumbfounded, his mouth was ajar, and he couldn't believe he was trapped. By her! While he tried to keep a calm face, his eyes were giving his panic away. Or maybe his desperation. How could she know? She should be curled up in a ball of mush, crying and whimpering in her despair.

He approached her slowly, like he was a deer creeping up to steal a drink from a brook. Between them was a small coffee table upon which was set a doily and some Polaroids, but he couldn't imagine what they were, given they were turned upside down.

Her voice was stern but had a tremble in it. "Gerald, sit down now. You have done some terrible things to my children. How could you? You should be ashamed. But we'll get to that in a minute. We have a few things to discuss first."

Gerald? I am in the dragon's lair, the place where I can finally slay the beast. But she has the drop on me. She knew it was me. She knew I was coming. Focus.

Jerry realized that he was being led to his own slaughter by the spider creeping along the web rather than being on the hunt to slay his dragon.

Mildred gestured to the paper and Polaroids on the table. "Let's get to it, you son of a bitch. Pick up the first picture. I think that will help you understand what we are dealing with here."

And why did a woman who was experiencing so much grief and

humiliation look like she was about to eat him alive?

He reached over and plucked the picture from the table. Quiet. Even the fire seemed to pause for effect. Jerry leaned back in the chair as the picture struck him cold. He could feel Mildred's eyes narrowing on him like a fox spotting her wounded rabbit.

Jerry didn't understand it. He was looking at himself. It was him. The same smiling kid was still sitting on his mother's mantle back home. He felt like he'd had too much to drink. The room started to spin. What the hell was this?

Jerry was certain she meant to kill him, but not until he was to learn something. Why would she have a picture of him? Something that she felt made her righteous in her kill. Or rather, as he leaned forward to scoop up the doily, be told something by this wicked woman. Jerry expected her to shoot when she was good and ready. He needed to come up with a plan, and fast.

Jerry slowly turned the paper over in his hands. It was dainty paper, like something rich folk used to create a feeling of wealth and time. He recognized the paper. He was confused. He was not himself given the gun pointed at him only a few feet away.

His lips moved slowly as he absorbed the letter. The beautiful cursive was all too familiar to him. It was his mother's handwriting, but who was Lizzy? Jerry's heart was racing and he read the note twice to be sure he wasn't missing something.

Dear Gerry,

I think of our last time together every day. Seneca was calm and gentle like you, the breeze was just enough to keep the heat off, and the occasional spray from the wake as we scooted back and forth all day felt like light rain on a spring day. It was the most romantic day of my life, and I *didn't want it to end.*

Making love that afternoon under those shady trees was a wonderful way to say goodbye. I felt like I was in an Audrey Hepburn movie, and I wanted it to last forever. But I understood your obligations and responsibilities, so I think I was ok with ending our time together that day. It has been hard, and as you can imagine, lonely at times.

But you left the most precious gift a girl like me could ever imagine. Here is our baby boy. You can see yourself in him. His eyes scream right back at you when you look at him. He is happy and healthy, and so am I. We have made a comfortable life here together, and the house was all we needed. Thank you for your generosity.

You know where we are if you ever change your mind.

Love,

Lizzy

"I don't understand," he said, his voice but a whisper. "Who is Lizzy, and why do you have my picture?"

Mildred smirked. She was clearly savoring the moment. But while she had a fierce expression, her tired eyes gave way to a tear.

Little did Jerry know he was about to experience his own version of despair. Jerry knew he was at her mercy—for the moment. She was behaving like blue bloods would. Do unto others; don't let them do unto you.

CHAPTER 80

Abby stepped in front of Sky just before she plowed into the police officer standing in front of the emergency room door. The two women collided just as Sky started her next rant.

"Fuck it. Give me the radio. I'll do it," Sky said, pointing at the police officer standing just behind Abby. "If you won't call it in, I will."

"No, you won't," Abby said. "Our Uber will be here in two minutes, and you can't afford to get arrested tonight. Calm down."

An older man in the waiting room looked up from his chair and let out a soft "Mm-*hmmmmm*." The rest of the patients in the ER nodded in unison, grateful for the one-act play unfolding before them but uneasy about the direction of its plot.

Sky took a step back from Abby and gave her a long stare. The shock from the museum was gone.

"I *am* calm," she said. "Because I know who did this and why. So do you. He's going to kill Millie next and then, who knows? My folks? Whoever he decides looks like a 'blue blood'? It could be anybody."

"Miss," the officer began, "we're—"

"You're *worthless*," Sky snapped. "That's the only thing Millie got right in all this. If you people were any good, you'd have Jerry Sharpe cuffed and stuffed in a squad car right now."

Abby gave the officer a knowing, and rather pleading, look.

"We're working on it," the officer said slowly. "I suggest you two get some rest."

"Duly noted," Sky said, "but your incompetence now requires us to do a lot more than that. When my next story hits, you'll know it. You'll *all* know it." The officer's face stiffened, and he took a step forward. Abby rolled her eyes.

"Sky," she said, "apologize to the officer."

"No." Sky bolted toward the emergency room door. The officer stood aside and let her pass.

"Sky—" Abby pleaded as she tried to follow. "Where are you going?"

"If they won't stop Sharpe," Sky said, "I'll get his next victim out of the way!"

Abby's heart sank as she saw Sky staring at her with that hawk-like look in her eyes, until her Uber sped away.

CHAPTER 81

Jerry's steel blue eyes connected with his own in the picture. Then he slowly raised his eyes to meet Mildred. She was literally on the edge of her seat, no longer dangling her little feet. She was drilling her hateful blackened eyes into him, ready to pounce. She was ready to eat. To kill. Jerry tried to understand what he was seeing. Mildred was savoring the moment, watching him take a beating and flop about.

Jerry stammered. "What the hell? Is this a joke?"

"Are you really that dense?" Mildred was clearly disappointed that Jerry didn't make the easiest deduction in the history of the world right away. She pointed a gnarled finger at his chest. "That is you, and the letter is from your dead mother!" She took another breath. "Don't you see? You are my husband's son!"

"But Lizzy? My mother's name was—was Beth. How could this be?"

Like a gambler at the Indian casinos up north, Mildred snapped up and swiftly turned the final card over in front of her flailing foe and tossed it to his side of the table.

She didn't have to say a thing. Jerry knew this was her last play-ing card. He slowly scraped the picture off the table. There she was. So young. She was beautiful, and she was embracing a younger ver-sion of the late Gerald Hawthorne and leaning on a boat on the beach. Jerry's heart fell to pieces in his chest. His breath escaped him. His eyes connected to Gerald's in the grainy photo. Then across to the photo next to Mildred, then back to his picture. Then around again in a dizzying spin of mind-splitting tag.

She was right. It was all there. But how? Why didn't she tell me? She said dad died before I was born. Why would she? Jane. Jane had to know. Was that what she was trying to say? Mom?

Jerry looked up. He thought he heard himself whimper under the elephant parked on his chest. Jerry's and Mildred's eyes connected. Jerry began to realize that Mildred was where he was hours ago. She was now the one taking pleasure in crushing him because of what his mother and Gerald had done to her. She was enjoying watching this grown man become a blubbering idiot.

"Your mother tried to tell you in her own way, but you weren't bright enough to pick up on it. You must have taken after her more than I thought. Your name. Jerry."

Another arrow caught him in the chest.

"He would have never let you in as part of this family. The shame would have been too much to bear. He could not, he would not, take the ridicule from his friends, siring a trashy little whelp. Laying with a common whore. He would have never let you play with your broth-ers and sister."

Jerry looked up. My brothers and sister? Jesus. Arrows were not enough anymore. A spear seemed to thrust him back again into the chair.

Jerry was getting wild and losing his grip on the moment. "What? Who?"

Mildred stood up defiantly, scooped up the letter and pictures and tossed them into the fire. The frail letter disappeared instantly, and his portrait curled into black. His mother's picture bounced off the log and onto the brick floor just in front of the fire.

"No!" Jerry stood up to grab the picture but Mildred stepped in between him and the fire.

He towered over the puny woman, trying to intimidate her with his size. She could have been mistaken for a middle school child next to him. He shook off his fog and gathered himself enough to reach into his pocket. He ripped out his only faithful friend and dared his tormentor to shoot him.

But Mildred was prepared and steadfast in what she needed to do. "Oh, honey. It's a shame you never got the caliber of education my lovely children did. Never bring a knife to a gunfight."

She unloaded a shot into Jerry without giving him a chance to lunge at her.

CHAPTER 82

Shannon was lingering. She was ordered to have Mildred ready as soon as possible so she could get out of town. Two trunks, no more. But she slipped into Tyler's room. No, he didn't live there anymore, but he would stay in the room where he kept his things, mostly from his college and fraternity days.

Shannon had spent too much time in this room, sometimes on her back, sometimes on her knees. But she had fallen for him hard. He was a handsome man with a cute, crooked smile, much like his father's. He was kind and generous. She remembered how often he slipped her small gifts when he paid her a visit. She knew that he was coming home to her rather than to visit his wicked mother. She felt miserable having to mourn him in solitude. She had to fawn over Mildred and her children at the service, at the funeral, and that awful reception. She was constantly asking Mildred how she was doing, what she needed, and how she could be helpful in this terrible time. No one knew her pain.

At least she was able to attend the service and funeral, not as a beloved family member, but as staff.

No one asked her how she was holding up. How could they know?

Now the others were gone too. They didn't know about her. But soon enough, folks would. Tyler said he was going to tell his mother about her. But he never had the chance.

Her thoughts quickly returned to her lost love. He tried to emulate his famous father, but he didn't get the love and devotion a first-born son deserved. Gerald was a distant dad and seemed to be thinking about things far off. This only made Tyler work harder to win his affection. But Tyler failed at turning his father's love toward him.

Shannon straightened the comforter on the bed. She gently touched the pillow that she used when she laid next to him. She sat there for a moment, quietly taking in the room, trying not to cry for fear of Mildred turning the corner and spewing wickedness at her.

After a few minutes, she worked her way out of the room and crossed the landing. She noted that the house was quiet. Had Millie fallen asleep? The quiet in the house was horrible. She could hear a mouse breathe if it dared show its furry face in a grand place like this.

Shannon needed to get this work done so she could go home. Being in this house was driving her insane. She pulled the trunks from Mildred's closet. They were rather small, but they would do fine. She began to excavate Mildred's dresser, neatly stacking underwear and bras, as well as ample sleepwear. Shannon knew she needed to get the makeup bag ready too. She quipped to herself that there isn't enough makeup on this planet to fix that awful woman's sneer.

With most of the drawers emptied, she sat on the blue chair in the window to take a minute. She didn't have the energy she used to before.

Shannon reflected on the box and case splayed out on the table. They were not there the last time she was cleaning the room. She opened the case and instantly smelled the oil from the cloth left in the case. She recognized that smell. Her father had kept a gun after he had retired from the force. The oily smell was distinct and resonated in her nose.

The hair on her forearms stood up as she scanned the room. Gerald's closet door was ajar. Mildred had on several occasions noted that she couldn't bring herself to go in there since his death a year ago. Shannon poked her head in the gentleman's closet.

It had the aroma of a rich man. Bourbon. Cigars.

She looked past what might have been fifty suits. Directly under a gun rack was a pile of letters and small boxes tossed back into a trunk left ajar. Mildred had been digging, searching for something.

Shannon bent down to see what was in the box when she heard a burst of yelling then a loud crack of thunder ripping through the house.

CHAPTER 83

Jerry screamed and recoiled against the fireplace and tumbled to the floor. The explosion echoed through the house, and the smoke and stench instantly filled the room. Mildred had only fired the gun once before, and the power was more than she remembered. The gun flew from her hand and landed between them near the fireplace.

She was shaking her hand from the gun's power but ignored the sharp pain surging through her fingers. She tried to take in the moment as she towered over her bleeding victim down on the floor.

Jerry felt like another barrage of cannon fire was flung over the castle walls. His thigh was burning, and he didn't know what to do. Could he regain his footing? Could he focus? He was here to destroy her, but she was winning!

Mildred wasn't finished. "You still don't get it, do you, *Junior*? You are too stupid to put this all together. I discovered this abomination, this treachery nearly thirty years ago! How dare he lay with her? This whore. A poor man's hooker. How dare he cheat on me! I saw them together. I had to do something!" Her breathing was fast and furious, but she was drilling her eyes into his. "Our summer home was turned into a brothel because of her. I bided my time. I planned. And I finally got the courage to do it. I found your bitch of a mother. I found that shack you call a house that my husband bought her and visited when I wasn't around. I went there."

Jerry winced as he knew what was coming. He already knew.

"I heard her in the bathtub. It was perfect. I went upstairs and I stepped right up to her. She didn't scream. She just begged me to spare her. I took great joy in shooting her and watching her bleed to death in the tub. It was like shooting a dirty dog. And tonight, I am going to watch you bleed to death right here in my own house."

With the calmness of a windless day, the crow hovered over her prey. Her voice cracked when she attempted to drive home her last point. "And Gerald, I know what you did to my children. Imagine what I am going to do to you." She crouched to pick up the revolver.

He had to swing back. Hard. He couldn't cower to this rich bitch. No more.

Jerry reached deep down, looking for anything to regain control. His eyes turned gray as a thunderstorm as they bored into little Mildred. He mustered up all his energy and sprang with a massive, blood-covered backhand across the woman's face.

Mildred was flung like a rag doll into the coffee table and bounced into her chair face down.

His leg burned while he tried to keep his balance, but he now had the floor. He was in charge. He strained to enjoy watching Mildred trying to right herself from the chair. Her head shook and she rubbed her cheek as she cried.

He delivered a swift kick to her stomach, and she hollered out, but no one would rescue her tonight.

Jerry wasted no time. The training kicked in. He ripped off the tablecloth and wrapped it around his thigh. He then stripped an electrical cord from the wall and bound her tiny wrists together. He dragged the gasping woman close to the mantle, looping her bound hands over the sconce on the wall. She was now eye-to-eye with him, and her little piggy feet dangled a foot off the ground.

"You nasty bitch!" He kicked the revolver into the fire. He scurried around and scooped up his trusted knife and placed it under her chin, only slightly cutting into her neck, for now. A streak of red started to seep from her.

"You want to know pain? Yes, I killed your kids! It was fun! I gutted your beloved Tyler and dumped his sorry ass in the river. Didn't you see the pictures of his eyes being plucked out by crabs?"

"How, how could you? You monster!"

"Yes, I was the one who slashed your fucked-up kids. I left her with the fucking monkeys. Come to think of it, I'm not sure which was more fun. Fucking your dear Caroline before gutting her or burying my knife in Hunter's chest. They were some fucked-up kids all right. And they got what they deserved."

Mildred was still dazed. This monster had done unspeakable things. Jerry laughed as Mildred began to sob. The reality of what was done to her kids hit her smack in the chest.

Jerry strutted back and forth as best he could. The blood was still pumping down his leg and onto the carpet. He pressed up against Mildred's swaying body as she tried to speak through her sobs. She was trying to deliver a verbal punch, but it came through without the defiance she wanted.

"You wicked, evil man. You are weak and pathetic, just like your whore of a mother."

Mildred whimpered something else, but Jerry wasn't listening anymore. He was in charge.

Jerry delivered a punch in the gut that sent her banging into the fireplace mantle. He felt the crunch of her ribs. Mildred vomited and choked on her own fluids. Jerry didn't care whether she was in more pain from that nasty punch or from the horrific deaths of her children. He slapped her while she sputtered to try and find the right words. But there were none. He was circling the room and returning to punch his dangling victim. He was only beginning to truly understand what Mildred had told him. He ran his bloodied hands through his hair as he tried to think.

He thought about that terrible afternoon coming home from school, finding his mother in the tub. The house was so quiet, and when he found her, he couldn't believe how cold the water was, and the sticky texture it had. It was thickened with her blood.

Jerry felt hollow again. He remembered lifting her limp, cold body out and onto the floor and the bolt of death struck him down next to her, shaking her, screaming at her. He stopped pacing. It struck him in the chest like lightning. He couldn't believe it before. Reality hit. His eyes lowered onto Mildred, who was still swinging a bit from the last punch.

"You killed my mom! You *killed* her!" Jerry smacked her across the face like a boy being punished for stealing. "You *killed* her!" Again. One more time. He punched her in the throat and watched her gasp and throw up bile.

He wasn't getting the satisfaction he needed. His frustrations were bursting from him, and he kept pounding the woman. He was spinning, spiraling out of control. He turned, paced, and returned with even more powerful bursts of punches. She was like a heavy bag, dangling there taking his punches, his jabs, his right crosses. He delivered crushing shots and could feel the crunch of her bones. He brandished the knife in front of her swelling, blackened, and bloodied eyes, but she only leveled her gaze back at him, trying to destroy him with her eyes.

Jerry couldn't regain his composure. This wasn't giving him what he wanted. She wasn't begging him for mercy. He was losing it. He stepped up so close to her that their noses touched. Her blood-ied eyes looked back at him with complete disgust, and he could tell she knew he was out of control.

He whimpered a bit as he thought about his mom, then pressed up even closer. He tried to gather himself and tried to sound like he was in charge. He whispered and sputtered to her in as calm a voice as he could pull up from his twisted insides.

"I am going to skin you like a fucking deer."

Then, through her bloodied lip and swollen face, she began to chuckle, laughing at him, if she had it in her.

With blood splattering from her mouth, Mildred looked over the knife and into Jerry's agonized face. She tried to deliver a final blow of her own.

"That knife."

Jerry looked at his prized possession in his hand.

"Yes, that one. It was a gift from my Gerald. I found two more like it upstairs."

Mildred let some more bile slip up and over her ripped lips. "He was a great man. Flawed. But he was accomplished. But you. You pathetic bastard child. You are just like your mother. Nothing. You could never measure up to him. Never."

Mildred was now looking into those crystal blue eyes a part of her had long recognized. The man who was the bastard son of her once beloved husband was staring back at her, burning with unhinged violence. She steadied herself and spat blood into the face of her family's tormentor.

Jerry didn't wipe his face. He took a step back and straightened himself a bit. He didn't feel the leg anymore. It was done. He was done. He began to calm down. Or was it the loss of blood from the gunshot? He didn't know at this point. He tried to take the moment to regain himself. Tyler was fun. He was a dick, and he had earned his gutting. Hunter and Caroline were so fucking weird that his butchery was likely appreciated by others. And setting up his own gorilla diorama was a blast and was deeply satisfying.

But Mildred Hawthorne. This was what he had been working his way up to—he was throwing all he had worked for into this very moment. But it didn't feel right. He wasn't feeling the thrill. She wasn't behaving the way he wanted. She was supposed to be terrified, begging for her life, crying and whimpering as he did when he found his mom so long ago. She was supposed to feel the same despair. But no, she was defiant. Nasty. Going down with a fight.

Without another exchange, Jerry took a deep breath and locked into her swelling eyes. Time to finish this.

He tightened his grip on the knife and ripped the blade through Millie's throat, almost beheading the woman.

CHAPTER 84

The fire's pop and sizzle started to fill the room again but didn't quite overcome the gurgle or two from the swaying body dangling in front of it.

Jerry was familiar with the sound blood made when it dripped on the floor. Snow makes the same quiet sound. When you're hunting, and it's late at night and nothing is stirring, you can hear it. The snowfall makes a gentle, constant crackle. It makes you feel like time is standing still. As if the world is at peace. You know it when you hear it.

Is this peace?

He stood right in front of her with his arm still up from the slash across the throat. He wanted to see the life drain from her eyes. He slowly lowered his arm and watched as her bludgeoned head dangled by skin and muscle that he'd missed.

He didn't feel it. But as he gazed at his work, he realized something. She felt it. She felt the peace of death. A disturbing feeling of envy started to bubble up in his chest.

Jerry took a step back and quietly mulled his failure. Mildred looked like a marionette that was put away after the show, worn and lifeless. He snapped his wrist to whisk blood off of his beloved knife. The streak of blood swept over the books on the shelf.

He lost his place as a nasty surge of pain bolted up his leg, replacing the adrenaline pumping through him. He adjusted the makeshift tourniquet and looked over the tiny woman swaying in front of him. He took a step closer and realized he was standing in a pool of blackened blood on the floor. He could no longer tell which was Mildred's and which was his.

Which is blue blood?

As the blood mixed, Jerry got the irony for the first time that night. He emerged from his daze and scanned the floor for his mother's picture. In the scuffle, it had landed too close to the fire. Most of his mother was already burned away, and there was nothing left but the man. Gerald. *Dad.*

He tossed the blackened polaroid into the fire and watched it curl into ash. He was finished. He glanced around the room, noticing a few animal trophies on the wall. Hawthorne. His father. He had many trophies over the years. Was his mom one of them? Now Jerry had added his own trophy to the family wall. But at what price?

CHAPTER 85

Shannon was still squatting next to the trunk, cowering. Listening. That had to be a gun. Had to be. She mustered up enough courage to stand and she worked her way to the bedroom doorway. There was more yelling, and she heard Mildred cry out in pain.

Shannon smothered her scream and squatted frozen at the top of the stairs. She could smell the gunpowder as a cloud still hovered close to the ceiling. Shannon tucked behind the door jamb as she watched shadows and listened to the movements from below. The fire cast ghostly images across the little floor she could see.

Then she heard him. She didn't know the voice, but it was distinct. It was a foul voice that filled the room with venom. She could hear thuds peppered between his near screams at Mildred.

"You nasty bitch! You want to know pain? I was the one who gutted your beloved Tyler and dumped his sorry ass in the river. Didn't you see the pictures of his eyes being plucked out by crabs? I was the one who slashed your…"

Shannon didn't hear anything more. *This, this man. This man killed Tyler!*

She thought about what he'd done to her love. Her eyes flared as she heard Mildred scream out in pain.

Shannon had heard enough. She spun and marched into the bedroom. She knew what had to be done.

CHAPTER 86

Jerry leapt out of his skin when a screech bellowed from behind him. Jerry turned, wincing at the pain in his leg, to see Skylar Nicholson trembling in the wrecked doorway. Her round eyes first met Jerry's, then they swept to Mildred's bludgeoned, nearly beheaded corpse dangling behind him, and then back to Jerry. He was surprised at the terror in Sky's face. Her mouth twisted as she saw her aunt dangling in front of the fireplace. Her hands and fingers were spread over her chest as if she was hugging air.

Then there were sirens somewhere in the night. Were they already on their way given the gunshot? Or was it just a coincidence? Did Skylar call them?

It didn't matter. He could not have asked for better timing. He could just keep going and complete a full night of revenge.

Jerry found the energy he thought was long gone and burst forward, limping toward Sky with his knife at the ready. Jerry could see the hunt he had been on many times before.

Skylar looked like a deer in the headlights. She didn't know she could run. She was glued to the tile beneath her feet. She wasn't going anywhere now. Her welling eyes were focused on Mildred. She moved her hands to cover her gaping mouth.

Skylar was now face-to-face with the most dangerous predator in the woods—a scene Jerry had watched on *National Geographic* too many times. The gazelle was giving up. It knew its fate. He was living the moment in his head.

Her eyes lost their glow, and there was a fait accompli in her body language—it was too late, there was nowhere for her to go. He was slower than he wanted to be. The leg dragged along like an anchor, and it made him feel like he was in slow motion.

CHAPTER 87

Jerry was advancing as fast as he could. He knew he had lost the opportunity to do her the night he killed Chris. It was time to set things right.

Jerry advanced with his knife in his right hand, pointed at Skylar, and his left was trying to hold his leg together. The searing pain was slowing him. The leg felt like an alligator had clamped onto him and wasn't letting go. He had to finish this. Now.

Jerry knew Skylar wasn't going anywhere. The shock had consumed her. He tried to stay focused, leveling his eyes with hers, making sure she didn't get any ideas.

Skylar's eyes were dancing and frantically searching for something that might save her life. "What have you done?"

Jerry knew she didn't have anything else to say. She was consumed by the hulking, blood-soaked killer lurching toward her with Mildred's battered and ripped-up body swaying behind him.

Jerry wasn't interested in a confession. He wanted more. He wanted this to be over. He bore down on Skylar and smiled as she instinctively raised her arms above her face to ward off the attack.

Jerry reached back over his head with the blood-soaked knife to drive down on her with whatever he had left. He stretched to reach her as he howled for her to die.

An explosion erupted from behind him, and his eyes widened as he watched blood and bits of bone spray in front of him over Skylar as she cowered to the floor. Jerry howled and twisted from the force of this agonizing blast. He felt like he was stabbed in the side with a hot poker. Grasping for a nearby table, Jerry managed to catch himself and remain standing.

He tried to twist his torso to see what the melting sensation was. His hand worked its way down to trace his shredded body, feeling the heat from his insides and the protruding rib bones. He tried to outline the baseball-sized, half-moon crater on his side to gauge the size of the hole. *What the fuck was that?*

Through the smoke-filled room that now smelled of death, Jerry watched as a dark-haired woman swiftly advanced down the stairs toward him. She moved with speed, with determination, and she was as angry as a mad dog.

She knew how to handle a gun. It was leveled at him like she was holding a guitar. She lifted and settled it into her shoulder as Jerry desperately reached out with his hand while the other clutched his side to keep his insides from spilling over his feet. He was hit, but the blast was from too far away and was not direct enough to drop him to the floor.

Jerry saw the next one coming. A second shot rang out. He saw the flash, and he instantly felt the heavy thud delivered into his shoulder. He was thrust backward into the wall, crashing over the end table and smearing the once milky-white walls with his own body parts and chunky blood.

Jerry slumped to the floor, bits of his flesh raining down on him. He coughed, spat up blood, and vomited. He was able to inch his hand up to poke at his own chest to assess the damage. He looked down over the burning hole in his side and in his last few seconds of life, was glad he wasn't wearing his Armani.

CHAPTER 88

The shotgun's thunderclaps shook Sky to her senses. There was blood, skin, and other human debris splattered all over her hair and cheek. She didn't know what to do. She wasn't sure whose blood was whose, and panic was racing through her.

Skylar pushed herself up on her rear and peered through the smoke to see Jerry slumped up against the wall like a rag doll. It looked like someone had thrown paint against the wall. There was a chunk of him missing, like a shark had taken a massive bite out of him. She could smell the burnt intestines as they oozed out in front of her.

It felt like there was a light mist of flesh and blood lingering in the air as they stared at each other.

Sky was only feet away. His feet almost touched her. She watched as the once noble congressman tried to understand what had happened to him. Sky couldn't look away when he tried to focus on her with his steel gray eyes, but they were fading. Fast.

Sky leaned forward to watch him sputter, cough, and leak all over the floor. She tried to clear her eyes knowing there was blood, bone and whatever else she could only imagine covering her face.

She shuddered and stared at the man in front of her. She had seen so much death tonight, but she had never seen anyone die before. She never imagined seeing anyone get blown to bits.

Sky watched Jerry use every ounce of effort to lean his head back against the muddied wall. He wasn't looking at her anymore. He was looking for the one with the shotgun.

His killer? What? Who? Who shot him?

She tried to retreat behind the nearest chair but froze as Shannon emerged from the billow of smoke above. With power and authority, Shannon stepped over Sky and stood over the wreck that was once Jerry Sharpe.

Shannon ejected the two empty cartridges and reloaded the two barrels again like an old pro. The two women locked eyes. Shannon looked calm as the gun smoke curled around her. Sky watched as Shannon lowered the weapon toward her and lingered, contemplating.

Then, with no further hesitation, Shannon turned and leaned into Jerry.

Skylar watched as she cocked the gun and stuffed it into his throat.

Jerry's body looked like an electric shock zapped through it, thrusting against the wall from the barrel's heat. Shannon raised the gun and aimed between Jerry's eyes.

A meek voice bubbled from under the mess.

"Tell Jane…"

Shannon lowered the gun and watched her lover's killer crumple to the floor. The gun smoke was heavy in the air as silence filled the room. Shannon calmly leaned the shotgun against the gory wall and turned to Sky who was still on the floor, trembling.

"Now it's over."

Shannon reached out her hand to help Sky to her feet, and the women embraced. The silence was like snow in the woods. You could hear it, but it didn't make any sound. Except that familiar crackle.

CHAPTER 89

Jane Robertson pulled a yellow pansy out of its plastic tray and set it gently into the hole she had dug next to her husband's headstone. Most people in Montour Falls—indeed, most Americans—spent Memorial Day thinking about how many people might come to the local parade, or to a barbecue afterward back at the house. But Jane's husband was a veteran, and she would not let a solemn holiday be sullied by such concerns. From the year they were married, through the year of her husband's death and on to the present day, Jane came here over Memorial Day weekend to tend graves. No exceptions.

Not too long now, sweetheart, she thought as she pressed potting soil around the flower. *I'm just going to spend some quiet time in town from here on out. Ask the Lord to take me when He's ready. I'll wait.*

She finished her work and was preparing to move to the next plot when she noticed a silver minivan slow to a stop on the thin, paved roadway nearby. It was packed full, with a car-top carrier tied to the roof. Jane took her sunglasses off, saw who was getting out of the vehicle, and smiled.

"Sergeant Matteo Polzinetti," she said, and pointed to her left. "Location E6, over by the fence. He fought with Patton's army and was your great uncle, if I am not mistaken."

"That's right! Hello, Jane," Henrico said. "I just said to Susan that I thought it was you out here, and sure enough. You know all the graves, don't you? How do you do it?"

"It's not that hard, really," she said. "I've been coming here for forty years, and the gravestones never move, so do the math." She smiled, and her smile faded as she looked at the graves in front of her. *Johnathan Robertson. Elizabeth Sharpe. Jerry Sharpe.*

Jane stood up, took her work gloves off, and walked over to Henrico. "Listen," she said, "I'm sorry about what happened—with the Chamber, and the paper, and all that. It wasn't fair. You didn't do anything wrong, and now—"

"It's okay," Henrico said. "The town needs summer tourists way too much. It's a problem, all these blue bloods invading our town each summer. I knew putting that in print would not go over well. But it's true, and we all know it."

"Still," Jane said. "It's not right. That's not how things are supposed to work around here."

"Well, the folks up at the *Post-Standard* noticed, and I'll land just fine with them up in Syracuse. Felicity is in college nearby, so Susan is happy. We're on our way up there right now."

"That's nice."

"And, well, how are you settling in? I hope it hasn't been too difficult." They stared at each other for a moment.

"It's hard," Jane finally said. "It's really, really hard. I miss them dearly."

"It's not your fault," Henrico said. "You know that, right? What happened—to Beth, to Jerry, to all those Hawthornes—none of that was your fault. You did the right thing by all of them, Jane. You did."

Jane looked down at her muddy boots, then at the gravestones, and then back at Henrico. "Thanks," she said, "but it would be easier to stomach if it were my fault. Then I would deserve to be the only one left."

Henrico took a step forward and put his hand on Jane's shoulder. "I'm sorry, Jane. I don't know what else to say." Jane took a deep breath and exhaled.

"Nothing else to say, Henrico," she said. "Or do. Have a safe trip, and come back soon to visit, won't you?"

"Of course," Henrico said. "We'll see you soon."

"Good. Love to Susan and Felicity."

Henrico got back into his minivan, shifted from park to drive, and slowly left Jane to tend to the dead on behalf of the living.

CHAPTER 90

Sky walked out of the NBC News building into the kind of spring afternoon that, if one had the presence of mind to remember it, would make Washington D.C. bearable in July. From where she stood looking across the street, she could see the Capitol building staring out across the city, urging more people to come out into the sun.

She looked to her left and considered walking a block to Union Station, where she knew a bartender who served those hesitating to either enter or leave the city. A slow breeze and the smell of spring flowers dissolved the thought. *Nope*, she thought to herself, *going indoors right now would call down punishment from a just God. Go home, Sky, and take the win.*

She closed her eyes, looked skyward, and let the sun bake her face before she turned to her right and walked toward her silver Corolla parked a few blocks away. Her phone rang. She smiled before picking up the call.

"Hello, stranger," she said.

"You should talk," Henrico said. "I've heard your voice more on TV and voicemail lately than live on the phone."

"Yeah," Sky said as she put her earbuds in. "Sorry about that. It's been crazy. I just finished recording another interview. They gave me an hour's notice. Can you believe that?"

"Don't apologize. Congratulations. This is what happens when you nail it."

Sky weaved among the crowd of office workers as she crossed D street. "I know. But it was Eric and the *Thread* guys who really came through. I can't believe what they managed to dig up. In the end, I was just the one who wrote it all down." Another warm breeze. Sky slowed down a bit to enjoy it.

"It's a team game," Henrico said. "That's how it goes. Hey, I have a question for you. And I hope it's not too delicate."

"For me? Never," Sky said.

"When we first met, did you know that the Hawthornes were so…"

"Corrupt?"

"Yeah."

"Well, my father had told me as much. But I never thought they were so good at it. I mean, anyone can buy off a Senator for some earmarks. But paying off the D.C. Police, the Capitol Police, *and* the FBI? That raises eyebrows, even in this town."

"I'd bet," Henrico said, "and it explains a lot."

"It does," Sky said. "The cops weren't merely incompetent. Millie was paying them to slow-walk anything having to do with the family, even if that thing was a plot to kill them."

Sky reached her car and leaned against it so she could continue to soak in the sun.

"Ballsy," Henrico said. "And once *that* story broke, the floodgates probably opened. Especially with a thousand sources texting you all the details."

"Exactly. Everyone's all righteous and blowing whistles now that it's safe to do so. Anyway, thanks for calling me back."

"I always have time for Skylar Nicholson. What's up?"

"The *Times* called."

"Of course they did," Henrico said. "What did they offer you?"

"Whatever I want," Sky said.

There was an awkward silence.

"Oh. I see the problem."

Sky stood back up on the sidewalk and started to pace. "That's why I called you—you're the only one who gets it." Another long silence.

"You still there?" Sky said.

"Yep," Henrico replied. "What does your gut tell you?"

"That I don't want the thing that *the entire fucking universe* is telling me I should want. That I always wanted or used to want. That I had, then lost. Shit, is that crazy?"

"Not at all," Henrico said. "It sounds downright sane."

"Well, it won't sound sane to anyone else."

"What? Because you're not driving yourself crazy going after the next thing, and the thing after that, regardless of the consequences, until you keel over?"

Sky smiled. She had called the right man.

"That's what runs this town, Henrico," she said, "that's the fuel for the engine. It's what I've been taught to do since I was in diapers. I'm surrounded by it. I have to live by its rules."

"Do you really believe that?" Henrico said.

Sky groaned. "Would I have called you if I knew the answer to that question?"

Henrico chuckled.

"What's so funny?"

"I think you do have the answer," Henrico said, "but you don't like it."

"Go on."

"Don't try that," Henrico said. "Uncle Henrico isn't going to hand you a solution here. That's on you. All I can tell you is that, believe it or not, sometimes where you are turns out to be the best place to be."

Sky stopped pacing on the sidewalk. Before she could respond, her phone buzzed. She fished her phone out of her pocket and checked the home screen. It was a message from Eric.

Daughter of Turkish ambassador found dead in the map room of the GWU library. Students sending content inbound. On it?

"Sky," Henrico said. "You still there?"

She smiled. "Yes, I am. Thank you, my friend. That helped more than you know."

"Any time," Henrico said. "I gotta go. Let me know where you land."

"I will," Sky said. "I will."

Sky hung up the phone, hopped into her car, and started the engine while typing left-handed into her phone.

On it. Sky.

CHAPTER 91

Shannon O'Donnell pulled one hand away from the papers on the lawyer's conference room table and laid it on her belly. The child inside kicked softly, as if he shared her surprise and confusion.

"I don't understand," she said. "I didn't come here looking for money. I just wanted to find out who else to tell about the baby. He's going to want to know about his family someday, and right now, I don't know what to tell him."

The thin, tall man with perfectly combed hair and wire-rimmed glasses leaned back in his chair. "We appreciate that, Miss O'Donnell, but Mr. Hawthorne's estate plan is clear. He modified it in this office a few weeks before his death. If you will turn to page six..." Shannon's mind raced as she turned the pages. What was this all about?

"It clearly says," the man continued, "that Tyler Hawthorne designated you as his beneficiary."

"I don't know what that means," Shannon said. The young lawyer looked down the table to the managing partner, who woke from a daydream and laid both of his palms on the mahogany table.

"It means," the gray-haired man said, "that the dollar amount at the bottom of that page will come to you each year for the rest of your life. I'm sure you will agree that it is an adequate amount for both you and the baby."

Shannon gasped. Ten million dollars. Every year. *He loved me,* she thought as the tears began to run down her cheeks. *He wanted to take care of me. Of us.*

"Is this for real?" she said.

The old man put on his best lawyerly, father-knows-best face. "Yes, Miss O'Donnell. It is quite real."

"I don't know what to say."

"There's more," the partner continued. "The baby you are carrying, when he turns 18, will inherit a majority share of Hawthorne Enterprises. The corporation's by-laws stipulate that in the meantime, his interest be represented by a trust, which must have as its sole trustee his closest living relative."

Shannon looked at the older man, then at the young associate, and finally back to the older man again.

"And?" she said.

"That's you, Miss O'Donnell. You're his mother. Welcome to Hawthorne Enterprises."